Being
Wicked

Being Wicked

LACY DANES

APHRODISIA

KENSINGTON BOOKS
http://www.kensingtonbooks.com

APHRODISIA BOOKS are published by

Kensington Publishing Corp.
850 Third Avenue
New York, NY 10022

All Kensington Titles, Imprints, and Distributed Lines are available at special quantity discounts for bulk purchases for sales promotions, premiums, fund-raising, and educational or institutional use.

Special book excerpts or customized printings can also be created to fit specific needs. For details, write or phone the office of the Kensington special sales manager: Kensington Publishing Corp., 850 Third Avenue, New York, NY 10022, attn: Special Sales Department, Phone: 1-800-221-2647.

Aphrodisia and the A logo Reg. U.S. Pat & TM Off.

ISBN-13: 978-0-7582-2059-2
ISBN-10: 0-7582-2059-6

First Kensington Trade Paperback Printing: February 2009

10 9 8 7 6 5 4 3 2 1

Printed in the United States of America

To my wonderful friends, Eden Bradley, Lillian Feisty, and Shelli Stevens, thank you for supporting me through all of my life's chaos. I love you dearly.

To Eric, thank you for pushing me to do better in life and for supporting the time I need to write. You are a constant influence. Hugs and kisses.

This book marks a learning transition in my personal and professional lives. Life is a juggling act for me; kids, day job, writing career, dating, time to write, time to research, and time to simply be. After writing this book, I found the balance needed to survive.

Kisses,

Lacy

1

The Intersection

Somewhere on a road in England, 1828

God preserve those with good souls. . . .

The muscles of her back ached as another jarring rut tossed her head against the hard wall of the carriage. She clenched her teeth together and held in a squeak. What a harebrained idea this was. . . . Bless the Lord, she was small.

In the end, this impropriety would only turn to good. She would prove both their relatives and the townsfolk wrong—in her mind, she would. No one could *ever* know she'd done this.

Brian was a proper gentleman—not the rogue bent on pleasure. His trips to the capital were for his new responsibilities, not to squander the family money and sow his oats.

His sullen, tired look of late had concerned her and a small doubt spiraled its way into her head. The carriage rocked to a stop. Had they made it to their destination? Wherever that was. She didn't think she could last much longer confined in this box. She peeked out the crack in the top of the bench. Her brother did not move, but the carriage lurched to the left as someone clambered on board.

"By Jove, Cunnington! Could you be any later?" a gravelly voice sounded through the muffled carriage seat.

"Only a touch, St. Jerome."

A loud, deep laugh erupted.

St. Jerome! Surely, her brother did not associate with that rake! She closed her eyes and imagined Brian helping her learn French. No, she surely misheard. She opened her eyes, pushed up from the floor of the carriage, and placed her ear to the crack in the seat.

"Are we to pick up Amelia or will she be meeting you at the rout?"

"No Amelia. I let her go," St. Jerome replied.

"Oh, you mean her handsome legs and even finer skills are available?"

Lilly smothered her gasp into her bicep. She had never heard Brian talk in such a way. Maybe this was all for show because that scoundrel St. Jerome was present.

"Quite so, but not for you, louse. With your family looming over your every move, she would ruin you." St. Jerome chuckled.

Oh, dash it! It was St. Jerome. The mill had been churning for the past week with his most recent, not so quiet, break from Amelia, his mistress. But what in all of England was her brother doing associating with such a rogue? Maybe he was out to save St. Jerome's soul. But from the sounds of it . . . that was the furthest thing from his mind. Her chest tightened.

Could the townsfolk have been right? Was her brother on a path straight to damnation?

No! She shan't let all those lies turn her against him. Oh, if they only knew the true him—the one that played with the kittens in the barn and sat patiently while she painted his likeness for the umpteenth time. He couldn't be only after loose virtue, stiff drinks, and cards. She strained to hear their conversation as the carriage rocked to a halt and another male entered.

"We are three . . . ," said a jovial voice she didn't recognize one whit.

"Indeed. We are off to the ball for some excellent liquor, and even finer pleasure." St. Jerome's laughing tone raised every fine hair on her neck.

God preserve her. They were headed to a ball. How in the world would she get into a ball uninvited and unmasked? Her brother would notice her at one glance.

The locals called her a pure beauty, but they were simply kind. Nothing of any significance claimed her features. She possessed the meager looks of their mother, someone that Lilly's pa had always scolded for not presenting herself well to anyone. *Make yourself presentable . . . if that is womanly possible,* " his angry voice bellowed at her mother. Each of his words had made her mother flinch and tears spring to Lilly's eyes. A lump formed in her throat and she swallowed repeatedly.

She had loved her father, though he was firm with her, and she had seen moments of his kindness to their mother. Those were the moments that she hoped for in her match. If she ever did make a match, she wanted someone who would be kind and gentle and teach her the things she needed to know.

She had yet to make her debut in town because of her mother's always failing health, and she had no real desire to put herself forth in such a manner anyhow. Being rejected for something she had no control over would simply be bothersome. She sighed and her stomach pinched.

No, it would hurt.

She closed her eyes as the carriage swayed to a stop once more.

"Who have you set your Abraham weeping for, Cunnington?" the stranger's voice inquired laughingly.

"Not one of your wicked girls skilled with the art of flogging, Devonton, that is for certain."

Chills raced along her spine. Lord Devonton! He was the worst rogue of all! Her heart sank to the pit of her stomach. Her brother sat knee to knee with two of England's biggest and most notorious rogues.

"Certainly not, Cunnington! One hit with the switch, and you would be crying like an infant."

The switch . . . that was true. Brian had cried and yelled like an infant when their nurse had punished him. His shouts grew louder and louder with each hit. She pursed her lips. Why would Lord Devonton wish a woman to birch him? Surely, he couldn't find pleasure in such an act. If true, the information would explain his reputation. An exasperated sigh pushed past her lips.

What was Brian doing with men of this ilk? He was a gentleman through and through. She could see how the townsfolk thought him scandalous when he consorted with the likes of these men. He plainly had another reason for befriending them. What could it be?

The carriage door opened and joyous music and laughter floated in. She cringed. There was no way she would be able to gain entrance to this event. A frown turned her lips. What was she thinking when she crawled into the blanket box? *Daft, truly daft, Lilly.*

The only coins in her pocket this night were her unnoticeable looks and that no one of this ilk knew her at all. Maybe she could sneak in the servants' entrance . . . but then what? Her attire certainly was not for a formal evening, and if she did gain entrance, she would never fit in with this set. Oh, and what would she see? His company on this ride sent icy fear straight to her heart.

She needed a plan.

The sway to the side and the sudden lack of noise, followed

by the lurching forward of the carriage again, indicated all had left the cab. The driver would pull over and stop on the street someplace and wait for her brother.

She would exit the carriage before they stopped and the footmen took notice of her. From this point on tonight, what came her way came.

Sweat pierced her brow and Lilly pushed up against the seat bottom and lifted the lid to the blanket compartment. She peered out—her heart in her throat—into the cab of the carriage.

No one was present.

She eased herself up with her arms. Her legs ached from the crouched position she held since they had left Rousemore Hall in Bedfordshire late that afternoon. Her body shook and she strained her body, which did not want to respond to her will to move. She concentrated all her energy on lifting her leg up and over the edge. She closed her eyes and gritted her teeth and strained slowly. Her leg lifted up over the edge and pins shot straight through to her toes.

Ouch! She lurched forward and landed on the opposite seat, her legs in searing pain. She sighed as the carriage swayed around a corner. This was her chance. She could not wait for the pain in her legs to subside. She grasped the door handle in her gloved hand and pushed it wide. The ground rolled by before her. She closed her eyes and sucked in a large breath. *Jump, Lilly, jump.* She sprang out of the carriage.

Her slippered feet hit the cobbled drive and slid straight back. Her arms flew out. Hands slapped into the hard, cold cobbles and a shooting pain burst through her knees.

Ouch!

She never was good at climbing or jumping as a child, and age had not improved that skill.

She pushed up from the cobbles and stood, staring at the side of a large country house and its stables, which surrounded

5

her. She grimaced and her gaze dashed around the stable yard. Footmen rushed about, but none of them glanced her way. She sighed in relief and her shoulders sagged. *Hide, you silly! They will see you if you shan't.* Bushes lined the edge of the house and she scurried to hide behind them.

No one had seen her escape from her brother's carriage. She pressed herself up against the rough stone house as branches of the boxwood scraped against the muslin of her sleeve. A tear leaked from the corner of her eye and she swallowed hard. Her body pulsed with the beat of her heart and she blew out a tight breath.

She was not in London. Sweat pierced her brow. What was she to do now?

She couldn't sneak off to Burber Place, the family London home. She was alight someplace and she had no clue where she was! Sweat pierced the skin on the back of her neck.

Foolishness, Lilly, foolishness. She shook her head. *Take a deep breath and get your bearing. You can always sleep in the barn if need be.* She inhaled the crisp night air and smelled the scent of horses, hay, and smoke from the chimneys floating on the slight breeze.

She would sneak into the house and find something to wear. She closed her eyes again. *What a blunder you have gotten yourself into. Silly, silly, Lilly.* A deep sigh escaped from her lips and she straightened her shoulders. No going back now. She was here and so was her brother. She would prove the townsfolk wrong.

2

The Intersection

She wished someone would have told her at that age what a messy thing marriage was. Grace narrowed her eyes at the group of young women who stood at the corner of the dance floor and blushed at the eligible men of the ton. White dresses, with satin bows, blushing cheeks, and batting fans. She rolled her eyes.

"Lady Wentland, may I interest you in a glass of lemonade?" The laughing note of deep, polished English purred by her left ear.

She sighed and rolled her eyes. "Well, Markus, only if it has a hefty shot of . . . what is it you call it, spirits?" She turned her head to see the deep blue gaze of her late husband's best friend, Lord Brummelton, slide down to her breasts and stare with the knowledge of exactly what they tasted like.

Warmth crept across her breasts and she swallowed hard. Her insides squirmed and she shifted in her seat. She hated the way the men her husband had introduced to their bedroom stared at her outside that sphere.

"Indeed, spirits. They are serving claret." His hand rose and his knuckles grazed the curve of her elbow. His voice dropped to a whisper. "I am heading to an event. A one-night ordeal. One I know you will enjoy, dear Grace. There will be people in attendance that you have not seen since Oscar's death."

She closed her eyes and heat spread through her . . . a one-night ordeal. It echoed in her mind, and as she opened her eyes, all the people in the room changed. The blushing girls in the corner slid into images of dancing girls dressed in barely anything as they teased and pleasured the men of the ton.

A warm longing slid down her arms and she held in a sigh of nostalgia. There was a part of her that had indeed enjoyed her marriage. Oscar had shocked her senses with futtering that she never knew had happened among her peers . . . or among anyone.

Markus's finger slid to her wrist and the images evaporated, like snow on a hot stove.

"I am uncertain, Markus. This is the first proper ton event I have attended this season."

"Grace." His eyes hardened with unrelenting determination. All of her husband's friends had *that look* when they believed something was right. How they all possessed the same expression, she had no idea.

She glanced down at her hands and then back at the tame and staid men and women chattering about nothing of any importance to her. After Oscar's death, she had longed to find a normal man. She desired to find a way to live out the dreams of her youth, married to a respectable man, but . . . She glanced through her lashes at the gentleman who stood two feet from her.

Lord Sutterley. His corseted waist and padded calves were obvious to everyone in the room. She cringed. Never would she end up with him. He fidgeted with his mustache as he glanced at her from the corner of one eye. Images of his mouth between her legs, and that mustache tickling her thighs as he licked her sex, made her stomach roil and she squeezed her legs together. No! Never!

She gazed back to her hands. The truth . . . a chill ran down her spine. The truth was, there was no reality in her childhood dream. Or the fantasies she used to share with her brother and their dear friend, Winston, in their youth. The idea of what they had all thought this world would hold simply was not steadfast, no matter how much she wished the illusion so.

She would not find what she longed for here or anywhere, but she could not, would not, end up in bed with Markus again, either. Not that he was untalented in that sphere.

The memory of his body pressed up against hers from behind, sweat from hours of long, intense futtering pooled between them, as he brought her to spend again and again. His arm muscles tightened about her, his fingers pinched her breasts. These memories wet her pussy on lonely nights. Markus was delightful. The problem was simply that . . . well . . . she promised herself she would have a different life and Markus was at the top of the peerage in what was Oscar's world.

She turned back to face the handsome black-haired man who had futtered her more times than she could remember as her husband watched from his chair. That damned chair!

Markus's lips curved up into a smile that said he knew he had won. "Thinking about the chair again, are you?"

She closed her eyes and sighed. "Very well, Markus. Which of the mistresses is holding the event?"

"Emma. She has been asking about you." He winked.

"Dear Emma." Her lips curved up into a smile as images of Emma and Markus's brother Rupert futtering in the hall at one of his famous parties filled her mind. Emma's legs wrapped tightly about Rupert's waist, her head thrown back, as he bit her neck and growled. Her small hands slapped and clawed at Rupert's back as he kissed her and thrust her against the wall, stealing her breath away.

Slick moisture tingled Grace's cunt and she rocked her hips backward in the chair, squeezing the walls together to relieve the blooming ache in her pussy. *Stop, Grace. Stop thinking about your wild longings.* "I have not seen Emma in well past a year. Is she quarreling as frequently with Rupert or has he moved on?"

"Rupert is now devoted to Cora. You will meet her tonight. When will you get past your stubborn thoughts on what you need, and go with what your desires tell you, Grace? I have never seen a woman more like a mule than you."

The icy, firm tone of his words slid like oil down the center of her back and between the globes of her bottom. Indeed, she was stubborn. The image of a mule pulling back against the ropes as Markus pulled and pulled quirked her lips up. She looked up into his eyes. The same intensity that shone in his eyes every time he caressed her cheek after they had futtered shone back at her—a gentle caring mixed with a firm determination.

She sighed. He was right. At the very least, she did long to see all of her friends again. She swallowed and stared back at the proper women her age that sat and laughed, talking about bonnets, and ribbons, and all the false things they pretended mattered.

"I will go, but only if you put me in my cups on the way."

He held out his hand to her and she wrapped her fingers around it and stood.

He stared down at her. "No problem, Grace. I have plenty of spirits in my coach, as you are well aware."

Indeed, he always had something in his carriage to soften the girls he brought to his home before they arrived. She hoped he had some of the chamomile and anise-flavored liquor that let down her inhibitions and pushed forth the longing to be bold and futter.

"Indeed, Grace. I know what kind of spirit you wish, though I do not think it wise going where we are. You should have your wits about you. You have not been touched since . . ." His jaw set firmly and his brows pulled tight together in a scowl.

"Precisely why I need to be touched, Markus. You want me to let go and follow my desires. Help me, but don't expect me in your bed." She cringed slightly as the words left her mouth. *That was entirely rude, Grace. Naughty girl. Markus doesn't deserve the backlash of disappointment that swirls in your life.* "Pardon, Markus."

"There is no need to slap me, Grace. I know you were only with me for Oscar." The muscles of his forearm tensed. "Much as I was."

Indeed, she was well aware of why Markus bedded her at the beck and call of her husband. Markus was indebted to Oscar and came whenever Oscar called. Chills touched the back of her neck and she forced that part of her husband's memories away from her mind. She didn't need to remember him that way.

Grace stumbled from the carriage and straightened her skirts. *Wonderful, Grace, now everyone will assume you are in your cups.* She smiled to herself. Well, she supposed she was a bit tipsy, but far from making a spectacle of herself.

Markus smiled at her. "I see the herbs in the wine are working well."

"I am relaxed, and a bit awakened—that is all, Markus." Why did she always feel like she had to prove to everyone that she was fine? She frowned. Why couldn't she simply let go and be what she was? Vulnerable, unsure of herself, and, well, a bit daft. *Enough of that, Grace. You have strong qualities, as well*

11

as your vulnerabilities. Was that true? Her brow pulled tight. She supposed that was. She simply needed to find out what those were and force them to the surface.

"Aroused, eh? I am glad to hear it, Grace. You need to remember what it is like to touch and be touched."

Grace sighed. Indeed. That was precisely why she had allowed Markus to talk her into this situation—this event she could pretend at.

She walked up the wide sandstone steps to the newly constructed manor house, which stood on the border to Chelsea.

The outside appeared to be a normal manor. Straight lines and perfectly spaced windows all cued up in rows across the front. A soft glow of candles radiated from the windows, where peering in was welcome by any who wished to see.

The inside was different. Anything but proper. As everyone in this set knew, this home was filled with the latest trends, as well as oddities. The owner was a wealthy Danish man who let the house for an extended visit to the capital and had taken a fancy to Emma.

Grace sighed. Emma did capture everyone's attention; so no surprise, she now resided in this masterpiece. Emma's petite stature and beautiful fair hair made her a sight to behold, but her many, many carnal talents kept the men at her side. All of Grace's encounters with her had been filled with passion and expertise. Emma's passion certainly came from all of the tutoring Rupert bestowed on her.

Though many said Grace was the one who drew attention—a talent she never wanted or had—she feigned it well.

She closed her eyes. A thud then a stifled cry, came from the right of her. She turned her head as her eyes shot open.

A young lady pushed to her knees and scurried into the bushes at the side of the house.

Grace hesitated. Did she witness a woman, a *lady*, jumping from a carriage? What was that woman about?

"Everything well, Grace?" Markus's fingers firmed on her elbow and he propelled her up another step toward the great rose carved doors.

"I'm fine, but I need to use the washroom."

"Very well. It is down the hall on the right side of the house, filled, I am sure, with all kinds of interesting things for you ladies to relieve yourselves in." He smiled a full-tooth smile at her. "I will let you know what room Emma has you settled in, when you return."

The right side of the home was the side where the young woman scurried into the bushes. Grace stepped into the house and turned toward Markus. He reached up and untied the ribbons about her throat that held her cape in place. The footman grasped back and lifted her cape from her shoulders.

She spun around. The entry dwarfed anything she had ever seen. The dark wood floor gleamed, and before her in the center of the space stood an enormous staircase. Intricately carved of deep rich wood, the stairs were the centerpiece of the room, which led to the second floor.

This home was indeed meant to impress. She headed to the right of the staircase and through the open door to the back half of the first-level rooms. Spotting two doors—the one to the right, with a red ribbon tied on the handle, and the one to the left, with a blue ribbon—she sighed and hoped. Red ribbon meant caution; it was a public place to futter. Blue was the retiring room.

She pushed open the door with the red ribbon to the right and entered the room. The smell of jasmine perfume and rose petals filled her senses and she glanced around. The room was beautiful—soft gold velvet chairs sat on blue carpet, gilded mirrors hung all about on cornflower blue walls. In the middle of the room was a large oval seat with a carved gold wood tree in the center. From the tree, straps of leather hung.

In her mind, she was pushed down on the gold velvet seat. . . . Her hands were pushed back against the wood tree and the leather straps tied tight about her wrist as a man, with gold hair, bit her neck and breasts. His hands spread her thighs wide as his rough fingers slid up her soft skin heading toward her core. She closed her eyes and moaned, savoring the fantasy.

Her nipples tingled and pebbled hard beneath her corset. She pulled her shoulder blades together and pushed her hard buds against the fabric. Tendrils of pleasure, as if from the wooden tree itself, curled about her body, tightening about her ribs, restricting her breath. Her pussy clenched and she panted. Her sensual desires pulsed alive and raged within her. The intensity of her need shocked her.

Grace, you need to straighten yourself up. No, what she needed was to futter. The herbs in the wine had taken full hold, but the act would have to wait. Something was amiss with what she had just witnessed. Though the herbs may have conjured that vision, she bit her lip. Doubtful. The herbs intensified lust, not conjured up escaping ladies. She forced her eyes open. Where was that fleeing woman?

The room stood empty. She walked to the only window in the room and drew back the covers. Pitch-black darkness stared back through the windowpane. She could see nothing.

Grace sighed, and the door to the room pushed open. A young woman, with mud spattered up her skirt, slid into the room. Her gaze darted around.

She came into the house? Grace's eyes widened. She would never have held the level of gumption to enter the home of a known courtesan at this woman's tender age.

"Good evening."

The young girl jumped.

"All is well, no need to fright. I sighted your flight from the carriage. I was actually looking out the window here"—Grace pointed to the window behind her—"to see if I could find you."

The woman stood stock-still, eyes the color of a deer's soft brown fur fixed on Grace.

"All is truly well. I do not believe anyone else saw you. May I help you?" Grace stepped forward toward the girl. "Truly, I will not harm you."

The young woman bit her lip. "I was not expecting to be here. I followed my brother."

Grace nodded. "I will not ask his name. This is a party filled with anonymous encounters . . . that may turn into long-term endearments." *Endearments involving more than one, usually.* Grace held back a frown as she reached the young woman's side. "If you wish to blend in, your attire will not do." Grace raised her hand and touched a strand of black hair that hung in a curl down the woman's cheek. "You will need a mask, especially if you decide to partake in any of the goings-on. You cannot have someone find out you are of class and breeding."

The young lady sucked in her breath. "How did you know that?"

Grace's lips turned into a smile. "Your clothes . . ." Grace ran her finger along the well-made muslin on the woman's arm. "Your hair . . ." She wrapped the onyx strand around her index finger. "The way you walk. It is all indicative of a lady."

"Who are you?"

"I am a woman who was once like you—a young lady of breeding and class with no experience in the world. My proper name is not important. Please simply call me Grace." Grace inwardly cringed that she just offered this woman her Christian name. Since everyone else here knew her as such, why should this girl call her something different?

The young girl glanced around the room, then at Grace. "What kind of event have I arrived at?"

"I hope it will be an event of education for you. You are at a ball for the underbelly of all of London. This is one of Emma Drundle's Cyprian events."

"Oh! Oh, no!" The doe brown eyes of the petite woman closed and reopened, glossy from tears.

"All is well." This young woman feared for her reputation. Grace's heart ached for her, but she deserved an education of what life was truly like before all her dreams shattered. She deserved to be educated about the enjoyment that could come with this kind of life.

A tear fell from the young woman's eye. Grace dragged the tips of her fingers along the woman's cheek and caught the petal-soft drop.

The strange girl squeezed her eyes shut. "My brother is here. This is all a big blunder. What is he doing?"

"I know exactly how you feel. If you do wish to stay, I will help you to understand. Everyone here is not evil or bad. When I was your age, I was married off to a man who was twice my age. An important man in society. I had no clue about what marriage was. I had dreams of what life after marriage was filled with, and it was all wrong. What people had filled my head with was . . ." *All rubbish.* She couldn't very well say that. She glanced at the young woman's fisted hands. "Let me show you. Do not give me your real name, but what shall I call you?"

The woman looked down at Grace's belly and bit her lip. "I don't know."

"Very well, I will give you a name for the night. . . ." Grace trailed her finger along the young woman's chin and lifted her head so her eyes met Grace's. "You will be Veronica for tonight . . . Miss Veronica." Grace rolled the name off her tongue and winked at the young girl.

"Oh, I can't play t-that part. . . . I—I—am not like that. I—I have . . ." The young woman's face turned a beautiful shade of red.

How delightful. The men here were going to devour her. Literally. She needed to prepare her for such an outcome. "Have you ever kissed a boy, *Veronica?*"

"Pardon?"

"You heard me, *Veronica.*"

"Oh . . . um" Veronica looked down at her shoes and reached up and twirled a strand of hair about her finger. "Once."

"Delightful, was it not?"

"But it is not right unless you are wed. Isn't it?" Her huge brown eyes snapped up to Grace's again.

"I realize this is a lot of information for you to absorb, but we need to get you masked and veiled and ready before someone walks in here and sees you."

Veronica sucked in a sharp breath. "Oh, dear."

"Come with me." Grace held out her hand. "I will get you turned about."

3

The Intersection

After trying several doors to apparently the wrong room, Lilly followed Grace into a well-appointed room with light blue and green cloth on the walls. She stood absolutely still a foot into the room. She inhaled a breath and tried to calm her rapidly beating heart. Her gaze darted around the bedchamber.

Off to one side was a large wooden bed, covered in deep bluish purple silk, and a swath of purple gauze hung by the headboard. In the middle of the room was a thick, circular grass-green pillow. The pillow was larger than anything she'd seen. Surely, it could hold five or so people lying down.

Lilly stared at the tufted cushion. After being cramped up in the blanket box for so long, stretching out on a divine pillow would be decadent. A sigh pressed past her lips.

What was she thinking? Her hands trembled and she shook her head. *Silly, foolish girl.* She needed to find her brother and then leave this house. Not nap here. She would be entirely ruined if it was discovered she attended this . . . this . . . ball? What a jest—could simply being here ruin her if no one knew of her folly?

She turned toward the woman who led her to this room. She stood, smiling at her. Grace. That was what she called herself. Lilly's brow drew tight. She appeared nothing like a Grace. She was more of an Olivia or an Elizabeth or a Helene. She was something classic, simple but sophisticated.

Grace certainly was a lady and all those things her name suggested, but she also was scandalous . . . Lilly fidgeted with the fabric of her skirt.

Were many of the women who attended these events ladies of the ton? Women whom she would admire and see as mentors when she finally entered society?

Green pins held Grace's brown hair away from her face. With each turn of her head, her hair shimmered red in the candle glow. Her eyes were not green and not blue. Beauty glowed about her, though not in a strikingly handsome kind of way. She radiated sincerity and goodness. Lilly's brows drew together. What a puzzle Grace made.

"This, I surmise, is Emma's room, Veronica."

Lilly swallowed hard; she would burst into flames and be sent straight to hell. She stood in Emma Drundle's bedchamber. Never, never, never in her life . . . she sighed as her stomach tensed in panic. *Lilly, calm yourself. The situation is as it is. It could be much worse, you could be. . . .* She closed her eyes. *No, there was no worse.* Society would outcast her and she would have to become an Emma Drundle. Her breath caught in her throat in shock and her hand flew to her mouth.

"Emma should have something here for you to wear, Veronica. Things are not as bad as you think. Though we certainly need to get you out of those clothes, you have mud spattered up your petticoats and you are dressed beyond proper for an event such as this." Grace walked toward the large clothes chest set against the one wall. She opened the doors and pulled out a crushed red silk cape. "This shall do nicely. We will find a mask and one of Emma's bloomers to wear with your corset and you shall fit in while you search for what you wish."

Emma's red cape? A corset and bloomers? Oh, no. Oh, no. Where was her soul about to head? "R-red b-bloomers? I have never worn such a garment." *Calm, Lilly. Calm. You have not burst into flames . . . and this woman wants to help you.*

"Red will have to do. Emma wears so much of it. Besides, it will go lovely with your black hair and complexion. Bloomers are comfortable and becoming fashionable." Grace pulled out a black-and-white mask made of fabric that had small crystals dangling from the eyes, as if tears.

It would cover Lilly's eyes. Half black, half white, the mask shimmered theatrically. Maybe this would not be so bad.

A white set of bloomers came next, which was embroidered with small black flowers about the knees. "There is something every woman should know. It is and will be hard to understand at this moment, but I want you to be protected if you should try any of what you see this night."

"Try? Oh, no. I could never partake in anything here. I will simply find my brother and leave as quickly as possible."

"You may be surprised, Veronica. Some of what you see may fascinate you. It is perfectly normal to wish to watch. No harm beyond education can happen from you observing."

That was true, and she did want to understand why her brother was here. Maybe, as she said, observing would be all right for a few moments.

"You said you have kissed a man. When you did so, I imagine your heart sped and you felt odd between your legs."

Lilly nodded.

"Have you created that sensation on your own, Veronica?"

Heat washed Lilly's face. *My God, how did she end up here talking about her private acts?* She fidgeted with her hands and bit her lower lip.

"I will take by the delightful rosy color that has infused your face that indeed you have. It is normal, and all part of how men and women find pleasure together. You need to understand, though, Veronica, men and women want to futter and the act is also pleasant for all involved."

She turned around and walked to a table where a bowl of lemons resided. She picked one up and walked back toward Lilly. "What do you know of bearing a child?"

"I watched my maid in the woods, and a local farmer's wife through the window once." Goodness, what was she about to talk about? She simply wanted to find Brian and leave. "Grace, I simply wish to prove to myself my brother is indeed not who the townsfolk say he is, and rather who I believed him to be."

Grace frowned. "Your brother is your brother. He is who you know him to be, as well as who he is here. Try to remember that as you venture into this house." She walked the last bit that separated them and raised her hand. Grace's fingers glided down Lilly's cheek and under her chin in a gentle caress—like none Lilly had experienced before. "Lemons prevent children, Veronica. Remember that if you so choose to participate tonight. Simply place half of one of these in your private place to prevent any evidence of scandal. That is all I wish to say to you."

"Lemons!" What was Grace talking about? "Pardon? I simply don't understand."

"I can show you if you wish. Or I can help you put one in and show you how to take it out."

"What?" Lilly's eyes widened.

"You will be touched here tonight, Veronica. If you don't want to stand out, you should let go of some of what you feel is proper and wrong. This is a night to see what your body and emotions show you as being true." Grace slid her hand down Lilly's shoulder to her corseted stomach.

Lilly jumped and stared at Grace's hands as she slid her fingers to her waist.

"It is better to be fully prepared than have regrets." Grace leaned forward. "What do you think, Veronica?" Her breath warmed Lilly's ear as she whispered.

A man would touch her as Grace's hands had. "Ummm . . . I—I don't know."

Grace turned away from Lilly and went to the window, where she stood and stared out at the night. "I wish I had understood more about our nature when I was your age. What it was like to feed your soul and simply be happy being human. Not what society told you was proper, not what your family said was your responsibility." Her breath came out loudly. "Our world is society, and even being here ruins you in our peers' eyes. For some, even if they themselves are here. It is truly such a shame."

Lilly stared at this woman. Her voice filled with longing, with compassion, with a desire for something that Lilly had no inkling what it was. Her legs wanted to carry her to Grace's side, to put her hand on her shoulder and tell her all was not so complex. Lilly couldn't move, though. She was grounded here in this spot by all the swirling fears and uncertainty about how she should act in such a place. She simply listened.

"I understand you look at all the people here and cast judgment on them. Most people do, but if you would simply open your mind a small bit for your brother's sake, you will see that this is what being human is. This is where adults play games like children do." Grace's hand rose and brushed her own cheek.

Is she weeping? Lilly frowned and stared at Grace. What weighed so heavily about Grace? "What do you long for, Grace? I can feel sadness in your words."

Grace didn't speak, simply stood still and stared out the window into the night.

Grace's words from the past hour floated in Lilly's mind. Grace so wanted to teach Lilly . . . yet Lilly feared the knowledge she wished her to learn.

Come now, Lilly, you said what came is what came this night. Dress, find Brian, and see what will be.

Lilly reached down, pulled the bloomers up her legs, then tied them about her waist. She never wore such a garment, and without a skirt to cover her legs, she fidgeted a bit. If only they were longer. She held back a giggle. *Surely, Lilly, longer bloomers would make all the difference.* She shook her head and rolled her eyes.

"I long for the love of a good man. One who knows and can feed the passions within. A man who is not afraid to do and be who he is," Grace declared.

Lilly stared back at her. Well, that certainly was a reasonable dream. Lilly tied the red cape about her shoulders and played with the edges. "That is not unusual, Grace. We all want passion and love. We should all strive for such things. I simply wish to achieve those in marriage, not outside it."

Grace turned about, her blue-green eyes big and round and filled with shimmering tears.

Oh, no! Stupid, stupid, Lilly. You have made her cry.

"I—I apologize if I said something rash or mean. I simply know what I want and what I believe in."

"No, it is not you. This is the first event I have been to since my husband's death. It is the first time I have come to such a place as a widow, alone, unwed. I had hoped to simply put my dreams aside and have some fun. It is proving to be a bit difficult to forget love was all part of the fun for me."

Lilly's stomach sank. "I am sorry for making you feel ill."

"It is not your fault. Our marriage was never what I thought a marriage would be. I did love him, though." She reached up and brushed a tear from her cheek.

Lilly frowned. She had loved in her marriage, yet she came

24

to places like this with her husband. Maybe she passed judgment on something she didn't understand.

"Let's look at you." Grace stepped toward Lilly. "You are stunning. All the men assume you know what you are doing here. You need to be prepared to be touched." She smiled a watery smile. "Be prepared to be shocked by the behavior you will witness this night, and if you feel you need guidance on how you might act, simply watch all the women about you."

Grace flourished the mask and raised it. Lilly turned about and Grace placed it over her eyes. The cool, thick fabric came down to the tip of her nose and covered her cheekbones. The ties ran over the tops of her ears, and with a few tugs, her deception was fastened.

Lilly inhaled a deep breath. Who was she doing this for? She was doing this for Brian . . . for Grace . . . and for herself. If she was honest with herself, she was a bit curious to see what the night brought. Hidden behind this mask, she truly appeared not herself. She could simply play the part. She pushed her struggles with being here to the back of her mind.

"Shall I show you how to place the lemon?"

Lilly stared expectantly into Grace's still-glossy eyes. *Play the part, Lilly.* "I see no harm in being prepared. I will not go as far as to need protection, but I should like you to teach me anyhow." The information could be useful when she did wed.

Grace smiled. "Indeed, Veronica. Every woman should know how."

4

Grace

Grace walked into the ballroom with her new friend, Veronica. Entirely transformed into a virginal tease, Veronica cautiously turned and headed in the opposite direction as Grace had instructed her. She was unrecognizable from the woman that Grace had found earlier. Her raven hair was pulled back from her face and half her face was partially hidden beneath her mask, which accentuated the innocence she possessed in abundance. The red-and-black bloomers, borrowed from Emma, were a perfect complement to the mask, as well as her white corset.

All the men in attendance were about to see a real treat—a virgin who would act as such. Grace hoped Veronica would listen to her guidance and watch some of what happened here this night.

Grace grasped a glass of claret off a tray as a man passed, standing back to take in the sights she had missed for the past two years.

Her lips curved up into a smile as her eyes settled on a group of women. All of them were masked and wore little clothing.

The woman in the center had golden curls that bobbed and sprang as she twirled with a tall, brown-haired girl, her short shift lifting from her body teasing a group of admiring men. *Emma.* Grace always enjoyed watching her. Her vibrancy for life and pleasure was evident in everything she did.

You are not here for the women, Grace, even if you do enjoy watching them. Not masked, she turned her clear gaze to the men in the room. She needed this to put her marriage behind her and soothe her powerful yearnings, but did she have the courage to do simply that? To simply feel and remember the sensations of being touched, of being desired? Could she do so and not have her emotions get involved? Oscar had always been there, watching from that damn chair. . . .

She closed her eyes and saw his brown hair and deep sable eyes filled with desire lock on hers as Markus slid his cock into her from behind. She trembled. She never removed her gaze from his during any of the acts he requested she do for him. She had loved him completely. She opened her eyes again and sighed.

What she craved could not be found here. Markus stood across the room, staring at her. He would watch her until she found a suitable man to tease—then he would find a plaything for himself. Maybe Veronica? No. Veronica was not for him. Markus would never approach, and Veronica would need to be taken, but with a gentle hand.

Time to tease, dear Grace. From afar, she could and would titillate Markus. That was safe. That she had been taught to do well. She smiled and tilted her head to the side. Her tongue slid out and traced her upper lip. The tingling of her moisture on the plump surface made her tongue retrace its path. She winked at him.

He inclined his head to her, then tilted it toward the two women teasing the men in the center of the room.

He wished her to tantalize him with Emma. Of course he did. She turned her attention back to them; there was a part of her that yearned for what he asked her to do. But only Oscar had ever asked her to do anything with a woman to titillate his senses.

Grace bit her lip at the echo of Oscar's voice. *"Flirt with them for me, Grace. I want to watch you,"* rang in her head. She swallowed hard. She couldn't bring herself to take that step forward and flirt with these women, to flirt with these men. Or could she? A shiver racked her body at the same time heat swelled in her womb.

In her soul, she wanted something different this time, and her heart battled for that one-on-one encounter she so craved. Everyone in this room futtered with their mistresses and protectors at some point. She wanted to do the act and not have someone watching her from *the chair*. She closed her eyes and the carved cherrywood object sat before her. "Leave me alone," she whispered beneath her breath, and the chair vanished.

She wanted to futter with the man she loved. Not simply have him watch her. Tears pushed to her eyes, but she refused to let them fall.

Come on, Grace. You can have fun and flirt and then settle in for the night with one, not two or three. You know it. You simply have never done this without Oscar. Without direction.

She inhaled a deep breath and pried her eyes open. *That's it. Look around the room, pick a protector you wish to entertain, and then flirt with Emma to win his favors for the night.*

She turned her head to the right, slowly taking in the crowded ballroom. Several groups of men and women stood laughing and drinking, but none of them gave her the prickles on the nape of her neck. Oh, indeed. She needed that reaction—that primal physical indication that simply by sighting someone, they would weave together well on the physical plane.

She turned her head back to the left and lightning struck down her spine and her bum clenched. She shook her head to clear her vision. Winston? Was that him?

With the wide shoulders and curl of blond hair over the collar of his fitted evening coat, it very well could be. But why would Winston Greydon be at one of Emma's events? He had never attended one in the past, and he certainly had always appeared a one-woman kind of man. Besides, last she heard of him, he was in India. It couldn't be him.

You still think of him after all these years as your perfect man. No man is how you thought them back then.

She sighed. It wouldn't hurt to see if she could attract the attention of this man—whoever he was. Even without seeing his face, he seemed someone she would be physically a good match for this night.

She stepped forward, in the direction of both him and Emma.

Men and women laughed, joked, and drank. They didn't notice her slipping through. The closer she got to him the bodies grew thicker, crowding her. She couldn't do this. Her lungs constricted and her heart sped as her feet slowed. No . . . no, she needed to do this.

Do this without Oscar.

She glanced across the room once more to where Markus stood. His blue eyes watched her. His face wore an expression she had not seen before. He worried about her.

As she neared the man who resembled Winston, Oscar's words *"Act like a cat playing with its food. Tease him, my dear"* assaulted her. A smile curved her lips. Indeed, he was her prey for the night and she would play with him as a cat did before she devoured him.

She purposefully brushed into Lord Kipberval—he was known for getting easily flustered—and tilted her glass, spilling some of her wine on him.

"Watch where you tread!" The stocky, black-haired man turned toward her.

"Pardon me, sir." Grace placed her hand on his forearm.

His gaze slid down her body, inspecting her in a glance. "My! You are a pretty thing. Sorry to have shouted, lovely."

"No worries, sir. I was simply heading out to the floor and slipped." Grace glanced sideways at the fair-haired man standing not two feet from her. He had turned at the yell from Kipberval and now faced her fully.

Eyes, so blue and intense, stared at her. The same blue that had sparked with laughter as they had discussed their plights in life and made up stories to run off and become gypsies together. She sucked in a startled breath as her heart hammered in her chest. *Winston.*

She beamed up at him. Her lips parted to speak his name with excitement.

His jaw angrily set and his eyes narrowed.

Anger? Chills raced her arms and she stepped backward, cowering away from his expression. His eyes hardened. She couldn't bear to look.

She tore her gaze from him and glanced around the room. Emma laughed out and her gaze jumped to Emma. *Indeed, Emma. Go to her. . . . Be the woman Oscar taught you to be. Winston is your past, and remember he, too, is not what you remember. He is a man, a man with as intense, carnal appetites as every man you have known.*

She stepped forward and onto the dance floor, mind spinning as her heart hammered in her chest. What was Winston doing here? And why was he angry with her?

The same arched nose and smile from childhood repeated in her mind and slowly faded to the wrinkles that now resided about his eyes and his mouth. *Happy lines,* which showed his age and indicated a happy life, most likely full of joy.

Though he was not smiling at her now. Anger and disappointment shone back at her. Her heart sank. Yes, it was disappointment. How dare he be disappointed in her? He was here, too. He stood in the middle of one of Emma's events. *What does he seek here? Why is he here?* her mind swung around, *Why is he here?*

Grace stepped closer to Emma as Emma swayed, shaking her hips sensuously in what appeared to be an exotic dance the likes Grace had never seen before. Emma was about to help her find out why Winston was here.

Emma lifted her head. Her gaze settled on Grace and she squealed, "Grace!" Then she walked toward her.

Grace's lips curved up into a smile. "Dear Emma, how are you?"

"I am delighted to see you. We have all missed you." She threw her arms about Grace's shoulders and pressed her lips to Grace's.

The gentle pinch of her soft lips against Grace's mouth slid through her veins. Grace relaxed and heard Oscar's words: *"That is it, Grace. Tease her. Show me how sensual two women can be, Grace. Show me how much you love me by doing this for me."* The proper Grace trickled from her body as if water poured from her hair, placing sexual Grace firmly into her role.

Grace's hand rose and grasped the nape of Emma's neck, pulling her more closely to her. Indeed, she needed to feel the soft curve of breasts against hers to know she did well. Heat spread through her limbs and Grace's nipples pebbled into puckered peaks. Oh, she forgot how good this felt.

She slid her tongue out and pushed it into Emma's mouth. Yes, this was what she needed to feel ... desire. . . . to be the sensual woman once again.

She opened her eyes and glanced in Winston's direction. He

stood no more than two feet from her, glaring down at her and Emma. Her body tensed and her gaze darted to Markus.

His smile reassured her, all was well, that she needed this. Just because Oscar was gone, the woman she had become had not died with him. Tonight would prove that.

Winston didn't say a word but towered over them, his heat mixing with theirs. His smell, the same crisp smell of the sea she always associated with him. Grace sighed deep in her heart. She had not realized how much she had missed him. Winston was home.

What the devil was Lady Wentland doing here? *Grace!* Every fiber of his being screamed for him to grab her by the arm, drag her from this ballroom, and spank her bottom for the scandalous behavior she exhibited. Indeed, yes, a spank to her bottom. Several quick, sharp slaps with his hand so her bottom was red and his hand stung. Or with a birch—even better. He smiled, then frowned.

No, Winston, don't even think it!

She was a true English lady, yet her actions screamed this act had happened for years. He swallowed the lump lodged in his throat and glared at them. Her lips pressed and nipped at Emma's.

Emma!

Lady Grace stood in the middle of the ballroom, kissing the most expensive courtesan in London!

Blood rushed through his ears, blocking all rational thought, and his fingers fisted. Grace's hands slid down Emma's back to her waist and fluttered there.

He held in a moan at the way she moved. So sensual, so graceful, so feminine. *His Grace* had grown into a sensual woman. No! What the hell was he thinking? Images of her as the innocent Grace, her brother, and Winston talking about every subject they could think of, including the act, came to him. Her brother, his best friend, would lock Grace in the attic if he knew she was here. Winston cringed—if her brother knew he was here watching her, Winston would be challenged to a duel at dawn. Blast and damn. This was not what he had expected when he agreed to stay in this house.

Grace's fingers pinched Emma's nipple.

His cock grew noticeably heavy. With teeth clenched tight, he glanced around the room. Damn it. Not the reaction he was hoping for as he watched her flirt and tease.

His gaze continued to assess the room. He needed to focus on anything but watching her tease. How many of the men in this room watched her? How many knew who she was? Most— if not all—of the men in the room watched them. Ice slid through his veins and his short nails dug into his palms as a wave of possession captured his mind and body.

He needed to get her from here, and then erase this image of her from his mind forever. Quite so . . . she was Lady Wentland. His Grace! The pure lady she was raised to be, and as soon as he removed her from this—this event—he would recapture that image of her. Her innocent ladylike teasing as a fresh debut— that was the image he wanted to retain in his mind.

He stepped forward and reached out toward her left hand, which gripped Emma's hip. *What the hell are you doing?* His hand shook, but he couldn't stop it. His finger traced the line of Grace's middle and index finger. Bubbles of sensation tingled up the tip of his finger and constricted his lungs.

Grace moaned and her passion-filled eyes slit slightly open, catching him standing only inches from Emma's back. Her hand slid away from his touch and down to the top of Emma's thigh. Emma rocked her body toward Grace, pinning her hand between their bodies.

A lump lodged in Winston's throat and he clenched his teeth tighter. His finger traced Grace's other hand and pulled her finger from Emma's body. The heat of them wet the tips of his fingers as the soft and slender length of Grace's finger rubbed, circling his knuckles, then retreated to grip Emma once again.

He slowly lowered his hand. She kissed this woman and teased him. He should walk away. He should drag her from this room and out into the hallway and talk some sense into her. She . . . she should not be here. His brow knit tight. She was utterly captivating. If he had not known her from childhood, Grace's actions this night fit precisely what he looked for in this house.

Damn it all!

He wanted her in his bed. In all his years in India, he never dreamed about the act of sin with Grace. Long talks with Grace, yes. Teasing her . . . taunting her . . . futtering her until she was spent and lifeless—that was a thought he had restricted to the parlors of the Indian dens, where they knew his tastes, because he had discovered them there. He never considered a blooded high-born English lady would possess the skills he wished to nurture. It was Grace.

He should turn right now and walk away. He could not touch her. India represented a lifetime of experience for him. Maybe all this time had also ripened his friends, who had developed a taste for the act that was different as well.

Emma slid her hands up to Grace's face. Her fingers slid into her hair, and in one move, her other hand slid back and lightly slapped her.

Winston's eyes widened. What was going on here?

Grace moaned, leaned in, and kissed Emma's cheek. Her tongue slid out and she licked a trail to Emma's ear.

Winston's feet would not move. He shook his head and tried to clear the image from his mind. *Emma slapped Grace, and*

Grace moaned. Grace likes to be slapped. Grace liked this kind of teasing and was doing it for him. The blood in his veins rushed south. No, no, no. *This is Grace.*

Winston closed the distance between them, wrapped his hand around Grace's bicep, and pulled her from Emma.

"What are you doing, Grace? You do not belong here." His voice came out harsh.

Grace stared up at him; anger, arousal, and tears shone back. She pulled and yanked on her arm as she tried to dislodge Winston's grip.

"Grace, dear, are you well with him?" Emma's firm tone slid through his fog.

"Let go of me, Winston." Grace twisted her arm in his grip, trying to dislodge his fingers.

"She is fine, Emma." Winston held his grip on Grace's arm and turned from Emma. Grace didn't resist as he pushed through the crowd, dragging her with him. Her slippered feet scuffed along the wood floor. They reached the edge of the ballroom.

"Winston, let go of me." Her voice was a meager whisper.

"Not until we talk, Grace." His mind spun. He wanted her to leave this place, and at the same time, he wanted to bed her.

"Let go of me."

He reached the hallway and spun her about. Her slippered feet scuffed on the floor as he pressed her firmly up against the wood-paneled wall in the entrance.

"What in the devil's sake were you doing in there, Grace?" His voice shook as he stared down into her upturned face. "Have you no idea who these people are?" He pushed a palm against the wood wall above her shoulder, and with the other, he continued to hold her arm.

"Do you, Winston? Do you? These people have been my friends for the past eight years. You have no idea how much time changes a person, Winston." She turned and tried to pull from his grasp.

There was pain in her voice. She was widowed. *She's been a part of this set for the past eight years*? Her words pierced his gut, and the urge to protect her bubbled through his veins. No matter how precisely she might fit his description of what he searched for in his personal temple goddess, he needed her to leave here.

She didn't belong in a place like this. Not his Grace. Yet, this is where she had survived the last eight years. He closed his eyes. *"These people have been my friends."* How? Why had she come to know this set of people? Damnation, he had no idea.

"Grace." He slid his knee between her thighs and up against the wall behind. His hand on the paneled wall reached up and grabbed her chin. He turned her head to the side and forced her gaze to the door. "You see that door, Grace? You need to walk out it. You have never belonged with this set." The heat of her pussy seeped through his silk pantaloons and dampened his thigh. God, if she didn't leave, he would end up carrying her up the stairs and into his bed.

He held her face pinned to the wall as his eyes slid down the column of her neck and the ridge of extended flesh that the position accentuated. He leaned in, and inhaled. Sweet, creamy arousal filled his nose. Arousal from her kissing Emma? Or was her wetness desire from his touch?

His tongue slid out and glided along his lips, then touched her skin. Salt and lavender coated his taste buds. He held back a groan as he pressed more firmly to the smooth skin of her neck and slowly trailed up to her earlobe, savoring the feast of her. Curling his tongue about the drop of flesh, he sucked the small piece of her into his mouth and pressed his teeth into a button.

Grace moaned. Fisting her hands into his coat, she sagged against the wall.

"Are you staying, Grace, or walking out the door?" His words, soft, as he traced the cup of her ear with the tip of his tongue. She tasted so . . . erotic . . . so sinfully tempting.

She said not a word.

And his will for sending her home faded with each sense that she titillated. He wanted her . . . here now, against the wall as everyone passed by, but he couldn't do the act with her here. *His Grace.* "If you are staying, Grace, you will not be going back into the ball. You will be joining me in my room for this night, and everything I ask of you will be taken without hesitation or question."

Her arms and legs trembled against him and she moaned.

Her reaction to his words was what he craved. He never would have considered she could be the one. The tremble at his words, and the moan that spontaneously erupted from her—when Emma's hand slapped her in the ballroom—indicated she enjoyed pleasing and firmness.

He swallowed hard. This situation was unfurling as if someone had searched his deepest fears and his wildest fantasies and meshed them into one. No matter, he always faced his fears, but only did so with control and determination. This called for nothing less.

"Well, Grace? The door or my room? Which shall it be?"

5

Grace

Grace swallowed hard, her throat working to find the words her mind could not. What had happened here?

Winston's body pressed her to the wall. *"The door or my room?"* His words rang as some unsolved riddle in her mind.

Her heart pounded in her ears.

What did she want?

She came here tonight to be desired once again, to feel passion once more, and to retire with a single person for the night.

Winston preferred her to leave. None of this made sense. Maybe he didn't prefer that. Maybe he wanted her in his bed, but his mind was telling him . . . *No!*

"Grace?" His thigh pressed up against her heated sex.

A ripple of dew waved through her cunny and her blood heated. She slid her tongue out and wet her dry lips, wanting more of the erotic sensation. "Winston, do you desire me in your bed? Or are you saying you would take pity on me and bed me rather than watch me play with others? Or is this some other game you learned in India?"

He pulled slightly back from her and gazed at her face. "No game, Grace."

"I—if this is simply pity, I will scream, and you will be removed from my body by one of the footmen."

Winston's free hand slid to her hip and pulled her toward him. The friction as her cunt slid along his thigh shot straight up her stomach and she bit her lip, holding back a groan.

His fingers then trailed her thigh and he lifted her knee into his crotch.

His stiff erection pushed against the soft spot below her kneecap. "Does this feel like pity, Grace?"

"Mmmm, you are a man, Winston. Men get aroused simply by seeing a woman's form." Unable to hold her body's reaction at bay, she trembled against his cock.

"No, you are wrong, Grace, and you just lost your chance to decide." He let go of her face and wrapped a hand around her shoulders, pulling her to him. Heat caressed her every pore. He hefted her up like a child and she laughed.

"Winston, what are you doing?"

"Making your decision for you, Grace," he answered, tilting her back over his shoulder and heading to the stairs. Her upper body hung partially down his back as he strode up. His hard shoulder pressed into her belly, and with each step, he made his intentions clearer.

Winston Greydon was about to bed her.

A smile curved her lips. He had turned into a sexual man. He certainly handled her as Oscar had—with presence, with knowledge, with ease. Maybe this time she should not be so easy to handle.

My goodness, Grace, you have known that about him all your life. Don't fear him. He was your friend.

Reaching the second floor, he turned to the right and down a long corridor. At the end, he pushed open a door and carried her into the center of the room. The dark wood floor, the only thing before her eyes, was a stark contrast to the whites of his stockings.

He tilted her and lowered her down his body. Every pore of her being sparked and jittered, as if igniting the coals in a fire grate. Her slippers hit the floor.

Winston stood, his body still pressed to hers. He raised his hand and skimmed fingertips above her ear and into her up-done hair. "Not speaking, Grace?"

Grace kept her head tilted down and looked up at him through her eyelashes. His eyes, clear blue water, flowed with desire and his lips curved up with confidence. Winston's expertise was evident in the way he held her; in the way he pressed her to the wall in the entry; simply in the way he brushed his fingertips along her skin.

"Very well, you will be making noise soon enough." His fingers traced her collarbone and the hairs on her nape stood. He turned and walked toward the other side of the room.

She inhaled a breath and savored the feel of his finger on her skin, then glanced about the room.

Amazing! The stories of this house said each of the rooms glittered with decadence, scandalous art, and erotic delights. But this room glowed with warmth and calmness.

This room reminded her of what she had read in books of India: the heat, the lazy afternoons lounging about, because the sun shone so bright, it made everything feel red and gold, like the walls in this room. Each wall was covered in a rich red, with golden and yellow patterns of birds and flowers.

She spun about, and on the far wall, opposite from where Winston now stood, was a large copper tub set into the floor. Surrounding the tub lay red and black carpets. A stack of towels and containers perched on the edge. Three large candelabrums stood about the tub with unlit candles. She inhaled, and humid scents filled her nose. What scent was that? Cloves and . . . She could not place it. She inhaled again—a soothing aroma nonetheless.

Turning back toward Winston, she gazed at the bed. The carved platform stood only three paces from the tub. It was low to the ground and covered in the same rich crimson as the walls.

At each corner of the bed frame, there resided an elephant head carved with elaborate detail. Their smooth, wide ears tapered down to a ridged and looped trunk. Images of ankles and wrists tied to each of the four elephants' trunks as Winston's fingertips trailed her body in a fire that engulfed her and made her eyes widen. Winston. She glanced across her shoulder at him.

He stood with no shirt on, no shoes, and only his trousers. His smooth chest held no hair, not like Oscar's. His nipples peaked on rounded muscles. Grace's fingertips pinched together as if rolling the sensitive flesh that tapered down his flat stomach to the edge of his pantaloons.

"Undress, Grace."

He didn't move, but his stomach muscles visibly tensed.

"*Undress* . . ." Reaching up, she pulled the tie to her shift and the shoulders loosened.

Oscar had never asked her to undress for him. He had always been the one to disrobe her. Doing so was one of the intimacies he could do, and she had savored every brush of his fingers, hands, and lips on her skin as he did so. She worried the inside of her cheek. How should she go about undressing for a man?

How would Oscar have wanted her to undress?

Like a cat playing with its food, she would tease Winston just a bit . . . before doing as he wished.

His eyes darkened and he stared at her, unmoving.

She rotated her hips and kept her fingers tightly on the strings to her shift. In her mind, music as exotic as the ladies of India, with their dark skin and hair, drifted in the air. Their bodies, covered in rich red and green silks embroidered with gold and silver threads, danced with her.

She pressed the balls of her feet into the floor and bent her knees slightly, then rocked her hips, as Emma had been doing in the ballroom below. With each rock of her hips, she slowly turned around in a circle.

Her hands rubbed the skin of her breasts, hard nipples poked the palms of her hands. In her mind, the women of India rubbed her breasts, then trailed hot hands along her naked thighs.

"Grace!"

Grace's eyes opened, and the beautiful, exotic images faded.

"You are a delightful dancer, Grace. I wish you to *undress* for me."

Her fingers shook on the strings to her shift. *Take a deep breath, Grace, and relax.* She swallowed and lowered her eyes from his.

"Grace. Undress now." The words were soft but firm, a reminder to listen to him.

She held in a frown. He didn't wish for her seduction. He wanted her to listen to him. She did want to please him. She simply had no idea how to go about such an act. Oscar's wishes were all she understood. Yet, Oscar had said all men at their base were the same. So why wasn't he enjoying the tease? He had not enjoyed the teasing in the ballroom with Emma, either.

She closed her eyes and slid her fingers beneath the gathered shoulder of her shift. She would do as he asked. Her fingers glided along her skin in a light trace, which left goose bumps in their wake.

She imagined her fingers were Winston's slipping the cotton

fabric down her shoulder as her body trembled and her pussy clenched.

Oh, how she wanted him. Wanted his hands doing so to her body. The masculine trail of his heat on her skin. She trembled and shook with intense lust. Lust for Winston. She could not deny how he created passion in her.

She licked her lips but didn't dare open her eyes. Her heart beat in her throat as she slipped the other shoulder down to her elbow. She wished he would come show her what he wanted or would tell her from where he stood.

The crisp cotton caught on the pebbled flesh of her nipples, then slipped down to pool at her waist. The humid air caressed her naked breasts, as if his breath washed across her flesh.

She swallowed hard and pulled the sleeves down her wrists and off her fingers. The shift slid in a hushed whirl down her legs to pool at her feet. She flinched at how quickly the fabric left her body, leaving her breasts and sex exposed to his view.

She kept her head tilted down. Her eyes firmly shut. She stood and trembled, yet she was not cold. Not at all. *Relax, Grace.*

"The garters, Grace." His voice came from closer to her and off to her side.

He had moved!

She swallowed. Oh. Oh, what was he doing? She should look. Open her eyes and see where he was and what his expression was, but she couldn't. Her shoulders slumped. Her eyelids simply would not open so she could gaze upon him.

A fevered ache spread through her body. She didn't wish to know what he thought of her naked form. Her arms jumped as she fought the urge to cross her forearms over her breasts.

Why did she struggle so? On the one hand, she was shy because this was Winston; on the other, she wished him to devour her every inch. She ached for his touch . . . for his approval of what he saw.

She reached her hands down her belly to the top of her thighs, then slid lower over the soft roundness of her right leg. Reaching the gathered garter below her knee, she unfastened the silk and let the two-inch piece of cloth fall to the floor upon the heap of white that was her shift.

She did the same with her left leg and straightened her body back up to standing.

He cleared his throat, the sound coming from the other side of her. "Grace, roll your stockings down, one at a time. When you reach your slippers, leave them pooled at your ankles."

Was he circling her? What was he doing? The image of him inspecting her from every angle quickened her breath. She inhaled a shaky yet steadying breath, and then another.

The scented air in the room filled her senses and her muscles relaxed. *That is it, Grace. Don't be shy. Be bold. Be the woman Oscar wanted you to be. . . .*

That woman, so far, had angered and frustrated Winston. He said he liked her as the lady he remembered.

She was someplace in between now.

She was not the outgoing plaything Oscar wanted, nor was she the proper lady Winston remembered.

She was simply Grace.

She could be nothing more than Grace—plain and simple.

She leaned down and slid her fingertips beneath the edge of her stocking. Sliding the silk down her legs, she let it sit pooled on her ankle. She repeated the same with the other side, then stood back straight. She stood still with her eyes closed, her nipples ached and her sex throbbed.

"What are you thinking, Grace?" His voice was soft and

strong. The air swirled about her. "Do you enjoy displaying yourself for me?"

She trembled. Her legs shook. She adored his gaze upon her. No longer the innocent girl, she wanted him to ogle her mature, womanly form.

He circled her. Though she could not see his eyes, his stare caressed her skin, her hair, and her face. All his thoughts and his energy were on her. He looked her over from a very close distance, as if she were a piece of art he appreciated. She inhaled and smelled nothing but him.

"Answer, Grace."

What had he asked her? If she enjoyed displaying herself for him. "A mixture."

He laughed. " 'A mixture.' " The two small words held the remains of his laugh. "Indeed. You are unsure who you are, Grace? The perfect lady? The trained plaything? A mixture of boldness and shyness. Your body reactions show your struggle. The way you undress for me and keep your eyes closed. You are shy, Grace. Take down your hair."

She lifted her hands to her upswept hair. Her shaking fingers pulled out the first of the many pins. Each tiny piece of metal she pulled, her curly hair loosened.

She inhaled deeply, simply feeling him. The heat of his body enfolded her . . . closer . . . closer as he moved to her while she worked her hair, letting each pin simply fall from her fingertips as she tugged it from her heavy locks.

In a rush, it tumbled down, washing her shoulders and back in cool silkiness.

She swallowed as quivers of excitement rippled through her.

"Open your eyes, Grace." The smell of port and tobacco infused her.

She slit her eyes open, her gaze fixed firmly down. His bare feet in view. His fingers slid up her temple and into her hair.

The caress was so gentle yet firm, her head gently nuzzled into his palm. The fingers in her hair fisted and he pulled the hair taut. Slowly he tilted her head back. Her gaze studied his face.

He smiled at her. The blacks of his eyes engulfed the sapphire blue. Winston. Winston would show her . . .

Just what Winston would show her, she simply couldn't fathom.

6

Grace

Winston stared into smoky green eyes and the swirl of emotion—the struggle within herself about the woman she had become. He would help her decipher the struggle. Help her to understand who she was and where she could find fulfillment. He had known her all of her childhood.

He knew her true self, the playful wit they had shared as youngsters. That was still all there, but it had been turned into sexual energy. He would pull her back. Make her see she didn't need to use the act of seduction—the way she had with Emma—on him. She could be the woman, the *lady*, who wished to be proper, who wished to please, as well as the wanton she obviously was instructed, and loved, to be.

His stomach pinched. She would be his wanton desire. Winston narrowed his eyes. Indeed, he wanted to instruct her to please him the way he enjoyed and she would be easy to instruct. In the depths of her eyes, he could see the same innocent will to please, but she was not the same naïve girl he left. She had grown and now had experiences and desires of her own.

He tightened the grip in her hair and watched her body relax in a wave. Indeed, she always had pleased him. When they were youngsters, she had shown him hers, and in return he had rewarded her with a mystery she had asked him about. He blew out a breath through his nose. He couldn't remember the name of the book. All he remembered was the look of joy on her face when he handed the bound pages to her.

He had no doubt she would please him. "Grace, will you allow me to touch you the way I please?"

Grace's eyes lit up, the smoke of the green sparked to embers of a slow-burning fire. "Indeed." A shiver shook her body and the fire seeped through her.

Winston's breath caught. Grace's passions astounded him, her ability to give herself so quickly to him. . . . Every fine hair on the back of his neck rose in arousal. "Very good, Grace."

He let his grip of her hair loose. The long, silky locks caressed his skin as he weeded his fingers free of her curls. Calmly he stepped to the side of her, arousal pushing his longing to smell all of her, to taste her, to an undeniable pitch.

She turned her head in his direction, her eyes following him as he walked toward the bed. "Winston?"

"Yes, Grace?" He stared at the bed. Where would he begin this . . . this start of what would become them?

"When did you return from India, and why did you not contact my brother or me?"

India. She would love the heat there. The cold and damp of England had always given her the shivers. He wasn't too pleased with the rainy season here himself. "I returned a fortnight past." He glanced at her. The latter part of her question, he would not answer. Not now. How could he describe to her that he had not contacted her because his priority when he returned was to find a woman in England that was all he wished—the wanton he could train, the lady he could cherish. He never imagined Grace might fit his needs.

She bit her lip in the same fashion she had all the years he had known her. Her nervous habit that said she also had questions. Questions he would have plenty of time to answer, and would over time.

At this moment, he would instruct her, make her quiver and shake with need for him, and him alone.

"Grace, come. Sit on the edge of the bed." He walked to the bed, a semireplica of the ones used in Indian pleasures.

He liked the carved elephants instead of simple metal rings found on the ones in most of the pleasure temples there. The warm wood carvings made the room look more elegant and less punishmentlike. He never punished. There was nothing like hearing a woman moan—the rush of breath as she spent was what he enjoyed more than anything.

The air about him heated and the scent of Grace tightened his lungs. . . .

Grace.

Grace moaning.

His cock tingled and the skin tightened over the flesh beneath the cloth of his trousers.

He glanced over his shoulder at her. She stood an arm's breadth from him, auburn hair down to the small of her back and a mix of desire and fear in her eyes. So beautiful was the contradiction of Grace.

Her fear, no matter what fear it was, would only fuel her spend. Indeed. He would have Grace spending within moments of touching her.

Grace stepped in between him and the bed, then gingerly sat on the edge. She tilted her head up and stared at him waiting . . . expectant of a futter.

He kneeled down next to her. A quick diddle was not what he enjoyed. Teasing, holding off until the last moment was what brought him thrills.

His fingertips gently grazed down the outsides of her legs. Grace's muscles tensed beneath his fingers' touch. Reaching the stockings, slouched at her ankles, he lifted her left leg and pulled her green slipper from her foot.

He grinned.

Her feet were anything but dainty. In all the years he had known Grace, he had never looked at her slippers. With every tick of the clock, he learned something new about the woman, whom he thought he had known entirely when he was a young man.

He grabbed the thin material webbed between her toes and pinched it. She didn't make a sound or a motion. Sliding the other hand down to cradle her calf, his fingers pulled on the stocking.

He needed to hear her . . . the sound of her breath hitch.

The quiver of her foot beneath his hands . . .

Anything!

He needed to know physically she was affected by his touch. Mentally, her thoughts were already with him.

Ever so slowly the length tugged down her foot, and with each bit, he listened. Waiting . . . willing her to react to the stocking's slow caress.

He stared at the stocking as he pulled. The last covered parts of her body were revealed to him bit by bit. All by his doing, the subtle contrast of her pale white ankle, the arch of her foot, and her long fingerlike toes. The top band of the stocking reached the crease of her toes—

Grace's breath hitched and her calf beneath his palm trembled. His muscles relaxed and he sighed. He had not realized his muscles had been so tense as he waited for her response.

The stocking traveled to the floor, leaving her wearing nothing at all on that side of her body.

She blew out a long, broken breath.

The sound trembled through his body, and his heart sped. He shifted in his crouched position, adjusting to remove the next stocking. She quivered again. Anticipation built within her and him. The rush of air through her lips was the sound he wanted more and more of. The proof he affected her, and how deeply.

He set her foot back on the thick wool carpet and reached for her second ankle.

"No doubts, Winston?"

He stared up at her face. There was a pinch between her brow, and her eyes shone soft and caring. She worried, an insecurity or some such. . . . "No doubts whatsoever." He was not sure what she was asking him; the question lacked specifics, but at the moment, it didn't matter. This was what he wanted and he was positive about that. Nothing mattered but Grace trembling to the ministrations of his hands, of his words, of his will.

He trailed his hands down the outside of her opposite calf to the stocking gathered in a slouch of wrinkles. Her muscles jumped and she smothered back a giggle.

He remembered from their younger years, she was ticklish. He grasped her heel once more and slid the slipper from her foot. He dragged his fingers down to the top of her foot, gently tapping, then twisted his wrist to lightly pet the arch on the underside.

She squirmed but didn't pull her foot from him. He didn't look up at her, but he grinned. Oh, the fun he would have teasing her.

He gripped the stocking by her big toe and twisted the fabric. Each twist of the loose material coiled into a rope, tugging as it slid from her smooth ivory skin. Grace trembled, her legs shaking as the last section slid from the tip of her foot. An intense rush of breath tumbled from her lips.

His eyes narrowed. There were so many questions about her

to which he didn't know the answers. Questions to which he was not sure he wanted to understand the answers. The thought of her in another man's bed . . . the thought of her as she was down in the ballroom with Emma—these were at the edges of what he could bear to think about Lady Wentland.

He held her foot extended out from her body, his hand firmly clasped about her ankle.

He stared at her foot; he knew he shouldn't consider asking this, but this was Grace. As young adults, they had talked about everything. He had to know some of what happened in her marriage. "Grace, I can tell you have been instructed more so than a typical English wife. What I don't understand is for what purpose?"

Her body tensed. "I don't understand what you ask, Winston."

He glanced up to her jade eyes, which were filled with fear.

He inwardly grimaced. He shouldn't have pushed. Not yet. "No matter, I will discover all your newly formed secrets." And he would. He would pair each one with one of her old ones. Like her kiss with Tommy, the butler's son. Finding out her new secrets would not be hard; he would simply do so, one touch at a time.

"Grace, I am going to fill the bath. We will clean each other." Winston stood and walked to the large tub, which was set into the floor. The smooth copper shimmered with water. Thank heavens he had the servant fill the tub with boiling water when he arrived. The water should still be warm, and the coals on the underside kept it nicely heated.

He ran his finger along the edge of the first container's lid and opened it. A mixture of cloves and lavender resided within. Taking a large pinch of the spices, he dropped them into the steaming bath.

He glanced over his shoulder to see Grace watching him.

She sat in the same position that he had left her in, legs parted and hands on each side of her.

He could see all of her—from her rounded shoulders to the slope of her generous breasts tipped with a dusty coral hue, down her smooth stomach to the accentuated curve of her hip. He wanted to drag his tongue over her body. The sweet salt of her skin would tingle his taste buds. The curled hairs at the apex of her thighs glistened with moisture. Moisture he had created, but had yet to touch. He licked his lips. Nor had he tasted. He needed to taste her, to slide his greedy tongue down between her sex lips, spreading them wide so he could flick her bud and lap at the honey spilling from her core.

"Come, Grace."

She stood with a smooth motion and walked toward him. Her muscles were like soft butter that slightly jiggled as she stepped. She turned out to be a beautiful woman, like the heavenly creatures in paintings that hung on the walls of museums. She was what men adored and women aspired to be. His cock grew heavy in his pantaloons. She would be his after this night— his to explore, cherish, and adore.

"Winston, I am confused."

"What about, Grace?"

"Why did you not simply take me there on the bed? I saw the desire in your eyes. Why do you wish to bathe me?"

Winston smiled contentedly. She was his straightforward Grace. "My intimate preferences all come from Indian traditions. One of them is bathing—cleaning each other so that you can touch and taste each other's essence without the tastes of other elements. Smell and taste are so much a part of the Indian culture that it is also in the way they futter."

"We will bathe each other?"

"Quite so. I will also shave you."

Grace's eyes widened. "Shave me?"

He grinned. "Indeed. Don't be frightened, Grace. I have shaved a woman's mound and lips. When in India, I also gave up having a personal valet for bathing and shaving. I preferred to have my woman or myself shave me. There is something intimate about the act."

"Oh." The muscles of Grace's throat worked.

She struggled with some emotion—possibly a memory. "You may still leave, Grace. But if you walk out my bedroom door, I cannot permit you to stay at such an event without me."

"I came to this event with friends, Winston, and I shall leave with them. Not when you tell me to."

Winston slowly stood to his full height, his throat constricting about his words. "No, Grace." His fingers slid into her auburn locks and clenched. He bent her head backward and forced her gaze to meet his eyes. "I want to instruct you, Grace. To teach you how to please me. Is that something you wish?"

Desire swirled in the depths of jade and she bit her lip.

"If you don't want me, Grace, I cannot permit you to stay. I want you in my bed, Grace. I will move the earth to keep you safe. I cannot watch you with another."

A tremble racked Grace and she shook against his body. Deep in his chest, he held in a moan. She wanted him, but still she fought that urge.

"The water may be hot, Grace, but not too deep. I will keep you safe, step in."

7

Lilly

Lilly stood at the edge of the ballroom. She couldn't tear her eyes away from Grace as she kissed and touched another woman in the center of the room. Lilly's heart pounded in her breast so hard, she feared the pulse actually moved her body. She inhaled, trying to steady herself, and smelled a heavy tart scent. What was that smell? She inhaled again, and the hairs on her neck stood in a wave of heat.

Grace's hands fluttered along the woman's shoulder and hip. *Stop staring, Lilly.* She pulled her gaze from Grace and glanced about the room.

Men and woman flirted, touched, and laughed. A man bent a woman over a chair and lifted up her skirt. *Oh!* Lilly squeezed her eyes shut and turned her head in another direction.

She surely didn't need to see a woman's large, round bum at this moment. This entire day needed to be a dream she awoke from in a moment and did not have any recollection of.

A chill raced across the exposed skin of her chest and her hands slid over the tops of her breasts in an attempt to cover them.

She cringed. Her behavior this night would cause her mother to roll straight to her grave. *Sorry, Mama.* If her father were alive and caught her, she would be birched, and soundly. She straightened her shoulders. An educational experience. She continued to glance about the room, not allowing her eyes to settle for too long on any one particular person.

She recognized several of the men in the room. Some wore masks; others did not, as if daring someone to say something to them.

Good Lord! She closed her eyes as a man near her wrapped his hands about a woman draped in red silk and squeezed her breasts from behind. The woman squealed and turned in to him, kissing him forcibly on the mouth.

The Marquess of Brummelton.

He was known for this kind of behavior, and his brother worse. He had, on occasion, visited her father before he passed. She always thought he had kind eyes and a soft, sad smile. How a man with such a soul could have a reputation as scandalous as his, she never would know.

She glanced around the room again and frowned. Brian was nowhere. Maybe he left? *No, don't be silly, Lilly.* She sighed. Her gut tingled deep down that he was here. She simply needed to find out what the respectable reason was for his presence—a plausible reason that would counter the sinking feeling in her gut and would ease the suspicions tangling in her mind.

Possibly, this act of his was some arrogant man's game to prove his bottom to his new peers. She would find him and see his purpose. If it was as the townsfolk said . . .

Her heart sank down and hovered above her stomach. Such an odd feeling to have little faith in a man she had known all her life—or had she? This certainly was not the acts of the man she had played with in the gardens at Rousemore Hall.

He was here, surrounded by debauchery, lewd men, and

scandalously easy women. Never would she have imagined Brian associating himself with such lowly activity. Something had changed when he went to school. *This* had changed. Or was this part of being human, part of growing up? She frowned as Grace's words made her think. She had grown up simply. Maybe this was what people did when raised with more adventuresome parents.

A woman dressed in a thin, translucent material twirled before Lilly. She was thin and tall, with large nipples on her breasts. The woman's gaze kept snapping, over and over again, to a man located over Lilly's left shoulder.

Lilly turned her head to the left. Vincent St. Jerome stood no more than an arm's reach away and stared directly at her. *Her!* Not the woman twirling for his attention. His wolfish gray eyes held an intensity that made all the hairs on her arms stand.

He stepped forward and smiled.

Her eyes widened. Oh, no! He approached her. What did she say to such a man? A large lump formed in her throat and she swallowed hard. *Come here often? Sweet Jesus, Lilly, no!* His lip quirked up and she shook her head to herself. She couldn't.

His hand rose slowly, inching toward her face. "You have a—"

"No!" She turned around and hastily rushed in the opposite direction. Her heart hammered in her throat. There was no way she could converse with him. She headed toward the opposite end of the ballroom, toward a large arch that led into another room.

She glanced over her shoulder and he was gone. She let out a long stream of breath and her shoulders relaxed.

Stepping through the arch, and into the next room, women of various shapes and ages were all about. They catered to the men, who sat on couches or stood by the walls. Or was it the other way around? Did the men wait on the women?

They all wore hardly any clothing—corsets, bloomers, shifts, or some variation of the three. Lilly held back her breath. *My . . .* She squeezed her eyes shut for an instant. She wore the same. As she glanced around, no one looked at her strangely. She appeared as if she were one of them.

Oh, how she had acted in the ballroom had made her stand out. They all expected her to act experienced, as these women did. Every fiber in her wanted to run. Her legs trembled with the conflict of staying versus fleeing this foreign world where her brother and so many others were comfortable. *Come on, Lilly, you can do this. Give Brian a chance, as Grace said.* She stepped farther into the room.

Men stared at her, some leered. She was a lamb who wandered into a pack of wolves.

Smile, Lilly. She forced her lips up into a smile. A man with blond hair swept back into a queue down his back stood and came toward her. She didn't recognize him. She would have to talk and flirt with him, or everyone would see her as the impostor that she was. Her throat grew tight and her heart thumped as if a galloping horse were in her breast.

"Good evening, ma'am."

"Indeed."

"I am Lord Barkington. What shall I call you?"

"Veronica, sir. It is a pleasure to meet you." She swallowed and tried not to show her unease. *See, Lilly, you can do this . . . just play the part.*

"Well, Veronica. Are you interested in a little conversation? Maybe some wine?"

He says 'Conversation'? Oh, um. . . .

She glanced over at the footmen, who stood about with silver trays and carafes of wine perched on top, and her throat went dry. Wine would be nice. The sweet taste might improve her fortitude and fix her resolve to remain as long as it took to find Brian. Indeed, one glass would set her nerves well.

"Yes, please, Lord Barkington. A glass of wine would be lovely."

"Very well, Veronica. Have a seat on the settee and I will fetch us some." He turned and caught the eye of one of the footmen. He waved his hand and nodded his head, and as she sat upon the soft velvet of the large settee, a tray with wine and pastries was set before them.

She watched as his long, thin fingers grasped tiny pastries and put them one at a time onto a plate. "These tiny bits will help keep your wits about you as you imbibe in some strong, sweet wine."

Her stomach growled.

Maybe this was a good thing. She could eat, have a glass of wine, and maybe Brian would simply walk right past her.

A shadow crossed her lap and the little hairs on her neck tingled. The air about her radiated with heat and swirls of the sweet smell of the fresh, upturned earth. She trembled as if she had stepped out of this dream and into the calm of her early-dawn walks through the woods.

"You are the most stunning creation I have set eyes on this night. Pure innocence ready to be tainted."

She closed her eyes and let the words roll over her. She had never once in her life been called "stunning," and now another person had used that very adjective about her this evening. This was a night of pretend for her, was it not? Was she stunning? She had no idea how to play that part.

"Pardon me, Veronica." Lord Barkington's voice snapped her from her peaceful dreaming. "St. Jerome."

St. Jerome . . . she couldn't look at him. She looked up at Lord Barkington.

"Your wine, Veronica."

"Thank you, my lord." She reached her hand out to grasp the glass and her arm trembled.

"It appears you need more than a little wine, my dear." St. Jerome's voice sent odd yet delightful twinges straight through her belly. Indeed, he was the scandalous rogue.

She wrapped her fingers around the stem of the glass and pulled the cup toward her lips. Consuming vast amounts of wine was an excellent idea. She inhaled and the cool liquid slid into her mouth. It tasted of rosy grapes, sweet tangy currents, and lavender. *Mmmm. A delightful wine.*

She swallowed and then looked up into Lord Barkington's eyes. "Thank you."

"My pleasure, dear ma'am." He stared at St. Jerome, then shook his head and sighed. "St. Jerome, this is Veronica."

St. Jerome stepped in front of her, and she turned her head to meet his gaze straight on.

His red tongue slid out and wet his lips. Then he winked. "You are certainly all I am hungry for this night, Verrrrrr-onica. Such a succulent name. You will be my dessert this night."

A gasp sprang from her lips. He truly wanted to shock her! She would not act that innocent part, but she had no clue how *not* to be innocent. She was innocent . . . though she had once kissed Timothy, the stable hand's son, and had seen the maid and the miller's son in the woods. Her cheeks grew toasty warm.

"Such a delightful, innocent blush, Veronica. I can only imagine the rosy hue of the rest of you at this moment. Will you show me more?"

Had he read her thoughts? She closed her eyes. *Don't be silly, Lilly. No one can read thoughts. He saw you blush.* She sighed and brought the images of the maid and the boy in the woods to mind. Her maid was pinned up against a tree, her skirts pushed up and her legs wrapped about his waist. He rocked his hips over and over into her as she moaned and clutched at his shoulders. What he actually was doing with his body and her maid's, Lilly had little education.

Lilly opened her eyes and stared into the eyes of a man who was sin and scandal and everything she would normally never converse with. *You can do this, Lilly. It is all a theatrical.*

"I am far from the newborn you see me as, sir. Though I am not the skilled courtesan you hope I am, either." Her stomach fluttered, but she kept her gaze locked with his.

"Indeed, Veronica. You are precisely what I want at this moment."

This moment indeed! Next week he would have another woman in his view. . . . Next week? No, give him five moments. She grinned and raised her glass of wine to her lips to cover her silliness. She gulped a large swallow.

All three of them looked at her glass. There only remained a small swallow in the bottom. Her lips quirked up slightly. *My!*

"I was thirsty, sirs."

St. Jerome looked to Lord Barkington and raised an eyebrow. "Indeed. Shall I get you more, Veronica?"

The wine had helped her a bit. "Indeed, St. Jerome. I shall love to indulge in another glass of excellent wine."

His lips curled up and he glanced back at Lord Barkington, whose eyebrows pulled together upon his stare.

"I shall return, Veronica. Barkington." He inclined his head and went over to another table.

He certainly was a handsome man. In his black-and-white evening attire, his clothing blended in with all the others in the room, but his eyes. . . . They were a gray like she had never seen—like a wolf, his soul was poised and determined. The way he walked, with long strides and purpose, showed his confidence. His determination to have whatever it was he sought, whatever it was he hungered for.

Indeed . . . hungered for at that moment. He grasped a glass and one of the carafes that was settled on the table.

"Veronica." Lord Barkington slid his ice-cold finger up the exposed flesh of her bicep.

Her skin tingled and she jerked her head in his direction. "Yes, Lord Barkington?"

"Are you in negotiations with anyone here?"

"No, this is my first night at such an event. I don't particularly know exactly what I am looking for . . . yet."

"Oh. So you are perusing, are you then? Looking for the best arrangement, for the best protector. That is a smart thing to do." He paused and watched her intently.

Arrangements? Protectors? Who did they think they were fooling with talk of such things? All of the men in this room searched for a quick—her face grew impossibly warm—quick join with a woman.

"Don't throw all your talents toward the handsome ones, Veronica. Word is, St. Jerome will marry soon and that will pull his attentions from whomever he protects. If he protects anyone once he weds."

"Pardon, sir? I don't understand. I would imagine he will always have a mistress."

"Doubtful, he has always been a one-woman kind of man. Amelia was his mistress for seven years."

Her eyes widened. Impossible! She let that information swirl into her mind. Her idea of a man she always thought of as a scandalous rogue was maybe false? *No, he is a rogue—no matter. Simply look at how he's talked to you thus far tonight. Though it is possible he had not had a different mistress every day.*

"Pardon, sir. But all the past weeks gossip about him and Amelia and their breakup was stated to be over his dalliances." Lilly stared at Lord Barkington intently.

"St. Jerome never futtered other women. Amelia was his outlet and he didn't want to be with anyone besides her. He does have women friends, though, and Amelia is intensely jealous. She will have a hard time finding a new protector because of her jealous rages. They were all present to all of us in this set. I considered her, but you are so much more my flavor, Veronica."

She looked up at St. Jerome as Barkington continued to babble on. He stood at the table staring at her, and she tilted her head to the side. Could it be possible? Had she and everyone in the ton misunderstood him?

His gray eyes stared at her as if he were a wolf that wanted to eat her, as he had stated only moments before. He had come here with her brother. Maybe he knew where Brian was to be found.

"Veronica, try one of these delightful little pastries."

Lilly turned her head back toward Lord Barkington. He held out a small white sugar-covered treat. His hand rose toward her mouth and she opened it as the pastry touched her bottom lip. Her gaze went back to St. Jerome as he stood in the exact same place, wine in hand, and simply studied her.

She closed her lips around the sweet and chewed, but didn't taste its delight. Her mind spun. Had she misunderstood everything that was society? What was right and wrong?

Had she somehow simply taken what others said as true—without forming an opinion of her own?

St. Jerome walked toward them once more. She swallowed and watched him the entire way to the settee. She stared up at him. He held out the carafe of wine.

"Hold your glass out, Veronica, and I shall refill it for you."

She held up the glass and he poured. His eyes fixed on the glass. She watched him. He stopped the flow of wine when it was about half full. He looked first to Barkington, then back to her.

"Have you reached an arrangement with Barkington, Veronica?"

"No!" She glanced back at Barkington. "We were talking about arrangements, but I am new and particular as to what I will be arranging with anyone. It certainly will not happen here this night." She had no clue what arrangements meant, besides you futtered and did it whenever your protector asked for it. She needed to get out of here with her reputation intact. She reached up and straightened her mask.

"You should take that off. We would love to see your beautiful face fully." Lord Barkington's hand headed toward the ties to her mask.

"No—"

St. Jerome's arm stopped him. "I like the mystery. Leave it alone."

Lilly visibly relaxed, then raised her glass to her lips and downed the entire contents.

8

Lilly

Vincent St. Jerome looked down on this innocent beauty. She was a puzzle he planned to figure out. She dressed like a skilled courtesan—yet, as she said, she was not skilled. Emma had taken her under her wing, that mask was unmistakably Emma's. He remembered it from the last ball she held with Rupert. Her blond hair upswept with ruby pins and the delicious red corset she wore. Amelia had raged about his comment on how stunningly Emma had presented herself that night. Letting Amelia go had twisted his emotions. She simply was not right for him.

At times Emma did play an innocent well, though she also played the seductress, which was more of her natural inclination. Veronica played innocence well . . . and he had a feeling she probably had seen little of the underbelly of the upper class. She was what he looked for this night—a distraction whom he could teach a thing or two. Then he would wed his bride and teach her all he wished her to know.

"Veronica, it seems you indeed are parched tonight. I am thinking, though, that possibly you might wish to see some more of this lovely house, if you have not."

She glanced at Lord Barkington, then back to St. Jerome. Barkington was such a scoundrel. Proper on the outside and an evil man within. Veronica was far too untutored and sweet to enjoy anything he had to offer her. His mind twists would have her sobbing within two chimes of the clock.

He set the carafe of wine on a table beside the settee and held out his hand to her.

"I have not actually. Only one of the bedrooms," she replied.

A bedchamber is all? Well, he would show her the secrets that resided within. Her fingers slid into his hand and a jolt of sensual energy slid up his arm and his cock twitched. This would be his last tryst with a woman other than the one he chose as his bride.

"Actually, if you wouldn't mind, St. Jerome, I am trying to locate a gentleman friend of mine . . . so a tour would be wonderful."

"A gentleman friend?"

"Oh, no, not that way. He truly is simply a friend and not a carnal kind of friend. More like a girlfriend in a sense."

"Interesting. A girlfriend that is a man, and a gentleman no less. I can't wait to see who this *man* is."

Curiosity pulsed through him. He was acquainted with most, if not all, of the gentlemen here tonight. Who was Veronica? A woman of her quality who was here with one of the rogues as a friend! He didn't bite that hook. If that were true, she would not have gone unnoticed by him until now.

He turned her about and they headed out into the main hall. The small feel of her as she strolled beside him calmed him, and an indescribable need to protect her washed through his being. He shook his head. It would figure he would find a woman he wished to protect and nurture when he couldn't.

Well, for this night . . . he could teach her. Start her off in this circle right. Point out the men who had strange tastes and the ones that simply wanted a companion because their marriages were so horridly matched.

It was proper to set her out in a positive direction. Finding one's way in this set of amours when you had little experience or knowledge was enough to send any new unaccompanied miss scurrying into bed with the first rogue she came across— simply for an anchor and guidance. He smiled to himself. Lucky rogue indeed.

"I have heard so many things about this house, both splendid and scandalous." She swayed slightly to the right and bumped into him.

His lips curled up into a smile. *Two glasses of wine? Indeed.* He had thought Barkington might have slipped something into the first glass, but he was unsure. He still was uncertain. Besides, the slight sway to her walk indicated she might simply be a bit tipsy. That was fine. Tipsy he could work with. . . . Erotically charged he could not. He liked his women when they truly wished to bed him, not because some herb influenced them.

"What would you like to see the most, Veronica?"

She timidly looked around the hall. "I am not sure, St. Jerome. I am honored that you are my guide. What would you suggest?"

"Lovely Veronica, what I wish to show you has nothing to do with the building per se. I would like to show you what to look for in a protector. Though I think that in doing such, we will most likely see most of the house and may possibly find your *female* gentleman." His lips curved up into a smile he had not felt in weeks.

She smiled and bumped into him in a playful manner he had not experienced since his teen years. She was indeed a bit in her cups.

He slowly slid his hand around her shoulder, pulling her closer to him. She didn't pull away or hesitate.

"Is this all right, Veronica?"

She looked up at him from the crook of his arm. Confusion swirled in the depths of her eyes. "Yes, I guess so." She continued to look up at him and a shy smile curved her lips. "I have never walked this close to a man before. It feels . . . nice."

She certainly did play up the innocence role perfectly. He looked at the wall—two paintings down and three red flowers to the right and the handle should be.

"What are you doing?"

"You will see, lovely Veronica."

He slid his hand until he hit the white painted handle completely hidden in the pattern on the wall. He pushed it down and pulled the narrow, tall door open. Looking down into beautiful brown eyes, he grinned, then winked.

"Ready to venture into the world of the unknown?" He smiled a smile of complete wickedness. "Turn back now, innocent Veronica, or abandon all hope for a sheltered existence!"

She bit her lower lip and glanced into the glowing corridor, then back at him. Their eyes held and her chest expanded as she inhaled a deep breath and let it out slowly.

She was nervous. "I promise, Veronica, I only wish to teach you. Show you what is what—that is, unless you tell me you wish for more."

She looked back in the lit doorway. Glanced from the corner of her eye back to him then stepped inside.

He blew out a long, frustrated breath. This was going to be one long and torturous lesson with a vixen who had no idea she was one.

9

Grace

Grace stared at the tub and the water swirling with spices.

She inhaled deeply and the scent of cloves and lavender filled her nose. He didn't talk about the bath when he said such words. He referred to himself. She sighed. . . . He wanted her to take the leap and be his. The steam from the water indicated the temperature was, as he said, hot. The bath would help to relax her.

Or would it? Winston had something planned. He said he would shave her. Was that something exotic he had learned in his travels? Little did he know, the most exotic thing he could do for her would be simply to futter her. To start the act and have him be the only one who touched or joined with her.

She tilted her head to the side. Really, she didn't care what he had planned. She wanted this experience with him, on this night, and she was more than willing to take the risk and step into the deep, or not so deep, hot water.

Grace grasped Winston's forearm and the muscles tightened to rock beneath her fingers. As a youth, he had been strong but lanky. Now he was defined, robust, a grown man in every way.

She gazed up at him and steel blue eyes liquefied into the bluest of ocean depths. She swallowed hard. He truly desired her. This was not simply a wish to remove her from the scandalous nature of her acts downstairs. How long had amorous feelings lived deep within him? Her hands trembled. She was more than terrified to ask that question.

She stepped down into the tub, her gaze never breaking the connection with his intense blue orbs.

The water slid up her skin like the finest velvet, warm and soft but not scalding. When her foot reached the bottom, the water came to the apex of her thighs. She lifted her other leg down and stepped fully into the tub. The warmth of the water sapped her energy and pulled her deep into its emotional depths. She relaxed, wanting nothing more than to float in the comfort Winston would show her.

Winston smiled down at her, and then turned away. Her hand slipped from his forearm as he walked toward the bed. Grace's gaze traveled along his shoulders to the column of flesh that led south, disappearing into the waistline of his pantaloons and the round swell of his bottom.

His bum . . . she imagined digging her fingers into the taut flesh as he lay atop her, his prick buried deep in the silk depths of her oiled cunt.

Her tongue thickened in her mouth, and her throat tightened. She would feel him deep in her this night. She would feel him to her soul. . . . Her heart swelled in her chest. *No, Grace. This is not about love. This is only about desire. You know that.*

He grasped a burning candle on the stand by the bed and turned back toward her. His muscles bunched in his arms and her heart leapt, lodging into her throat. She couldn't breathe. *Stop it, Grace. He simply picked up a candle. There is no need to be emotional from such an act.*

He reached the first of the three candelabrum set around the tub and set to work lighting each one. The room radiated to light.

Winston turned toward her and his gaze slid down her body. She looked down to see her figure fully illuminated in the water. *Oh!* She fought with her hands to cover her body from his view, then closed her eyes. *Come now, Grace. . . . Why are you so shy in front of him? Most of the people in this house have seen you barely covered. Why is this so different?*

She kept her gaze tilted down, reopened her eyes, and stared into the water. Spices floated on the surface and also gathered on the bottom. At each end of the copper tub were benchlike seats that would allow two people to sit facing each other in the tub with their knees bent in the middle. Would he be joining her in the tub? She hoped so.

"Grace." Winston's hand appeared into view. "I want you to first put one of your feet up on the bench by me, then your other foot up on the bench by you."

Grace's head tilted up to see his face. "Pardon?"

"I will not repeat myself so you have longer to absorb and think of what to say." He wiggled his fingers in front of her. "Give me your hand and I will assist you."

Grace stared back at his hand. Each moment she had spent in Winston's presence was different from the last. Nothing that happened in this tub would be what she thought would have happened. She swallowed hard. She had no idea what he was going to do to her. Chills raced along her skin and her heart sped. She was thrilled and scared all at once.

"Grace." Winston opened and closed the fingers of his outstretched hand.

He wanted her to spread her core open for him above the water. A quiver racked her body as the fever of his words took hold.

She closed her eyes and imagined his thick fingers sliding

73

along her oiled labia, then parting her. Tingles of wetness coated the walls of her cunny and she opened her eyes and stared at his fingers. Those fingers would frig her. "I can do it myself." She could stand on her own as he inspected her.

"Very well." Winston retracted his hand.

Grace lifted her right foot and placed it on the first bench. The water only covered halfway up to her knee. The coolness of the air tingled her wet skin and goose bumps rose along the exposed part of her leg.

She turned and looked at the bench at the opposite end of the tub. It was not far, but how would she accomplish this?

She stepped up fully onto the right-end bench and then stepped across. Her foot hit the other side and stuck. She turned toward Winston, but she still refused to look him in the eye. She stared down her body. My God, her pussy was gaping open. She flaunted her sex directly in Winston's view, while daring him to touch her.

"Indeed, Grace, you are exposed to me. Fully pouting open like a flower in bloom."

The laughter in his voice rushed warmth through her veins.

"Such a pretty blush, Grace. Strange, isn't it? That blush was nonexistent in the ballroom. Why is that, Grace?"

" 'Why'?" Her word came out a whisper.

"There is no need to repeat the question, Grace."

She swallowed hard. *Why? Because I have had a fancy for you all my life. Because you are a man that intimidates my heart. Because you are a childhood friend that knows only the pure Grace, not the one used by her husband as some breeding stock to be passed about....*

"Because I like you, Winston." Indeed, that was true, and so much less complicated.

"And you held no fancy for Emma? That, I do not believe, my dear—"

"No, I do, but that is different. That was for attention."

"*Attention?* I don't think so. You knew what you were doing and were enjoying yourself. There is no need, Grace, for you to put on favors as such, unless you find pleasure in them." He stepped closer to the tub, his eyes level with her breasts.

Her nipples pointed and her breasts swelled. *Oh, please let him touch me. Let him breathe a long, hot breath against the tips of my nipples. Or graze his hands over the curve of my hip.* She held her breath and closed her eyes, waiting. But nothing came.

"Grace, you see that ring above your head?"

" 'Ring'?"

"No repeating, Grace."

She had not realized how she repeated things back to people when she was uncomfortable. "Pardon me." She looked up. Hanging from the red-and-gold-painted ceiling was a six-inch metal circle. She nodded.

"Reach up and grasp it with both your hands."

She glanced back at him, then at the ring. Images of her holding on as he did . . . oh, as his hands slid up her inner thighs and parted her folds. His thick fingers glided into her well-oiled pussy as she dangled, quivering and open to anything he willed.

She swallowed hard and raised her trembling left hand up to the ring. Her fingers wrapped the curve. To grab the loop more securely, she would need to raise up on her tiptoes a fraction.

"Grasp the metal with your whole hand, Grace. You need to be stable."

Her throat tightened again and she slid the rest of her hand through the slick metal and pulled her body up onto her tiptoes. She wavered, tottering back, and grasped the ring with her right hand to hold her balance.

"Very, very good girl, Grace."

She hid the side of her face into the soft underside of her right arm and watched him with her left eye only. She couldn't believe she was doing this. She had told herself she would do as her body wished this night and ignore caution. This was only the beginning . . . of a night that promised to be exceptional.

Winston stepped down into the tub, leaving his pants fully on.

Why would he do that? They would stick horridly when he went to take them off.

His fingertips lightly brushed the inside of her knee.

Her leg muscles jumped and a rippling of sensations rose up her leg and through her sex. Her button throbbed with acute precision, and her need to be touched by him slickened her folds.

His fingers slid up the inside of her thigh, stopping at the crease to her pussy. She stood completely open to him, yet he went no farther. Her mind focused intently on his finger on that spot—the pressure, the exact size of the tip of his finger, and the throbbing underneath. His heat pierced straight to her core.

"Close your eyes, Grace." His low, demanding voice caused every fine hair on her body to rise, and her eyes fluttered shut.

In her mind, his fingers slid along her delicate netherlips and into the weeping flesh of her sex. Spreading her hole with his fingers, he probed her deep, hitting that spot that made her whimper in delight and gush with honey.

It had been over two years since a man touched her that way, and longer since a man she cared for touched her. Oscar's words played in her head: *"I can no longer caress you, Grace. The torture of doing so and not being able to fulfill your needs is destroying me. I will simply watch you."*

Her throat tightened. The last time Oscar touched her, she

had spent from the single touch. She wanted Winston to touch her that way, and she never wanted him to stop.

Her muscles tightened, willing him to touch her deeper, but his fingers stayed . . . curling in the tight curls of her mound. He gently traced small circles through the hairs as her muscles twitched against the caress. He leaned to the side and she heard him pick up something.

His fingers left her and then touched her at the top of her curls. A smooth, cool substance touched her skin and slid, with his fingers coating her skin. His touch furrowed through her hairs and a delicious aroma of jasmine filled her nostrils.

She wanted to open her eyes, but Oscar had told her to always obey when told to do such a thing. *"Simply feel, Grace. You don't need to see to use your senses and feel what I am doing."*

Feel. Yes, that is what she wished—to simply let go this night and feel with all her being all that this man could create in her . . . all his touch and will could make her cold body feel.

A shiver raced across her skin as his hands continued to massage her mound and the crease of her thighs. His fingers slid down the join, tapping and wiggling through her hairs and along the outside folds of her sex.

She focused on the light and teasing touches as his hands smoothed on a substance, its aroma smelled of bergamot spice. The scent opened her nostrils, seeped into her twisting mind, and relaxed her thoughts.

All her body did was feel . . . the intensity of their passion, the need for him to ease the ache in her tingling flesh.

His body was so near, masculine heat radiating from him, as his fingers maddeningly massaged through the hairs on her mound and his touch glided along the outside of her sex. She focused on him and all he pressed upon her—the sound of his breath, the smell of his masculine odor, the feel of his fingers in the oil.

If she could only taste him as he touched her, then all her senses would be evoked. Her legs shook and trembled, partially from the strain of holding herself, but mostly from the desire he unleashed and now slowly tamed.

His fingertips left her and she heard the water in the tub move.

"Grace, I need you to hold still."

Her body tensed. She would not move.

His fingers pressed to her hip bone as flutters filled her belly. The touch pulled her skin, and then something dragged through her hairs, leaving a slight burning sensation on her skin. Her breath caught in her throat.

He shaved her as he said he would.

She swallowed the captured breath. She had heard of people in the East not having any hairs. He conclusively preferred to have smooth skin over the tickling bristles of a woman's mound. The blade made an interesting scraping sound as the hair separated from her body.

The blade lifted and she heard a splash of water; then the metal pressed to her again and again. Her hands gripped the ring above her head with a tight grip as her body perched like a teetering paper house in a strong wind. The sound of the blade traveling over her mound and the coarse hair sent shivers down her spine. The muscles of her bottom shook and she gritted her teeth to stay still.

"Almost done, Grace." His hand smoothed down her belly, sending a tendril of pleasure straight to the core of her sex. His hand continued down, a finger pushed one lip of her sex to the side. Chills raced up her spine and she dug her fingertips into the palm of her hand. The blade followed his finger's path. Gently but firmly, the sharp edge glided along her charged skin.

Every nerve in her body held taut as she dangled on tiptoes, holding herself open to him.

His fingertip pushed the lips in the other direction, smoothing the heated skin against the blade's trail. The edge of the blade touched the skin at the top of her lips on the opposite side. My God, she wanted his fingers inside her. A moan burst from her lips and her chest heaved.

The blade stopped and his fingers pushed her lips more firmly over the opening of her cunny. "Shhh."

The blade then continued down the edge of her pussy as he shaved from her mound, down to the curve of her buttock, and then the blade lifted from her skin. His fingers still held her cunt lips to the side, and warm water from the bath splashed on her skin.

Her muscles jumped and more water splashed up against her. His palm rubbed and held the soothing damp heat to her newly naked flesh. He cupped her mound and his fingers pinched her lips closed. "Your pussy is beautiful, Grace. Lush." His fingers continued to hold her closed and the tips wiggled against her opening. She shook the sensations shooting straight to her soul.

She wanted the tip of his finger to curl into her sex—not hold it closed. Her hips wiggled and she rubbed her mound into his hand. Small pulses seized her sex and she whimpered as the muscles of her cunny wound tight.

"Are you ready to come down, Grace? Or would you prefer this?" He spread her lips wide, then speared his fingers up into her cunt.

The force of the entry made her pull on the ring above her head, lifting her up and off her tiptoes. She gripped the metal loop. Spasms erupted through the flesh of her womb. She screamed and fluid gushed onto his hand. Her legs shook and she moaned as her pussy continued to throb against the invasion of his fingers.

He wiggled his digits and prodded her flesh, holding on to her hips and buttocks as he pushed into her opening, hard. Her arms and body relaxed, and she gave herself up to him, allowing him to do as he wished with her body.

"Indeed, Grace." The arm that was wrapped about her buttocks held her tight. "Let go, Grace. I will not let you fall. Ever."

She believed him. Her fingers slipped from the ring and she slid slowly down his body. With his fingers deep within her womb, he eased her into a cradled position in the water. Her body submerged in the fragrant warmth, she trembled and opened her eyes.

Winston stared at her. His eyes deep pools of sapphire need. "Grace. Dear Grace. You are mine."

10

Grace

Winston stared at Grace and shifted until he sat on the bench closest to the candles' flicker. He wanted to see her. The light glow of the candles off her ivory skin was beauty to behold. Every crevice of her shimmered with dewdrops from the tub.

His legs shook as he slowly stretched them out before him. She weighed less than any of the women he had lifted in India. Yet, not one bone was defined on her body—only softly padded flesh covered by the creamy English white he had missed so much. Sandy tones and deep onyx hair had surrounded him in India, and though he found them beautiful and exotic, he longed for a simple English miss. Well, simple in looks, but complex in mind and spirit.

He pulled an image of Grace as a young woman to him: The time he watched her, lying in the field on her belly, playing with the grass. He had stood in the trees and frigged himself, watching her from behind. His body tingled as he rolled the skin of his cock up and over the crown. He closed his eyes and savored that image. If she knew he had done such then . . .

He sighed. She probably would have laughed and hit him playfully, scolding him for not letting her watch.

He trembled now the same way he had that day, but it was her laughing, her smile, her fingers trailing along his elbow, that captivated him.

She quietly lay in his arms after spending in a gush down his fingers and wrist. His hard prick twitched in his pantaloons. He wished his phallus lay lodged in her as she spent.

His chest tightened and he rested her bottom in the crook of his legs. The soft plush contour of her ass cradled against his hard thighs. The scar he so detested—concealed in his pants—rubbed against the underside of her legs. What would she think of his leg? The large, raised red flesh with pits and swells that gave him the shivers when he simply thought of the ugliness. In casual encounters, concealing the flesh was easy, but any future with Grace would require she see the disfigurement. Habit left him in the tub with his pants on. He held in a chuckle.

Her head nestled into the crook of his neck and her lips mouthed a gentle kiss against his collarbone.

He needed to see her face. He lifted her up. "Slide your legs on either side of mine."

She slid her legs so that she straddled him, her face with his. She stared at him with dream-filled eyes. Oh, the dreams that filtered through: passion, companionship, and love. He could see their future shimmering there in her smoky green eyes.

He reached up and weaved his fingers into her long hair about her shoulder. "You are a woman, Grace."

She lowered her eyes in seductive shyness.

His pulse soared.

God, he needed to be inside her. He reached down and unbuttoned the flap to his pants. "Pull me free, Grace."

Her hands trembled, but she didn't hesitate. Her fingers foraged into his wet trousers and pulled his cock free. He grasped her shoulders and lowered her toward him as he gradually reclined them down more and more into the water.

Her hands braced on his chest as he slid down so water hovered below his chin. His arm snaked about her and he pulled her forward. Her breasts were pressed to his bare chest. Lips parted, her tongue slid out and moistened the surface.

He gazed at the shine, longing to taste the sweet pout of her lips. Maneuvering his hips, his cock slid along the heat of her slit, and he popped his prick up behind her. His pego stood straight up along the crevasse of her ass. He rocked his hips, the crown gliding on her soft skin. A groan rumbled deep in his chest. He rubbed his prick down between the plush globes.

Her snowy white skin burned in contrast to the ivory color. A drizzle of wetness wept from his cock and he groaned as his sac tightened. He needed to be within her steamy heat, to feel the walls of her bottom clench tight about him.

His hand fisted in her hair and he turned slightly onto his side. He studied her face, her eyes, and in their depths, he saw his aphrodisiac—trust. Pressing with his fist against her scalp, he pushed her head down into the water above his shoulder. She struggled slightly, then relaxed as if floating on her own while swimming in the lake. His other hand guided his cock into the tight ring of her ass. He rocked his hips up and the tip penetrated the tight pucker. She tensed and her body shook. He let the hand fisted in her hair free.

She burst up, panting, and slid fully down onto his cock, the tight silk of her pucker wrapped his length in intense heat. "Mmmmm." He smiled up at her. Her face dripping wet from the tub, her eyes fully dilated in arousal, she quivered about him. She arched her hips, and her tight sheath gripped and choked down on his length. She whimpered.

"Shhh, Grace." By God, she was beautiful. She defined sensuality.

Her body trembled again as she moved her hips and body in tiny degrees. Pressing her sex and anus fully down onto him, she tightened her inner muscles about his cock. Ripples of ecstasy slid up his belly, making the hairs on his neck prickle.

Oh, she liked this. He held in a moan as his eyes fluttered, savoring the feel of her. He rocked his hips up a fraction.

"Are you well, Grace?"

Her eyelids fanned across her cheek. "Ummmmhummm."

"Was that a yes, Grace?"

"Yes."

"Good."

He thrust his hips up harder, then rocked them down. The tight, smooth skin of her bottom sheath grasped and held him. The water about them rippled and lapped at his sides. Her eyes closed, her plush lips opened as air jittered in and out.

She trembled again. Her leg muscles and her bottom gripped him as if holding him dearly.

Amazing. Utterly amazing.

He never would have guessed that his Grace, the woman he had known since boyhood, would enjoy this act. He stared at her, self-control bubbled below her surface, and that control she held made him want to shock her—push her and see where her boundaries were. His pulse jumped and he clenched his teeth.

The urge to take her out into deep, emotional depths—and see how much they could keep each other afloat—surprised him, grounded him, and gave him his purpose.

Hold on one minute, Winston. That idea turned him into a scared pup that ran beneath his bed until the thunder passed. His heart sped and sweat pierced his brow. How did this woman have such power over him?

He traveled the world and experienced all manner of women.

One look from Grace and he shook with insecurity. How was it possible she so quickly engaged his mind *and* body?

Her fingers gripped his chest as a stronger tremor shook her. Would she be the kind, sweet Grace he knew, the one that opened up and told him all, every little secret no matter how odd? Or had life changed her? Scarred her on the inside ... twisted her up so intensely that her fear was one of those scars, much worse than the one on his leg?

He frowned and the flesh on his leg grew warm. Her despair and insecurity, which he had sensed as she had gazed at him, said that life had done just such to his sweet Grace.

Some he encountered in India had never recovered from emotional scars inflicted on them. He needed to go slowly but didn't want to.

"Grace, I want to do something with you. . . . One of the things I found in my travels that I truly enjoy is the sound of breath rushing in and out as someone spends. The tone alone has, on many occasions, caused me to spend. Will you do as I ask, Grace, so I can hear your breath?"

She trembled again and forced her green eyes open. "Winston, I will do as you wish of me."

He rocked his hips up again and studied her face. Her eyelids fluttered and hung half closed across her velvet eyes. She watched his face with a mask of passion etched on her features.

She snagged her full lower lip between her teeth in a sensual plea to do what he had asked—to reach bliss for him. The water gently trickled from her long hair, down her face, and onto her breasts. It was a trail his tongue wished to follow—to capture her salts and feast until he needed to drink from her, to sate his body's thirst.

His hands slid down her hips to the swell of her bottom and he gripped the soft cheeks, pulling his cock out to the tip. Tingles warmed his sac and his stomach muscles tightened.

She shuddered and whimpered at the long, slow stroke. "Grace, when I push back in, I want you to hold your breath until I say you can breathe. Do you understand, Grace?"

"Yes, Winston."

He pushed back in, ever so slowly; the tiniest bit by bit, her skin slid down him. Oh, the silk warmth of her bottom could be his undoing. She sucked in her breath and quivered, her fingers flexed and pressed into his chest. His sac twitched.

"Good, Grace, now hold it." He clenched his teeth together. She aroused him so damn fast. *Think of something else for a moment, Winston.*

Two plus two is four.

Four plus four is eight.

He continued to press into her, watching her face and her body. Her chest did not move and her face was set in concentration. As he requested, she held her breath. The hairs on his neck stood and his heart raced.

Eight plus eight is sixteen.

He pressed fully into her pucker.

She trembled. He pulled back out, then increased the speed as he pressed back in. Her silk skin gripped him with each stroke, and sent drawn-out ripples of rapture to his balls, pulling them up close to him.

He pulled out and she moaned and shook, struggling to hold her breath. "You can breathe, Grace."

Whoosh . . .

The air rushed out of her lungs and through her lips. She gasped, her chest heaving in and out as her body shook, close to spending. The muscles of her anus clutched at his cock and she jerked.

"Hold your breath, Grace."

She sucked in air and held her upper body as still as possible as he continued stroking her with his cock. Each press into her, she tightened about him. He watched her shuddering and concentrated on her muscles tightening about him. She would spend soon . . . and hard.

"Grace, I am going to count backward from fourteen, and when I reach one, you can spend."

She nodded and the muscles of her stomach tensed.

"Fourteen." He stared up at her face. "Thirteen."

She whimpered and arched her hips back in an attempt to get him to move his cock within her.

"Twelve." He reached one of his hands up and pinched her nipple.

She whimpered and her eyes squeezed tightly closed. The flesh of her labia throbbed against his stomach as she neared erotic bliss.

"Eleven, ten." He pulled his cock slowly out. "Nine." He pressed back in.

Her legs shook to each side of him. All her muscles twitched as she struggled to hold her breath. She concentrated on the sound of his voice and the numbers. She would erupt on him soon.

"Eight, seven." He continued to cup her breast and stroke her bottom with his prick. "Six."

She whimpered again.

"Five. Four. Three." He slid into and out of her silky warmth with each number. His balls heated and his head grew light. He could not allow himself to come yet. "Two. One."

Her breath came out in a rush, and her chest heaved as she gasped and sucked in air.

Her eyes locked on his, her entire body shook, thrashing in the water, as she came apart about him. The slick, silk muscles of her bottom clasped him and she rubbed and rubbed her clit against his stomach.

She inhaled and inhaled again. Slowly she steadied herself.

The ripples in the water subsided. He blew out a tense breath. *Count to thirty, Winston, or you will spend in her as you exit her body.* He didn't want to reach his bliss yet. Not in her pucker. When he spent, he would do so in the oiled sheath of her cunny.

Erotic Grace . . . her whimpers as she had struggled to hold her breath made him want more than this. He wanted to make her whimper and moan . . . scream and cry out in bliss. Amazing she was here this night; while he was barely convinced to stay here this weekend by Lord Brummelton. He would later thank Brummelton for being so persuasive.

For right now, he would concentrate on Grace. He would make her shatter in delight once more; and to do so, he had the perfect thing planned.

She looked down at him and trembled, the muscles of her legs jumped once more. Her brow pulled together to form a wrinkle between. Her eyes grew glossy with tears and her lower lip trembled.

Damn it. Maybe he would strangle Brummelton, something was wrong here. "Grace." He reached his wet hand up and touched her face. "What is it? Tell me, Grace. Tell me, how are you feeling?"

11

Grace

Grace stared down into eyes that had floated in her mind since the day she wed and found out her husband's secret.

Oscar was impotent and had never joined with her this way.

He watched . . . watched from that damn chair. She wanted to burn that chair . . . had ordered the task done several times . . . but could not, in the end, have the order carried out.

She wanted to tell Winston—to tell him this was the first time she had joined with a man she cared for. The emotions welled up in her and she wanted to huddle into a ball in the warmth of his arms and cry. Cry all the deep, sorrowful sobs that resided in her soul. Never had such vulnerability flowed from her. The strength of her will to give herself over to him and disappear from all she had known sent her stomach aflutter.

She worried the inside of her cheek. She couldn't bring herself to lay on him and weep. Her need to be strong—to bury her pain—won out, and fear was the victor. Allowing herself to be vulnerable to anyone was impossible. The walls that she constructed as protection to this world stood strong. She was not prepared to let them crumble down.

What Winston did to her was beyond anything Oscar instructed her in. Her spend was the most powerful she had ever experienced, and all because she simply held her breath and focused on Winston as he futtered her hard.

Her mind floated in every direction. *He may love you. . . . You could wed and have all your dreams become reality . . . lust, love, and companionship all in one man. He is a man. . . . He was here. . . . There would be others.* She mentally shook herself. Her emotions intensified all too fast and confused her.

The wall she had constructed so carefully about her emotions cracked. All the years of pain welled up in her and pushed at the mortar. The restraint bowed beneath her pain's pressure. She wanted to fall into a puddle, here in this tub, and tell her onetime friend everything. Yet, she couldn't. This was by far the most stupid thing she could have done.

He was more skilled than Oscar, and if he was . . . that meant he would expect all the same things from her, or similar . . . maybe more.

She could not, and would not, allow herself to be shared as if watching another man take her was joyful in the best of ways. Oscar showed her how to be wicked, and doing so had twisted her and him into a shell of what they could have been.

She wanted the love of one man. She wanted to cuddle up each night and futter one man, and know he would be the only one in the act with her. Her throat closed off and she swallowed convulsively.

"Tell me, Grace."

She looked down into his eyes and nothing but compassion shone back. He reached up and rubbed his fingers across her face in a benevolent caress, which made her heart crack.

No! Grace, don't. You are not prepared to let him in, not

tonight. This night was about uncomplicated things, desires, and touching again. If you tell him, things will get complicated. Tell him another time. She inhaled deeply and curbed the intensity of her feelings. She only needed to know one thing from Winston this night. She opened her eyes and stared down at him.

"Did I please you, Winston? Did you spend?" She had never been able to tell when a man spent in her and she needed to know she had brought him pleasure this night. Knowing she had brought him that bliss was all that mattered.

Her heart pinched . . . and all the years of wanting to share her feelings with him—to joke with him and hug him—bloomed warm and steady in her breast. She loved him . . . and if she could not allow herself to be his, she needed to know that she had pleasured him as he deserved.

Her heart beat a mind-maddening pace as she waited for his answer.

"Grace, I don't spend quickly."

"Pardon? I don't understand." Her eyes widened and her heart sank. He hadn't? How, with all the passion of this experience between them, could he have not? In some way, she had disappointed him. Her throat tightened and a tear escaped her will's grasp. The warmth spilled down her face and she closed her eyes. Another brick from the wall cracked.

"No, don't! *Don't!* There is much more pleasure for me if I hold my spend until I can no longer, Grace."

The tears continued to trickle down her face as she let the bricks holding her emotions in check crack and fall, one by one. "What more pleasure can there be between two people in this act than spending in bliss?" She choked out the words and her will grasped with all its might for her emotions and tears to stop.

"Grace, I want you to stand. I will get us some wine and we will talk. We need to talk, Grace."

91

She nodded her head. Didn't he realize he could simply call for wine to be brought to the room? *But if he leaves the room, you have time to think, to steady, to regain your strength.*

She inhaled a deep breath and raised her chin. "Very well, Winston."

She stood and water ran down her body; the air chilling her skin to match the slow frost that crept up and about her heart.

Gooseflesh lined her skin and she shivered, not caring much about the cold.

"You are cold. Go lie on the bed and wrap yourself in the sheet. We will talk when I return. I won't be long, but I feel we need some wine."

Wine. Indeed.

She walked to the bed, slid the blanket back, and pulled it about herself.

He stood from the tub and water slicked off his tanned skin. His pantaloons clung to his curves and he walked across the floor, each step leaving a shiny spot on the dark wood.

He reached up and pulled the handle to the carved wood cabinet. The muscles of his arms flexed and he glanced over his shoulder at her. The corner of his mouth inched up.

The image of him as a young adult looking such a way before he told her something forbidden and wicked played in her mind. . . . Sneaking in to watch the town's girls as they relieved themselves in the woods. My God, how many times had he told her that story simply to make her laugh? She couldn't help the smile that curled her lips.

He pulled a fresh pair of breeches from the door. His hands grasped the edges of his trousers and he shimmied his hips, pushing the wet cloth down his legs and stepped out of them. He turned his backside toward her.

He had developed into a well-muscled man. The skinny legs of boyhood were gone and solid, well-formed flesh replaced them. Her hands pulsed with the need to reach out . . . to run her fingers along the column of his back and knead the muscles, relaxing him and bringing him joy.

She had always found such great pleasure in touching Oscar that way. Winston would enjoy such attention, too. She missed those quiet shared moments when . . . Her throat tightened. She wanted so much to let her love free again, to believe all she had thought of this man in childhood could be reality. Her dreams of Winston could take form and be her future.

She swallowed hard. Those dreams could never be. He had gone to India and had learned things that exceeded Oscar's carnal appetites. She would lock this memory away and be happy with that, and her childhood fantasies.

"I will be only a moment, Grace. Stay warm." His deep tone pulled her mind from her faltering.

She should run. The need made her muscles twitch, urging her to stand and dress while he was downstairs, then fly away.

She couldn't. . . . She loved him.

That would simply never do.

12

Grace

Winston strode down the hall. What in damnation had happened to her in her marriage? Not spending brought tears to her eyes? He shook his head and sighed. Damn Oscar. What the hell had marrying a title done to *his* Grace?

He would not leave her again. She needed him and his protection, his guidance, his will, in order to bring her back to the playful woman who showed no fear. And he needed her. The years in exotic places had taught him well the arts of the act, but he had dreamed of teaching an English miss all that was possible. Grace had vividly frequented his dreams then. Now he saw the potential and the reason why. He loved her. Had for years. He stopped in his tracks as the air was sucked from his body. How could he have been so blind to the need and the emotion?

They both needed wine and lots of it . . . but, in truth, even more than a Dionysian feast, they needed one another.

Winston needed to be with Grace, and Grace needed to trust him and share her fears—fears she was holding tight to her heart.

He spun about and went back to the door. He could have

sworn that shaving her and the tub had built her trust in him, but she struggled. They needed to talk while she was in a space where he had control. Wax . . . would be his tool—his words and emotions would show her he meant no harm.

He pushed open the door. She sat, legs hanging over the edge, the blanket wrapped about her, and stared at him with calm blue-green eyes. Nowhere in all of his travels had he seen eyes like Grace's. They possessed life and vitality, joy and sadness. They truly were the windows to her soul.

"Stand, Grace."

She unfolded herself, the blanket dropping from her shoulders to the bed, and stood. Her soft, curved form was womanly perfection—from the fluid flesh of her thighs, to the gently padded swell of her stomach, and her bottom.

She was exquisite, not only in form, but in spirit. He walked to her and grabbed a silk cravat he had earlier placed by the bed for this purpose. "Put your hands behind you and look downward."

She did so without hesitation.

He walked to her and slid the silk about her elbow. Holding the fabric in place with his right thumb, he wrapped her arm once. Then he pulled the silk taut and over to the other arm, wrapping that one in the same fashion, too. He pulled the cloth taut and ran a fingertip down the inside of her arm. Gooseflesh rose on her skin in his finger's trail. A good sign she was enjoying this. "Do you trust me, Grace?"

"Yes."

He frowned. He was not sure he believed her. He wrapped the cloth around both arms in one loop and continued down in a spiral fashion, weaving the cloth between each arm and around both, until he reached her wrist. There he looped the cloth back and secured it by weaving it in and out of the already laid strips.

"Move your arms, Grace."

She wiggled her arms in an attempt to pull them apart.

"Good, Grace. Now try up and down."

She did so and her right arm slid.

"Can't have that now, can I, Grace?"

"No."

He slid the end free and readjusted the wrapping. "Again, Grace."

She pulled her right and left arms, trying to dislodge them. They held firm.

"Wiggle your fingers for me, Grace."

She did so with ease.

"Very well." He stepped back to admire her. Her arms thrust back behind her back, the way her shoulder blades contracted in a line leading to the white bind, which he had created on her, was art. He had only begun. He would make her front just as appealing—not that her breasts weren't already.

He stepped around to the front of her. Her shoulders thrust back, her breasts stood out in two luscious mounds. Her damp hair hung over one shoulder and down to her waist.

He stepped close to her and stared down into her face. She refused to look up into his eyes. "Grace, look up at my face."

She slowly turned her face up and the liquid heat of her stare shot straight to his cock. That look! Pure animal desire. The lust shimmering there made him want to topple her over and do wicked things to her all night long.

He ran his finger down the curve of her jaw. Her body trembled and arched toward him. "Good, Grace."

He stepped away from her and grasped one of the candles from the stands by the tub. He stood before her and held the candle up into the air, staring at her breast. Her chest rose and fell with each aroused breath.

He tilted the candle, spilling a drizzle of wax onto her breastbone. Her breath hitched as the sting of heat hit her skin, rolled down the slope of her breast to her nipple peak, then off onto her stomach. A single drop hung in cool, solid form from her breast's tip. Beautiful.

"All well, Grace?"

"Yes, Winston." Trust swirled in a mix of emotions in her eyes.

His heart flipped in his chest.

"Grace, why do you fight trusting me?" He spilled a larger splash of wax onto her skin. The question was an obvious one, and he kept his expectations low on the depth of her reply. She didn't trust him, and more time would be needed for less simplistic answers.

She shuddered in arousal, and her breath hitched once more, as the hot liquid ran down her nipple and followed the same path as the first.

"It is not the trust in you that I fight."

He moved the candle over and let another line of wax run down her opposite breast and crest her hard bud.

"What is it then, Grace?"

She shuddered and trembled, then bit her lip.

"Spread your legs farther apart, Grace."

Grace spread her legs more than shoulder-width apart. Her cunny throbbed and ached. Oh, how she wanted him to touch her. The wax on her chest amazed her. The tingling sensation—though nowhere near her pussy—sent quivers rippling straight to that spot.

"What are you struggling with, Grace?" He drizzled a long stream of wax across her chest.

The instant of sting, followed by soothing warmth, then hardened into an uncomfortable tightness. Aroused heat pumped through her. Her head grew light and all she could think of was Winston and the sensations assaulting her body, mind, and heart.

"I struggle with fears from my marriage."

"Good, Grace."

He drizzled another line down her breast. The wax sent heat straight to her core. She sucked in a deep breath and closed her eyes as her cunny pouted open and throbbed with need.

"What happened in your marriage, Grace, which you fear here with me?"

"Oscar shared me, Winston." Her throat closed off on her breath and she convulsively worked her throat. "I will never give myself to another who has that need again."

"Good, Grace." A single touch from one of his fingers slid down the center of her open pussy.

"Oh. More. Please, more." She rotated her hips to show her desire for him to enter her. Her head tilted back and a groan from deep in her soul pushed out through her parted lips.

"And what do you fear with me Grace from that experience?" His tone was calm and his finger traced back and forth in her folds. Ever so softly, his touch wound her muscles tight.

A sting of wax hit her on her stomach. She flinched, the sensation stung more . . . but, oh, how she wanted to feel the drip run down her mound and crest, spilling over into her folds and harden there. The crack of the wax with each motion she made would arouse her most sensitive flesh. She moaned as Winston's finger traced up to the new line of wax he poured on her skin.

"If you wish more, Grace, answer." His firm voice made her tremble.

Oh, yes, she wished more. "I fear never bringing you pleasure in bed. I fear you sharing me and simply watching me. I fear you wanting to watch other women. I fear I will not be enough, all on my own, for your appetites."

"That is all I need to know *for now,* Grace." A long drip slid down her lower belly and hit her freshly shaved skin.

She sucked in a sharp breath and gritted her teeth. My goodness, that stung!

"You enjoy wax, Grace. Would you like more?"

"Yes, Winston." Being bound and helpless to him released in her the vulnerable woman she feared. Confessing her secrets to him, while in this state, filled her with hope. Hope she could be vulnerable with him in more than the act. Perhaps, she could indeed turn to him and cry.

He gently grasped her arm and turned her toward the bed. "Bend over the bed and support your body on your shoulders. Turn your head to the side. Keep your legs spread."

Grace obeyed. She heard him strip away his pantaloons and walk back to the tub. . . . To get another candle maybe?

The wax on her chest and breast cracked and peeled as she moved. The slight tugging made her itch. Oh, how she wanted to scratch at her skin, but her hands were bound.

She wiggled, rubbing her shoulders on the bed, trying to get any relief she could. She frowned. She couldn't move much.

She was helpless to Winston. She smiled and her muscles relaxed. She trusted him here—in this private, intimate space.

It was her heart she feared giving over to his keeping. The strange organ pinched in her breast as her emotions pushed and banged against her ribs, demanding to be heard. She utterly couldn't allow him to enter there.

His hand caressed her bottom and gently pulled the cheeks of her bum apart. His cock pressed at the slick opening of her cunt. Her swollen lips pouted open, gasping to be filled with his hardness. Her mind, body, and soul focused on them joining—body to body, here and now, for this instant in time.

He pressed forward. The hot head of his cock glided into her effortlessly. She trembled and her breath deepened.

He slid forward all the way and groaned. Grace's pulse soared.

As he slid back to the tip, his legs tensed behind her while he slid all the way in.

She moaned. He moaned. He repeated the caress.

"You never have to worry about pleasing me in this, Grace. You are sensuality in human form. If I didn't enjoy the sensation of holding back my spend, I would have eased myself in you several times already." He thrust into her again and again. "I am going take my pleasure in you in moments and I want you to savor the sensation."

She pleased him in this, the truth of his words echoed in his tone. She trembled and shook. A burst of light bloomed behind her eyelids. *I please him.*

His cock glided effortlessly in and out of her oiled flesh. She grasped his prick with the walls of her cunny—her own bliss was just on the horizon. Her muscles tensed and her legs gave out against the bed.

"Savor the feel of my cock slipping in and out of you as it is now." He continued to stroke her and the sting of wax sliced across her back. She whimpered and the heat shot straight to her cunt. Her pussy gushed against his cock's onslaught.

"Yes. That is it." His fingers dug into her hip.

Another sting of wax cut across her back in the opposite direction. She inhaled a sharp breath, all of her muscles tightened and her mind swam on the colliding sensations. The pleasure of his cock, the pain of the wax.

"Oh! Grace!" Winston shuddered, pulled out, and lunged back in. Her body erupted. Her vision grew hazy and warmth filled her womb. His prick twitched inside her. He stayed pressed fully to her womb. She lay in a daze, panting beneath him.

The sting of wax slid down the crack of her bottom. The shock of the sensation overtook her and she shook uncontrollably. The hot warmth ran down her crack and through her netherlips to drip on the bed beneath her.

Drop after drop hit the same path. Each second was drawn

out as her mind captured the sensations . . . the hot sting, the hardening of them together. He coated her, and him, in wax. A physical tie of their bodies joined.

A tug came at her wrist and Winston slowly unwrapped her arms. He rubbed her arm in small, firm circles, fingers to elbows.

All the hairs on her arms stood. Her mind completely focused on the firm hardness of their join, and the sensations of him massaging her body. She relaxed in a haze of sensations.

Every motion he made tugged the hard wax where their bodies joined. He slid a hand under her stomach, lifted her, and rolled them on their sides.

"Grace, reach down between your legs and feel how solid we are together."

She slid her hand down over her belly and the remnants of the wax that still clung to her skin. Her fingers trailed her mound and slid deep between her legs. Smooth, hard wax coated the crease of her thighs and the join of his cock in her. She closed her eyes and swallowed deeply.

"That seal is more than us futtering, Grace." His breath warmed her ear. "We mesh on more levels than this, and you well know that truth. I never dreamed you had such fears as you mentioned, Grace. We will talk about each one of them in depth, Grace, but you need to know . . . now. I love you, and have for some time."

He loved her. Panic and joy clawed and fought in Grace's belly. Her lungs tightened.

His arms wrapped possessively about her. "Tonight, when I saw you downstairs in that ballroom, our stifled longing, desires, friendship, and love were pushed to the forefront. All of this here tonight simply proved we are more than compatible in the sinful act."

She fisted and uncurled her fingers in the blanket. *Calm*

yourself, Grace. This is what you want. Joy calmed her rapid heart. Indeed, she did want the love of Winston, but he didn't say he would never do all she feared. He simply said they would talk about her fears. She closed her eyes and sighed. Her insecurities grabbed hold once more.

No, she needed to think rationally, and now was not the time to think about love and complications. *Enjoy this moment, Grace, and when he sleeps, slip away and think about this rationally. Think this through. You always do better when you think about things by yourself.*

13

Lilly

Lilly stepped into the candlelit glow of the entryway, and all the hairs on her body tingled with anticipation. Strange, but that was true. Only hours ago she would have run, covering her eyes to avoid seeing what was occurring in this house.

Brian was here. She thought she knew all there was to know about Brian, but she was wrong. How had Brian come to such an event? Lilly frowned and Grace's words *"Open your mind just a little for your brother's sake"* assaulted her repeatedly.

Maybe Grace was right. Maybe she needed to see with her own eyes what the temptation was so she could decide for herself if the wrong he did was fairly judged. In fact, being wrong was all a matter of perspective.

She looked back at St. Jerome—his too short black locks, devilish gray eyes, and knowing smile. A major scoundrel. Heat bloomed deep in her belly. He appeared nothing at all like she thought he would be. Her gaze dropped to his mouth. Were his lips soft? Would he taste as good as he smelled?

She imagined tracing the contour of his lips with her tongue. *Sweet Jesus, Lilly, what are you thinking? You have always been a good girl!* That smile . . . she swallowed hard. That smile made her want to be bad. Wicked in fact.

A kiss. Indeed.

She licked her lips. He stepped through the door and closed it behind him. Grabbing one of the candles from the wall beside the door, he pressed up behind her.

So close. Her heart pounded in her chest. She would surely faint away in a fit of vapors. *Hold true, Lilly. Use your fortitude.*

The heat of him surrounded her and her corset stuck uncomfortably to her skin. There was barely enough room in the corridor for them to walk side by side if she stayed as close to him as she possibly could. Impossibly close. Her gaze slid down the side of his body, and tingles spread through her.

His warmth pressed against her and his breath quickened. *My—oh, my—he smelled delicious.* So close, yet she couldn't allow herself to taste him. Her heart leapt in her chest. The idea of his flavor flooding her taste buds thrilled her.

"As we walk along this path, Veronica, the light will diminish. There are other doors, where more candles will be lit, but those are few. It will be dark. We will be peering into several of the rooms where acts are going on."

Peering into rooms? The hairs on her neck stood and she glanced at St. Jerome. His mouth quirked up at one corner. She fisted and uncurled her fingers. "Doesn't everyone know about—"

"No. I have become a close friend with Lars Petersen, the owner of this house. I know a few of this house's secrets." His finger gripped her waist, and twinges shot straight through her stomach.

She inhaled and smelled his sweet, earthy scent. His essence radiated from him like a welcome breeze on a day when no relief from the heat was in sight. She relaxed in the balm of him. Did all women find a single sniff of him so soothing? Of course they did. That scent had to be why he had so many women friends.

Never in all her life had she thought people could be walking around in the walls of her home!

They walked along in silence and his arm slid about her stomach, pulling her close to him as he held the candle with his other hand. "I don't want you to trip."

She tensed at the closeness. No one would ever see her concealed behind the walls. Her muscles relaxed and she snuggled into him. No one would ever know what happened here in this passage.

These walls made her invisible to all here in this house—so feeling his arm about her, and what it was like to be so close to a man, tempted her beyond reason. In this moment, no one could see her.

They continued down the wall, the light fading behind them. The single candle he held in front of him illuminated a circle of the wood floor before them.

St. Jerome stopped and held the candle up to the wall over her head. In the wall resided a piece of black fabric draped like a curtain of sorts, hiding something from view. To the left of it was a black notch carved into the beam of the wall.

"Veronica, I am going to look into here. Afterward, I wish you to do so and ask me as many questions as you would like." His finger traced the curve of her jaw. "Until I look, I wish you to close your eyes. I want to make sure what is going on in here is something worth your seeing."

Lilly sighed, and then closed her eyes. "All right."

His arm brushed along her breasts as he slid the cloth to the side in the small space. Sweet Jesus, he touched her bosom. Tingles of heat spread through her breasts and down her belly to between her thighs.

His scent overwhelmed her. His torso pressed up against her

side and breast as he leaned in to gaze behind the curtain. A lump formed in her throat and she swallowed hard. What was she about to see? Could she do this and still be the same Lilly in the morning?

"All right, Veronica, open your eyes and look at me." His deep, sinful voice tempted her nerves like nothing she'd ever experienced.

The rogue. Her eyes opened like a sleepy butterfly stretching its wings. His face so close to hers. Illuminated by the candle, the roundness of his cheeks and the square edge to his chin, which dimpled in the center, were revealed. He was splendid to behold. Heat infused her cheeks.

"Veronica, you are an angel. All men will notice this trait and wish to capture the skittish beauty you are." His gray eyes held her to him. "Who, may I ask, is your friend? The one you are looking for?"

She mentally shook herself. "Pardon?"

"You had said you were looking for a man who was more like a girlfriend than a man."

Oh, sweet Jesus. Her brother! Please don't let her see him in one of these rooms. Panic flooded her mind. Her belly flipped and chills doused all the heat St. Jerome's closeness had created in her. "Um, Lord Cunnington."

He frowned. "Ah, I know him well, though I don't believe we will find him in one of these rooms. Do you still wish me to show you what is here?" Disappointment showed on his face.

"You know where to find Br . . . Cunnington?"

Damn, she nearly said his Christian name. No one knew it, besides those he held dear. She glanced at the opening in the wall, then back to hungry wolflike eyes.

"I know where to find him. He is in another part of the house, finding his particular brand of pleasure."

She came here only to find her brother. She forced her eyes closed and inhaled the essence of St. Jerome. Each fine hair on her arms stood and she shivered in pleasure. Sweet Jesus, he tickled her senses without even touching her. She couldn't resist absorbing all the sensations swirling about her. This night would be a dream soon enough.

"I can always show you what lies in these rooms and offer my advice, then get you to Cunnington, Veronica." His soft voice held concern.

She opened her eyes and stared into a face filled with desire. It was an expression she longed to see a man show toward her. She licked her parched lips. His gaze dropped to her mouth. Her tongue repeated the path. *Please. Yes, please. Kiss me.*

He inhaled and his shirt and waistcoat pulled tight over his chest. His hand rose, and with the pad of his thumb, he pressed to the moist surface of her lower lip. Dragging it down, he traced along the line of her mouth.

"Touch my thumb with your tongue, Veronica."

A jolt of pleasure washed through her, tempting her to simply feel this night. Indeed, she wanted to taste his skin. *Lilly, taste him. You will regret not doing so. Besides, how could tasting his skin be bad? Be wrong?* After all, it was simply his thumb, not some scandalous hidden bit of his body. Her breath quickened. No one would ever know.

She slid her tongue out and touched the edge of his fingernail, then slid up the smooth surface to the salty tang of his skin. Her chest tightened and her breath whooshed out over his hand. The salty taste faded as she licked and licked his skin.

More . . . yes . . . more of his taste. More of him.

She wrapped her tongue about his thumb in quest of more of his flavor. Pulling his thumb into her mouth, she closed her lips about his digit and her eyes fluttered shut. *Oh, scandalous behavior, Lilly. You should stop now.* Saliva pooled in her cheeks and she circled the plumpness of the tip with her tongue.

He slowly moved his thumb out and then back into her lips' grasp. She would savor this. This last bit of his flavor she would cherish. She licked the circumference, then grabbed every trace of his taste down to the join in his hand.

His chest labored in and out, and with each inhale, he touched her torso with his. The delicious contact elicited a moan from deep within her.

Slowly he pulled back, and the tip of his finger glided from her lips. She opened her eyes; her mouth remained parted and she stared at him.

"Shall I show you, Veronica?"

There was no need for thought. She wanted to learn all he would teach her. "Yes."

"In this room, there is a woman tied in a position that has left her open wide. Her cunt is exposed and vulnerable to whatever these men wish to press upon her."

Cunt? Such a scandalous and forbidden word! Yet it rolled right through her thoughts without restraint. How could such a word hold her so captivated?

He placed his hands on her shoulders, about the red cape, and turned her so she faced the saucer-sized opening in the wall.

In the room, a woman lay on her stomach on a bed. Her buttocks and cunny faced toward them.

Rope was tied about her wrists, secured her back, wrapped her thighs, and spread her legs wide. Her sex lay open and shimmered with moisture.

The woman's sex became vividly etched in Lilly's mind. The red flesh pouted open, the nubbin at the top longer than Lilly's, with neatly trimmed hairs. The position the woman was forced to hold exposed her bottom hole clearly, too.

Lilly's bud throbbed between her legs and she shifted her stance slightly. Her hand itched to slide down her body to trace her bud with her fingers and see how different hers was. *No, Lilly, simply because you are hidden does not give you full sway to do more than watch.* She fisted her hands at her side to hold them still.

A man slid a piece of cloth over the woman's eyes and tied it. Another man stood to the other side of the bed and harshly stroked his phallus.

Goodness, didn't that hurt? Lilly's eyes widened.

His small hands slid down the long width of his prick, and pulled back the skin, exposing the bulbous end. He rocked his fingers, then pulled the skin back up over the head. Circling the crown with his index finger and thumb, he slowly moved up and down.

Her brow pinched. How did that feel? He obviously liked touching himself there. Just as she enjoyed touching herself, but she could never do that in front of someone else.

The flesh between her legs tingled. Or could she? Sweet Jesus, she must be mad. She stood here as if this was something proper and normal to be thinking. To be feeling this way in the presence of others, including a man who stood so close that her body hummed his name. She sighed.

The man who tied the blindfold began to rub down the woman's back, gently massaging.

"The man touching her is Lord Brenton. His wife is one of the coldest women I have ever known. She won't allow him in her bed. He comes here to be touched, to find comfort in a woman who will permit him to tie her."

Lilly nodded. Lady Brenton had severe melancholy. Even in her limited access to the ton, Lilly had heard the stories.

"The woman he has tied is protected by the man who is

standing to the side of the bed. He has been her protector for some years and loves to watch her with other men, as long as he can participate."

Lilly's eyes widened. He enjoyed watching her with other men? How could that be?

"Lord Brenton may be a good option for you as a protector, if you find what he does to her appealing. We will watch for a moment." St. Jerome stepped behind her, placing her between him and the wall. He leaned in over her shoulder and watched through the wall as she did. His face next to hers. His chest pressed to her back and his thigh to her bottom.

She tensed. The rake he was shone through as his breath warmed her ear. "Being tied up can be pleasing. Some women really enjoy not having a choice in what happens to them," he growled into her ear.

Oh, Lilly, what are you doing? His heat enveloped her and she trembled, wishing once again she had more layers of clothing between her bare skin and the temptation that was St. Jerome. "Do you enjoy tying women?" She glanced at him from the corner of her eye.

Glint of the wolf sparked in his eye and his lips curved up. "When the mood is correct for it, I do, though I am not one who enjoys acts that deviate too far from the norm. Simple pleasure, and bringing my partner pleasure, is what I desire."

His heavy voice relaxed her trembling. She leaned her temple against his bicep as she watched the scene unfolding. *That's it. Relax, Lilly. This is what you wished to see. Open your mind.*

"Sweet, tender Veronica." His breath warmed her ear. "Watch and see if you are intrigued by anything."

She focused back on the scene. Lord Brenton crawled up behind the woman, his fingers slid into her sex, and the woman cried out.

"Oh, yes, please. Please fill me and stretch me."

"You're a naughty little dove, aren't you, my sweet?" The man who stood by her head stroked his cock, then slid his fingers into her hair. "You want your pot filled and stretched wide?"

"Oh, yes, please. *Please.*"

Lord Brenton slid his fingers deeper into her and then continued to thrust in and out of her with ease.

Lilly's eyes grew impossibly huge. Never had she even considered doing anything like such to herself. She simply rubbed around the outside, caressing the bud until her body exploded and her vision flashed. What sensations would gliding her fingers into her soft flesh hole create? The flesh itself throbbed. Indeed.

Her fingers certainly were nowhere near the size of a man's. She would surely remember to slide one of her digits into herself the next time.

The woman cried out and her legs pulled apart farther as more wetness slid from her.

"You unclean dove. You want his pego in you. Stretching you as you suck on mine?" The man by the woman's head spoke challengingly.

"Please, yes, two pricks in me . . . one at each end. Oh, yes. Please."

If humanly possible, Lilly's eyes got even larger. She swallowed hard and glanced down.

"Veronica, have you ever done anything like this?" St. Jerome's calm voice washed over her.

She should tell him yes. She would be lying to him, but what was the point really? He would never see her again. She glanced over at him. No, it was important he be enlightened on some of her limited exposure. "I have little experience."

St. Jerome's fingers slid into her hair above the mask she wore. "Indeed, I know."

Lord Brenton kneeled behind the woman. His thing was

much longer in size than the prick of the man at the woman's head. He grabbed the woman's hips and lifted her bottom slightly up off the mattress. Her knees still wide, she no longer lay, but she kneeled before him. Her shoulder pressed into the mattress. His bottom flexed and they both moaned.

What was going on? Lilly could not really tell what happened from this back angle. Had he slid his prick into the eye of her cunny?

The flesh of her pot throbbed and she shifted her stance. Her back and bottom brushed against St. Jerome, who stood so close behind her.

"Mmmm, I see you are aroused by watching them futter. I can smell desire on your skin."

He could smell desire? Is that what she smelled every time she inhaled his scent? His attraction to her?

"I want to touch you, Veronica. I cannot offer to be your protector, but there is no denying we are fond of each other."

She stiffened. He wanted to touch her. In what way? Like the men in the room were touching this woman? A shiver of charged pleasure fluttered through her veins. Why was she even considering letting him? She had gone daft!

"Do you wish to stay and watch more, or shall we move on to another room?"

She glanced back into the room. The man who stood at the woman's head continued to stroke and caress her hair as Lord Brenton slid his prick in and out of her.

Lilly wanted to watch more, but the urge to have St. Jerome touch her trickled through her. Scandalous! She couldn't allow herself to do more than what she had already done. She needed to step aside from this and walk for a bit. "Let's move on."

St. Jerome's hand slid about her waist and he turned her to face him. She gazed up into eyes filled with rampant need. His lips crushed down on hers. Wet tongue thrust deliciously along the slit of her mouth. She parted her lips and let him in.

Lilly, you ought to resist. Where had her good sense gone? The moment she tucked herself into that carriage, her good sense vacated. This act would only lead to . . . St. Jerome touching her private places! Oh, what would his fingers touching her delicate skin do to her will?

Her tongue slid out to taste him. Wine, and a sweetness that was all him, tangled her taste buds. Her stomach twisted in fear and excitement. His kiss was better than any wine she had tasted. Her head spun and her knees shook.

He pulled back and she reached out for him, fisting her hands in his coat. She opened her eyes, panting for more of him.

He smiled at her. "Indeed, Veronica, there will, without doubt, be more this night."

14

Lilly

Vincent held all his muscles taut and pulled himself from Veronica with paper-thin control. He wanted to taste her breasts, her stomach, and her cunny. The smell of her arousal as she shifted her stance shot straight through his nostrils and into his veins. His heart sped to a gallop and his cock bulged. In the seven years Amelia had belonged to him, simply kissing her never aroused him this way.

Tempting Veronica.

Sweet Veronica.

By Jove, what was he thinking? She deserved to know to-morrow he would attend the Woodlandslys' musicale and start his quest for a bride. He could not live the dual life most of the ton did. He would be true to his wife.

Veronica would have to find another protector, someone who would be gentle with her. Her inexperience shone clear from her body's reactions. She most likely had few encounters with men altogether. Vincent's position was to simply guide her in that quest. He didn't want to resist her. . . .

He wanted to relish her . . . to undress her slowly, and press kiss upon kiss along her exotic skin. And he would. He was no saint and could not persist in *not* having her for this night. He sighed. She needed to know their encounter would be simply that . . . a memorable encounter. Nothing more.

He entwined his fingers in hers and picked up the candle he had set in the groove. Her hand grasped tightly in his, he pulled her down the narrow passage toward the next room. His heart pounded in his chest like a randy lad's before he had his first woman.

Rounding the corner, he hesitated. Lord Devonton would be in the next room. The room held a Berkley horse and Devonton's woman of this calendar was Mistress Gertrude. Vicious Gertrude, with a birch in hand, scared Vincent straight to the grave. He never understood Devonton's odd desire, but they were friends nonetheless.

He hesitated by the curtain and his tongue grew thick. He didn't want to show Veronica the twisted ways of Devonton. "Veronica . . . sweet Veronica. Do you wish to see the extreme wickedness that happens between men and women?"

She stared up at him and her large brown eyes grew wider.

"Maybe not tonight?" He smiled down at her.

Whack!

The sound of birch whizzing through the air and hitting flesh echoed from behind the curtain. A man moaned deeply.

Veronica flinched and stared at the curtain. "I—I think it is better that I not."

His shoulders relaxed. "Very well, we are on to the next room."

He had no idea who would reside in that room. The space was one of the more tame and beautiful ones. A replica of a room Petersen had discovered on a trip to the East. Reds and golds, carved woods, and a tub that was sunk into the floor. The space certainly set the mood for wicked futtering.

They plodded down the dark path toward the small, steep stairs that led to the final rooms upstairs. If Veronica had worn a skirt, the climb would amuse indeed.

He glanced down at her waiflike form and the white-and-black bloomers tied about her waist. The slit in the center of the fabric, though not visible, was there. His fingers ached and he wanted to have her traverse the stairs in front of him. To reach his hands up under her cloak and separate the damp cotton slit, then slide his fingers into her velvet depths. Would she be weeping for him? Her soft, inner flesh swollen and waiting to cradle his cock? Or would she be liquid slick?

He would want to stop, linger, feel the sensations of the intimate caress, but he would tell her to keep striding up. Her bottom rocking against his palm as his fingers slid in and out of her weeping flesh as they went. His cock grew heavy in his drawers.

Candles blazed at the foot of the stairs, but no light resided on the climb itself. He held the candle up at the foot of the stairs. "Take the candle, Veronica. I will follow behind you, in case you should slip." *Randy lad. You simply want to watch the sway of her bottom, even if you don't touch her flesh.*

Her meek brown eyes stared at him and then at the stairway. Soft fingers slid about the candle in his hand. The hairs on his forearms stood in a wave that shot straight up his neck. He shivered in arousal.

"St. Jerome?" Her gaze held his.

His gaze dropped to her lips, wanting to taste her once more. "Veronica." *Stop it, Vincent. Show her what she needs to see.* He released the candle into her soft grasp. "After you."

She hesitated, not taking her eyes from him. "Are you well?"

He could have lied, but honesty seemed vital in this moment

here with her. "No. I am not well, Veronica. I desire you, and cannot have you. I have not felt this way about a woman since before Amelia."

Veronica's eyes widened in astonishment of his confession. "I—I am sorry, St. Jerome." Her gaze dropped to the ground. "I—I don't know what to say, or do."

He held in a terse, annoyed chuckle by locking his jaw, then nodded his head. "Go on up the stairs."

Blast and damn, St. Jerome. You don't even know her. You are supposed to wed—not find a mistress to fall all over like a puppy dog.

He let out a terse breath and stepped into the stairwell behind her. The sway of her hips beneath the red cloak hit him like a fist in the gut. The image of his cock buried in her from behind as he requested her to wiggle and rock her hips invaded his senses. He envisioned his length coated with her cream, and the desire tightened his stomach.

He shook his head.

Out!

He could not allow himself to . . . want her this deeply.

Out! Out! Out!

He should turn around and tell her that he couldn't show her more tonight. He watched as she twisted around the tight corner, up the next flight. He couldn't. Responsibility pulsed through him. How the hell had that happened in only an hour in her presence? Veronica, and Veronica's education as to who was who, and what was what, was his ever-winding, horrific path for the night.

It was not her education of what his cock would do to her, or how she should move, whimper, and moan against him. His cock twitched.

He reached the top of the narrow stairway and she waited,

holding the candle waist-high with both hands. She appeared as one of those angels painted on the walls of churches that he had seen in Italy. He smiled at her, then stepped closer and wrapped his arm about her shoulder. He stared down at the candle flicker. Her hands shook.

"What is it you wish, Veronica?"

"I—I . . ." She bit her lip, then looked up at him. Her eyes shone with uncertainty behind her black-and-white mask.

"What do *you* wish, Veronica?" he repeated softly, hoping she would feel comfortable enough to tell him.

"I desire you to touch me as we watch." The words came out in a rushed whisper. "Once. Here in this corridor." Her pink tongue slid out and wet her lower lip. "I—I want to know what a touch of desire feels like."

St. Jerome's stomach tightened. His heart jumped back to the gallop he had successfully calmed. *Just once.* He searched her brown eyes. There was no regret at her words. Once was all he could offer her. He would be foolish to deny her that pleasure. It was what she wished . . . once.

"Indeed. This once, this night, Veronica, I wish to feel your desire, too."

His hand wrapped about hers, which held the candle, and he pulled the warm waxy rod away. Reaching across the narrow hall, he placed the light in the notch beside the curtain, then grabbed her hands and guided them to his cock. He closed his eyes and moaned. Her hands trembled against his hard thickness, and he heard her breath quicken.

"Veronica, unbutton me. I need you to feel the heat and pulse of blood through my veins."

He opened his eyes and watched her hands, and she fumbled with each button. She did want this. Her hands trembled with excitement. He would take her slowly, to savor each brush of her fingers against his flesh. He would show her this room, and tease her, then take her when they moved to the final room.

She folded the flap down, then looked up at him through her mask.

"Pull me out."

Her lips quirked and her dainty hands slid into his pantaloons and along his thigh. Fingers wrapped about his width and she pulled him free.

"Oh!" Her eyes went round.

"Indeed. Touch me. Here." He wrapped his hand about hers on his cock. "Feel how much pressure I am applying to your hand about me?"

"Yes."

"Grip me like that as you slide the skin up and down over my stiff head."

Her arm shook and she gripped him firmly. She slid her hand down; his skin slid over the crown of his prick. Delicious feathers of sensation trickled down to his balls. She slid the skin back up, and his skin slid over the ridge. He groaned. "Yes, that is it." Oh, what a vixen! She knew exactly how to pleasure a man this way.

"Did I do it correctly?"

He smiled, his eyes lazy. "Indeed, just how I like it."

He widened his stance and leaned back against the wall. Her small, smooth hand stroked his large, thick cock. The difference in their sizes excited him all the more. He needed more pressure.

"When you get to the tip, slow your hand as you glide over the ridge."

"Like this?" She pulled the skin up his shaft and over the ridge of his cock. Hovering at the ridge, she squeezed slightly. His sac tightened and waves of sensation spread up his belly.

"Oh . . . oh, that is . . . very favorable."

Her small hand glided down him again, then back up in the same fashion, and his head grew light. He wanted to stay here in this spot and allow her to frig him thus until his custard sprayed all over her dainty hands as he pulsed and pulsed against her strokes. The image in his mind alone drove him daft.

By Jove, he needed to stop her and savor her . . . show her the rest, then take her as he wished.

Placing his hand over her fingers, he regrettably stopped her stroke, then shook.

"Turn about, Veronica. I wish to pleasure you with my hands as well." Indeed. It was his turn now. He reached out across the small space and pulled the curtain to the next room aside.

The small hole in the wall glowed with candlelight. When they peered into the luxurious, foreign space, a red-haired woman sat on the edge of the bed and kept glancing at the door. Even in profile, she was a classically pretty woman. She obviously awaited someone.

While she waited . . . Vincent would wait no more for Veronica. His mouth watered with wanting to smell her cunny, and rub his face in the scent of her neck. He hungered to taste every bit of her she offered to him.

"Give me your hands, Veronica."

She glanced up at him over her shoulder and raised her hands toward him. He grasped her right hand and placed it on the wall below the candle flickering in the notch of wood. He then wrapped his fingers around her left and placed it on the curtain, pulled to the side. "Watch, see, feel me."

He placed himself behind her. His arms caging her between his body and the wall, his prick pressed to the small of her back. Fingers wandered up her arms to her shoulders and the clasp of her cape. She certainly didn't need this. He tugged the tails of the red ribbon, then pulled the cape from her shoulders.

In a rush, the fabric fell down between them. Her body shook and her breath exhaled at the same moment, as if a bellows had gushed out air.

His hands ran over the smooth skin of her shoulders. Her skin was so soft, so purely white and creamy. He slid across her back. The fine hairs on her body rose in reaction to his touch and he stared at them as they glowed translucent in the candlelight. This would be an experience he would never forget. He would savor every tiny detail.

He trailed his hands down her sides to the curve of her hip. Her corseted waist stood so small and impossibly stiff. He wanted to unlace her and run his hands along the newly released skin of her hips, to squeeze the small swell of her thighs. Damn, she was small. A tiny slip of nothing. A woman, through and through—a nymph who outwardly appeared small, but who inwardly glowed with divinity, grand thoughts, and spirit.

He leaned in and his chest molded to her back. His hands slid across the silk of her stomach and traveled to her upthrust breasts. A finger trailed along the dainty lace edging.

Her breasts heated and her chest heaved. She trembled against him and fisted her left hand into the curtain. He smiled. His finger strolled in a lazy path to the vale between her breasts. Dew met his fingers as he dashed beneath the silk and into the cavern her flesh provided. She damn well purred, the sound so sexy to his ears.

He foraged deeper, slipping below the underside of her breast. Her pulpy flesh yielded to him and he cupped her. His fingers massaged the soft flesh. He needed to feel her nipple, to twist the puckered bud between his fingers and make her hiss like the cat she was proving to be. Pushing upward, he erected her nipple from the silk covering. The hard flesh poked above the edging and he pinched and rolled her turgid flesh with the fingers of his opposite hand.

A tremor raced through her and she gasped, "Oh," grinding her bottom back against him. He studied the side of her face; her velvet brown eyes closed, her dark lashes fanned her cheek. Between his thumb and his forefinger, he rolled her bud gently, then hard.

Her mouth parted slightly, and shudder after shudder slid through her. His cock twitched against the thin fabric of her bloomers. He shifted his hips from side to side in an attempt to open the slit in the fabric of her bloomers. He needed to feel the heat of her bottom against his balls.

She arched her back and pressed her bum into his cock.

His hand slid down her belly to the front of the slit. Fingers gathered the fabric and he pulled the cotton apart. His lips touched her neck and his tongue slid out to taste her. Her scent flooded him—a floral aroma, which he knew not, but drank in like the life milk he needed. The heady tang of arousal and the salt of her skin bit at his tongue as he mapped his claim on her. What was it about Veronica that shook him to his toes? Her smell, taste, and feel were nonesuch.

Sliding up her neck, he sketched the taste of her skin onto his memory. His fingers grazed the curls of her mound and flicked the springy texture. The skin of her mound was damp with desire. The urge to slide deeper and feel her oils, and the slick heat of her opening, consumed him. He needed to taste her cunny on his skin, and smell her for hours whenever he raised his hand. His desire for her claimed his actions and pushed him for more and more.

Veronica.

His palm pressed and held to her mound, rubbing the skin

and curls. He curled his fingers about her, his middle finger caressing her folds. She moaned as her right hand was pressed flat to the wall. His left hand pinched her nipples as his right hand glided along the oiled velvet of her sex lips.

Her hips rocked with each curl of his middle finger against slick folds. The motion was an invitation to sate his desire and finger frig her at the earliest opportunity.

"Veronica, I want this. . . ." He slid his middle finger into her opening. The finger disappeared into her cunny with ease. My . . . God . . . she was wet.

She tilted her head against his and moaned that same animalistic cat purr he couldn't resist.

He slid his finger all the way in.

"Oh . . ." She pulled her legs farther apart, then forced her cunny down on his probing. Her hips instinctively rocked against him in a natural futtering motion, which he was eager to experience with his cock.

He pulled his finger out, then slid his palm and finger up the folds of her cunny and over her large bud.

"Oh . . ." Her mouth opened and closed, repeating the single word. "Um"—she bit and released her lower lip—"more, please."

"Sweet Veronica."

"Stand, Grace." A deep voice came from the opening in the wall.

Vincent's gaze focused on the room. A tall, fair-haired man strode toward the woman, who had stood at his request.

"Please." Veronica rocked her hips against his hand. Her bottom rubbed against his cock. He didn't give a damn what would go on in this room, he simply wanted to futter her. He gazed at her face, not even a flinch of acknowledgment of the man who entered the room. Her every sense focused on him.

His finger slid back down her silky oil and into her opening. He stopped there and spread his fingers out, opening the lips. Then he wiggled his middle finger in and out, in and out.

"Oh! Oh!" She trembled and pressed against him. His lips pressed once more to her neck and he dragged his teeth along her pulse.

Her entire body bucked, and then her muscles relaxed. He slid his middle finger all the way into her. Her insides scorched, and her muscles clamped about the digit.

He pulled out and slipped the tip of his index finger into the opening of her cunny. His teeth left her skin and he licked the line he had scored on her skin. He wished he could mark her this way, every day for a week. He frowned. For tonight she gave herself to him, and him to her. No more than that.

He would take what he could get and cherish it.

"Veronica," he breathed against her skin.

"What are they doing, St. Jerome?"

He looked up to the room to see the woman standing, her hands clasped behind her back and wrapped with what appeared to be a cravat.

The man raised a candle up and slowly drizzled wax down her chest and collarbone. The wax ran down her, cooling in drips that hung off her nipples. The woman's body shook with arousal, even as she sucked in startled breath after startled breath with each fresh drip of wax.

"It is a sensation, Veronica. Some get a thrill from the sensations that rush through the body. It can be cold sensations, such as snow. Or warm, such as wax. Smooth, such as silk, or rough, such as wool. Every sensation elicits a body reaction."

"Sensations." She turned her head and kissed him on the lips.

The soft flutter of her lips along his relaxed his muscles. Her tongue, more sure than before, thrust in and tasted his depths.

He moaned.

She pulled back, a breath away from his seeking lips. "I enjoy the kind of sensation kissing and touching *you* creates in me."

His lips curved up, and he touched her forehead with his. "Quite so, Veronica, an intoxicating sensation that will only get better this night."

15

Lilly

Lilly had no idea how this could get any better. What she did know was St. Jerome was indeed intoxicating. More so than the cook's aromatic bread. She licked her lips and inhaled the earthy scent of him once again.

She really wanted to continue this improper behavior. She slid her hands down from the wall and turned to face him. Reaching for his shirt, she trailed her fingers lower, seeking out his hot, ridged flesh that boldly jutted forward from his body. She enjoyed touching the smooth, silky, warm skin stretched across his hardness. The echo of his heartfelt moan from earlier bounced back and forth in her mind: *"Mmmmm."* Indeed, she wanted to bring him more pleasure. Her hand wrapped about his hardness. . . .

"In a moment." He wrapped his fingers about hers to stay them.

Her sex throbbed and ached. She wanted more—more of him touching her. She wanted him to slide his fingers deeper into her body and ignite her blood in a spasm of delight. Each time he had pressed into her, she teetered on the edge, aching for the pleasure she sought on occasion when she was alone.

"Shall we move on to the only other room on this floor?" His eyes stormed as though a thundercloud of desire. A desire she wanted to dance in as he rained down, thoroughly wetting her skin in pleasure.

"I . . ." She couldn't tell him no, she wanted him to bring her bliss *now*. "That would be nice."

He slid his fingers down her arm and to her wrist. There he wrapped his fingers about her, forming a bracelet that she wished to take home with her. No man had ever told her she was beautiful. No man had desired her. Here she stood, though, in a dark crevice of a wicked house with St. Jerome, a man she had thought was the worst of rakes.

She rolled her eyes. Who was she fooling? He may be a rake, but he was a gentleman, too. It was that contradiction that confused her. He, as well as the others she had met tonight, confused her. Nothing was as she had thought on the surface.

He grasped the candle from the notch in the wall and let the curtain fall back over Grace and the man she was with.

Grace was stunningly beautiful undressed. She allowed that man to touch her, to press upon her sensations Lilly could not understand as being pleasurable. Wax? How could the sting against your skin make you shake in arousal the way Grace's body had?

If St. Jerome had wished her to experience such a thing, she would have considered it. Maybe that was part of the entire thrill. To do as your partner wished, simply for his pleasure. Sweet Jesus, she had gone mad.

The sensation of St. Jerome's hands on her breasts, on her stomach, and on her honeypot had sent tingles up her belly. Simply remembering re-created the amazing feelings—she swallowed the lump in her throat. Why did her mind wander back to that improper place?

She had let a man she was not wed to touch her private places with his hands. She had let him kiss and bite her flesh. She should be shamed for her thoughts and acts. Heat washed her face.

His touch made her feel light-headed. It made her glow from the inside out. How could that be wrong?

Grace's words—*"Let your body tell you what is right and what is wrong."*—slammed into the echo of St. Jerome's moan bouncing around in her mind.

His moan was right. His voice, the sound of his pleasure, was what she wanted to hear more of tonight. She wanted to experience *him* tonight. . . .

Doing so was wrong, though.

She bit her lip and thought of her family's reputation. Her brother was here. . . . He would duel St. Jerome if he ever found out he touched her thus. A chill crept up her spine. She couldn't allow them to hurt each other. This could turn dangerous.

The warmth of St. Jerome beside her warmed her soul, and just this night was worth the secret. This was a simple fancy she simply would indulge.

She could not deny how St. Jerome made her feel. This one time in her life she wanted to savor something that made her pulse speed and her legs grow weak. To not follow the good and dutiful etiquette her father had sternly yelled into her since she was eight: *"Be the lady you are being raised to be. Outshine your mother and present yourself well."* He was gone now and Brian was in charge of her fate. He would at least understand her acts, because he himself was here.

They reached the end of the corridor. He placed the candle into the notch in the wood and slid the curtain back.

Moans, sounds of wetness, and flesh slapping together erupted from the hole.

Her gaze jumped to the scene displayed in the oval.

"Seems we saved the best for last." His tone held a note of humor.

Two men and two women engaged in futtering.

A man lay on his side, a woman also lay on her side, licking and sucking on his long and sleek thing. Another woman's head was nestled between that woman's legs and she licked her as the last man slid his short, thick pego in and out of her cunny as she moaned.

Lilly's eyes widened and a shock rippled through the soft flesh at the top of her thighs.

Women and men did things like this together? She absorbed the scene before her.

"A sight to see, Veronica. I can tell by your reaction you have not seen such."

"No. I . . . no. I have of course seen art, paintings of women frolicking together. Rubens's *The union of earth and Water* comes to mind." The image of the vivid colors and the sensual smile of the naked woman standing as she conversed with the sea god and the merman came to life before her.

St. Jerome raised her captured wrist and placed her palm on the wall, then gently unwound his fingers. His body brushed against her side and the fluidity of his motions set her body aquiver, all the way to her toes.

By God, how did he do that?

Shaking, she tried to relax and concentrate on the scene before her. *Come on now, Lilly. This is what you wanted, to have this experience tonight, to feel more of the devious, devilish sensations he pressed upon you.*

She was positioned before him, his length pressed to her back. The muscles of his body captured her from behind. Her heart pounded in her chest, and the flesh between her thighs throbbed with renewed moisture. The thick ridge of his sex pressed to the crack in her bloomers. The heat scorched against the un-touched skin. Goose bumps raced everywhere. She was hot and cold, clammy and soothed—all at once.

His fingers grazed her nipple. Her breath hitched. Oh, in-deed. *Please . . . please touch me there again.* His touch headed down across her restrained stomach to the curls of her pot. She spread her legs apart.

She wanted his fingers to bring her the rapture that drove her mad. His finger slid, catching slightly on the lips, then parted her folds. The slickness of her inner cunny yielded to him. She pushed her bottom back against him and rocked. His fingers parted her opening and she shook.

The image of the man's fingers futtering the woman in the first room slammed into her as the sensations of being touched, just the same way, built her cravings for more. Her sanity fled. . . . In her mind, the woman's soft flesh pouted open as fingers slid in and out.

A finger slid inside her and she bucked. "Oh!" Her voice was so loud, she bit her lip to curb her sounds "Um . . ."

"More, sweet Veronica? Do you want more of me inside you?"

Indeed, she did. She wanted his fingers sliding in and out of her as the woman had experienced in that first room.

"Please."

He slid his fingers out and his hips pulled back from her body. His prick slid down into the crease between her thighs.

She stiffened—no, she was not ready for that. Nor did she know if she wanted to be. His fingers continued their flight, slipping back into her, building the ache she needed relief from so desperately. She moaned another loud sound and felt his smile against her neck.

"No need to be quiet, sweet one." The hot skin of his cock glided along the back side of her folds as his fingers spread her wide. With each press forward, the head of his thick thing touched her opening as his fingers slid in and out.

The smell of her own wetness clung to her. She squirmed, and all her muscles shook as moan after moan came from all about her—her moans, his, and the couples in the room, which she had no ability to even watch.

His lips kissed and licked her neck. She turned her head into his. Her legs trembled, threatening to give way, as the bliss coiled deep in her belly. Heat spread up her limbs and her head grew light.

He continued the same pattern with his hands. All her being concentrated on that one spot: his fingers slipping and stretching, the delicious twinges in her sex, the wetness—oh, the wetness—the sounds, the smell of her arousal, the earthy scent of him.

He slid his finger in again, and her entire sex throbbed. She was close to shattering, to seeing the blinding bliss, as her body crashed in ecstasy. His fingers spread wide, and as he withdrew, he rocked his hips forward. The head of his prick nestled into the opening of her honeypot.

She wanted more of his thing inside her. She pressed back against him. He met her press with one of his own. Searing pain sliced through her opening as he slid all the way into her.

"Sweet Jesus!" she screeched, and pulled forward to relieve the pain.

"Shh." He held her tight to him. "I know. Relax. Breathe and your body will adjust to me in a moment." His fingers slid to her button and circled it.

Her sex throbbed in pain, but the blissful ache burst back to flame.

Rocking his hips in small motions, he possessed her. His cock moved slowly in and out of her wetness. The drag of him against the lips of her flesh sent renewed pain swirling with pleasurable sensations deep into her belly. He was so impossibly huge inside her.

She had never in her life experienced anything like this. His hard length pulled to the tip, then thrust back in.

She shook and trembled. The pain was still there, but it mattered little compared to the sensation of being joined with a man. He moved his hands to her hip.

"Oh, sweet Veronica. You are gripping me so tight. . . . I am not going to last—" He shuddered and moaned behind her.

Last? Her eyes widened. He thrust harder into her. The sound of her wetness with each press amazed her. How did that happen? Was he weeping into her body?

He forcefully bucked into her. The burning sensation engulfed her muscles and she cried out. A shocking wave of bliss shook her being.

He groaned and held still behind her. His rock-hard thing pulsed within her, "Oh . . . my . . ." He pulled out and slid back in. "Sweetness!"

Her eyes widened. Oh! What was that? The sensation of being overly filled shocked her senses.

He held her hip and shook. His pego buried deep in her, he panted and gasped for breath.

Neither one of them said a word and his pego softened in her swollen flesh. Wetness dripped from her opening and down her legs.

Oh, my. She had given herself to him and he had taken her with vigor. Her legs shook as he slid from her body.

"Are you well, Veronica?" He grabbed her hand and turned her toward him.

Am I well? Good question.

She shook. Her lower lip trembled as sadness, elation, and fear overtook her.

"I—I am . . . I think." *What happens now?*

He stumbled back against the wall and pulled her to him. With his arms wrapped about her, she rested her head against his chest. His heart beat a hefty tune beneath her ear. She closed her eyes and absorbed the sound. The heat of him calmed her muscles, and his scent calmed her soul. She licked her lips.

This was all well. She had the lemon in and he would never know who she really was. His hand slid down her belly to the curls of her mound, and a finger slid into her folds.

Lilly tensed as a slight burn pulsed through the tender flesh. His fingers aimlessly wandered back and forth without entering her.

"Would you like to again, Veronica? This next time, we can do so in a bed, where we can touch our entire bodies, skin to skin."

Oh, my, how she wanted that! To feel his body entwined with hers would be divine, but she couldn't.

What she had given him—needed to be all she did. This one time with him. No more.

He circled her button and the muscles of her sex washed with pleasure. She needed to leave his company and she couldn't simply tell him that. Tears rushed to her eyes. She needed to leave this falseness.

The strain of the lies she had told, mixed with the intense pleasure and newness to all things physical between man and woman, was too overwhelming for her. She needed to leave.

"I would like to do it again, St. Jerome, but I need the washroom."

"Indeed, I imagine you do, sweet." He dragged a hand down her back.

She shifted her stance and a gush of wetness spilled from her sex and down her legs. She cringed. What was that? Blood? His seed? She was not sure she actually wanted to know.

"We will go. You can use the washroom. After which, we

can find a comfortable place to enjoy each other for the rest of the night. I am looking forward to seeing every inch of you."

Sadness grabbed at Lilly's heart, and the unused organ pinched in her breast. He would be disappointed in her flight from him, but she had no other choice. She would go and find her brother and then leave.

She glanced up at St. Jerome. Calm and relaxed, he had no inkling of what was about to happen. She couldn't very well ask St. Jerome to escort her to find her brother any longer. She ruined that chance.

She inhaled deeply. Maybe finding Brian didn't matter. She had seen what was in this house . . . and had learned a few things about what she herself was capable of when tempted. She enjoyed being a bit wicked.

She would leave this house, find her way back to Burber Place, and hope no one recognized her on her exit.

16

The Intersection

St. Jerome pushed open the door to the main hall on the second floor and Lilly slipped through to the large, elegant corridor. She glanced down at her white bloomers. Red blood stained the fine linen that hung between her legs. Thank goodness the red cape covered her from behind. She pulled the edges of the wool closed in front of her body.

Glancing over her shoulder at St. Jerome, she sighed.

His short black hair stood as neat as when he had entered the corridor. One sound reason to have such unfashionably short hair, it looked the same after vigorous encounters.

He smiled at her.

"The washroom is down the stairs." She fidgeted with the openings to the cape, clutching the fabric together.

"I will meet you at the foot of the stairs. I will scout us a room while you take care of your needs."

She turned to face him, taking in his likeness one more time. My God, he was handsome. His wolflike gray eyes, filled with adoration, glinted down at her. She reached her hand up and touched his cheek. "Thank you for making me feel beautiful this night." She slid her hand into his short hair. The soft bristles tickled her fingertips.

She would always remember him like this. The look in his eyes . . . the feel of his warm cheek and hair.

His brow pinched together. "Get washed up, sweet, wicked Veronica. A combination that is so intoxicating."

These would be the last words she ever heard from him. "Sweet" and "wicked" and someone else's name. Her throat tightened on trembling emotions, which she didn't know, and feared she could not hold back.

She quickly turned away from him and made her way down the stairs. A tear leaked from her eye.

She didn't dare look back. She swallowed hard as a torrent of tears welled to her lashes. Each step she took in the opposite direction of him felt wrong. Her will urged her to turn about and go to him, explain her situation and plead forgiveness. She couldn't. Brian would slit him with his sword from gullet to neck, if he found out.

She had no idea if St. Jerome watched her, but not knowing was much better than having the knowledge that he did not.

She made it to the bottom of the stairs and turned toward the right and the door nestled to the back of the entry. She would make it to the room where she had met Grace and then make her plan.

She pulled on the ornate brass handle and opened the heavy wood door. A woman walked straight into her. Reddish brown hair in a tangle clung to the distraught woman's face, and Lilly screeched, gaining her balance. The other woman sobbed.

"Grace? What are you doing down here?" Lilly stepped to the side of the doorway so they could have more privacy. Grace appeared in a state.

"Oh!" Grace sniffled as tears ran down her face. "I—um—I am fretting."

"Oh, dear, what happened? I—I saw you upstairs with that man. Did something happen? Did he hurt you?"

"You saw me?" Grace glanced at the door.

"Pardon me?" Heat infused Lilly's cheeks. "Indeed, I watched him drip wax on your breasts. You barely flinched. Is that what made you cry?"

"No." Grace shook her head, then looked down at the floor. "He . . . he loves me."

Lilly's lips turned up into a smile. "Oh, Grace, that is wonderful—"

"No, it is not!" Her fear-filled gaze shot to Lilly's.

"Pardon?" Lilly sat down on a small bench at the base of the hall. "You had said you wanted love with one man—someone who made you feel passion."

Grace sat down beside her. "Yes . . . though *not* with Winston." She chewed on the inside of her cheek.

Lilly stared at Grace, her long reddish brown hair hung in ringlets over her shoulders. Lilly was puzzled. "I don't understand, Grace. Do you love him?"

Grace stared at the wood floor. She glanced up at Lilly, then back down to the floor. "I have all of my life."

Lilly sat motionless and stared at Grace. Emotions of love and fear and despair swirled about her. If she loved him all of her life, he had to know. "Tell him."

"He is not a one-woman man." Hurt dripped from her words and she pushed her hair from her face.

"He certainly seemed to care for you, Grace. It was in the way he touched you, and adoration shone in his eyes." Lilly stared at her new friend. "Why does he scare you so much, Grace?"

Grace's lower lip trembled and a tear spilled down her cheek. "In my eyes, Winston is a perfect gentleman. Someone I should have married—a temptation I resisted but should have embraced. I see now what he is *really* like, and he is like any other man."

Something was amiss in Grace's thinking. Lilly scratched her head. "Pardon? You told me my brother was still the same man, even if he was here. Doesn't that hold true for your . . . Winston? Isn't he the same man you knew?"

Grace stared at her hands, then slowly looked over into Lilly's eyes. She tilted her head to the side as if considering her own words. "I suppose."

"Tell him. I have a feeling from the way he looked at you, he already knows, but tell him." Lilly smiled. Good could only come from Grace expressing how she truly felt.

"I—I shall." Graced glance down at Lilly's legs.

Lilly slid them closed as embarrassed heat rose to her cheeks, making her ears burn.

"I see you have decided to experiment. To live. Are you well, Veronica?"

"I fear I told a lie." Lilly looked down at her hands. "No, I did tell a lie . . . and I fear what the consequences of such a deception will be. I need to leave here, Grace." Tears welled in her eyes. "I have no carriage and I have no idea where I am." She glanced around the hall. Music and laughter came from the ballroom. She feared any moment St. Jerome or her brother would stumble into the hall and her lie would be told.

"Veronica, what happened? What did you lie about? I may be able to help you."

"A gentleman is most likely at this moment waiting for me at the bottom of the stairs. I told him I would spend the night with him. When what I gave him already is all I can permit myself to offer him." Her words tumbled out in a painful rush, and her tongue grew thick in her mouth. "I fear I may have fallen from my views of proper society . . . and have strange loving emotions for this man." She fisted her hands and shifted her hips in discomfort. "Which is preposterous! I have known him for all of a few hours, and all this night was filled with fantasy, temptation, and sin. I have begun a journey on a lie and I have no idea how to get back, or if I even can."

"Indeed, temptation and sin are all around, Veronica, though not simply on this night. Feeling connected to someone may only take a single moment. You may have more emotion in a single touch with one man than you ever do in a hug or a kiss with another you've known for years. I am glad you followed your desires this night. I also know, this being your first encounter, repeating the act this night is not wise. I will call my coach for you to the servants' back entrance."

Lilly stared at Grace, her wise words filling her with hope and calmness. "You said you didn't want to know who I was, but I think I would like to know you, Grace, outside of this night." Lilly's hand slid across the bench and grasped Grace's fingers. "You may tell them to take me to Burber Place."

Grace squeezed Lilly's fingers, which lay wrapped in her grasp. "Very well, Lady Veronica." She winked. "I shall call my coach and I shall call on you in the next few days. Remember, take the lemon out in the morning. Not before. And soak in a hot tub. That will ease the soreness of the first time."

"What should I do about the clothes and mask?" She glanced down to her legs. "The bloomers, I fear, are ruined."

"You shall need to wear them home, dear lady. What you do with them from there is your choice." Grace stood and continued to hold Lillys hand.

Lilly pushed to her feet on tired, shaking legs. "Thank you, Grace. Until we meet again." She leaned in and kissed Grace on her soft cheek and lingered. In one night, this woman had changed her life. Or had it all been some strange and fantastic dream?

Grace wrapped her arms about Lilly and hugged her, then

pulled back from the embrace. "Please remember, Veronica, you did nothing wrong this night, and no one, including your brother, shall ever know—unless you wish them to. Watch for the coach with the Wentland crest on the side." Grace stepped around Lilly and pushed through the door, which led to the main entry.

Lilly stared after her new friend. What a strange night. She came here determined to prove her brother innocent in all the townsfolk's gossip. Instead, she ended up doing the same he did here . . . or maybe worse. She cringed. No, she had barely done anything in comparison to what went on in the rooms.

Besides, she wouldn't tell a soul.

Who was it that Grace would find standing on the foot of the stairs? The curiosity of who had claimed the innocence of her new friend beckoned like a glass of the very best wine on a thirst-filled day. Whoever this man was, he had also claimed a piece of Veronica's heart.

Curiosity quickened her step. No one stood at the foot of the stairs. She frowned, then glanced up the stairs. Still, no one. She continued to the front door, and signaled the doorman.

"Indeed, ma'am?" The thin boy bobbed his head and a shy smile curved his lips.

"Please have my coach brought around to the back entrance." What was such a shy boy doing working in this house? Her brow pinched tight and she turned about.

Vincent St. Jerome descended to the bottom of the stairs. He turned and stared at the door to the back of the house.

Her brow pinched. St. Jerome? He was a fine gentleman—no matter what the town gossips said. Anyone who could stay true to Amelia after all her rages deserved happiness with a sweet young woman, a companion to share the rest of his days with.

She bit the inside of her cheek. He should know Veronica wasn't coming, and maybe—just maybe—he would catch her getting into her coach.

"She will not be here to meet you, St. Jerome."

His gray gaze spun to her. "Pardon?"

"Veronica, she left."

"Pardon?" His eyes widened and panic clouded his clear gaze.

Grace glanced down at his fisted hands. "She asked to be taken home."

"Home? Isn't she one of Emma's girls?"

"No." Grace pushed past him and stepped up onto the stairs. "She is a lady, St. Jerome." She glanced down and saw a small bit of Veronica's innocence on St. Jerome's flap. "Take a look down at your pantaloons. You may wish to think about heading out the back way yourself."

17

Lilly

Vincent St. Jerome stared down at his pants, and his head spun. *My God, what . . . what happened?*

Across the front of his pantaloons smudges of dried blood shone. She was a virgin. Or *had been* would be more accurate. A lady. He cringed. He futtered her as roughly as he took a seasoned mistress. Or nearly so.

Damn, he should have known by the way she pulled away from him when he slid all the way in. What had he done? He cringed as the scene played over in his mind.

Take it easy, Vincent. You have never bedded a virgin before. You knew you would have to soon, when you wed. You simply had practice. To the gates of damnation with that thought!

He had her. She gave herself to him. She was a respectable lady and she was his . . . his bride.

What luck! Here he was resisting her all night because she was not of blood—only to find out she most certainly could be his bride. His throat closed off. Damn it. Blood pounded through him. Who was she? Lady Veronica? That was not likely.

He turned toward the door that led to the back of the house

and ran. His feet moved as fast as he could down the short hall. He yanked open the door to see nothing. Not a damn blasted thing. Sweat pierced the back of his neck. He was too late.

Stepping through the door, he headed straight toward the back house and the large door that led to the back gardens, then spun about. Nothing. Where would she have gone? He stilled himself. His heart beat fiercely in his chest. The need to find her consumed him.

"You had said you were looking for a man who was more like a girlfriend than a man." His voice echoed in his mind.

"Um, Lord Cunnington."

Lord Cunnington. Indeed.

But would she have gone to look for him before departing?

Lady Wentland's comment about her urgent departure made that doubtful, but Cunnington knew Veronica, and St. Jerome knew where Cunnington would be found.

He turned and ran, leather soles slapping the wood floor, to the game room.

Rounding the corner, he entered the doorway to the large plush room. More than twelve men resided—smoking, drinking, and engaging in all kinds of games.

His gaze darted through the smoky fog to find Cunnington sitting in one of the large leather chairs, a cigar in his mouth, a half-full glass of brandy dangling from his hand, as he stared at the ceiling.

He strode around the hazard table. "Cunnington!"

"Ah, St. Jerome." Cunnington pulled his cigar from his lips. "Heard you went off with a pretty young dove for a little fun." He winked and the smell of brandy wafted about him.

In his cups. Damn. The drink was what Cunnington came here for, to escape and simply be. "Interesting you should mention that, I was hoping you could help me find her."

"Me help you find her? Where did you lose her?" Cunnington's lips curled up into a smile. "It is always a sad moment when one loses a dove." He scoffed.

Blast and damn. This was not going to be easy. Vincent glared at him, his patience nonexistent.

"Last bird I lost went off to Scotland with a rogue from Devonshire." He raised his glass of brandy to his lips and inhaled another large swallow. "Damn pity, too. Beautiful breasts on that one."

"Cunnington!"

"Very well, tell me."

Relief washed over him. He had forgotten Cunnington kept his wits—well, mostly—when he drank. "She said she looked for you. That you were her friend."

"My friend, you don't say? I don't have many women friends, St. Vincent. Can you describe her?"

"Of course I can. She is very petite, with dark onyx hair and the most innocent brown doe eyes. Thought she was one of Emma's girls, but I found out she is not. I need to find her."

Cunnington's brow pulled tight. "You described all the women in my family, St. Jerome. Well, besides the fact that they are looking for me *here*"—his eyes grew round with the emphasis—"and my sister is the only one I would call a friend." He raised the glass of brandy to his mouth and slurped a large swallow. "Now, if she was here with you, we would have something *very* serious to talk about, St. Jerome." Cunnington glared at Vincent.

His sister? No. Simply not possible. The consequences of what he had done would be so dire if she was Cunnington's sister. He stared at his friend in the same dark brown eyes as Veronica had, and his gut twisted. So be it. His sister. "Indeed, we would, wouldn't we? Are you sure you don't know anyone else who may fit that description?"

"Not I. Are you sure she said me? Maybe she was simply

trying to brush you over for my good old self. Where did you say she had gone?"

Brush him over? She certainly had done that. His panic and the urgency to find her slowly turned to anger. "Could be, Cunnington. Point well made." His sister. How would he explain to his friend that he spent the night showing his innocent sister the rooms, and had taken her for her first time standing in a hall? There was no easy way to broach this subject, and depending on Cunnington's mood, this would either end in fisticuffs or in a duel. Neither appealed to him. Cunnington was his friend.

Well, it certainly would not do to tell him now. Tomorrow, or the next day, when he could see with his own eyes that lady Veronica indeed was Cunnington's sister. Then, and only then, he would launch himself off that cliff. For now, he needed to get a glimpse of his sister to see if Lady Veronica and she were the same.

"You know, Cunnington. I have never seen your sister out in town. Do you keep her hidden away someplace? Allowing her no fun whatsoever?"

Cunnington laughed outright. "My dear old pa would not allow her to do anything. I hadn't really thought about it much, I suppose I should have." His brow pinched and he raised his glass to his lips, then stopped and lowered it. "You are in search of a bride, St. Jerome. Maybe you will simply wed her and save me all the fuss."

Indeed. Vincent laughed. "Every lady should have an introduction to society, Cunnington. What about the musicale tomorrow night?"

"By damn, St. Jerome. That is a fine idea." His lips turned down. "Why are you so interested in my sister, St. Jerome?"

Vincent smiled at his friend and ordered a glass of brandy for himself. "Really, Cunnington, you simply mentioned her and I realized I had never seen her. Seems odd to me, that is all."

If all went as he wished, he would find his lady, have a few sound words with her about deceiving him, and then announce talk to his friend about a betrothal after the event. The idea slid into his mind and soul.

A warm contentedness seeped into his gut. He enjoyed showing her around this house. Her reactions to his touch? Even stronger proof that they would be good together.

Lady Veronica, her small form, and her laughing eyes.

Her sweet innocence.

Innocence . . . he had taken, and would keep.

Lilly sat in her tub in the safety of Burber Place. No one had expected her arrival, but the servants were nevertheless kind. Her hands slid up her stomach to her breasts and grazed her nipples. The flesh between her thighs throbbed. She closed her eyes and pictured St. Jerome, his wolfish gray eyes glinting with desire, and his short, cropped hair, and his smile. . . . Yes, that smile.

Her hands slid down her body to the flesh of her thighs. Her mind wandered to the rooms they had viewed—the couples playing, Grace and the wax—all of the night flashed before her.

Her fingers slid to her slick sex. The water had eased the burning ache from the act itself, but had done little to quell the vivid urges that gnawed at her mind.

The memory of St. Jerome's sex cradled in her hand—the heat of his skin and the silkiness when she slid the skin up and down—came to her. Her cunny throbbed and delicious tingles raced through her muscles.

She slid her finger into her pussy and winced. The flesh burned and she moved her fingers to the inside of her thigh.

She should have told him. It was wrong of her not to tell him she was pure. He no doubt had proof of her innocence on him. She should have told him.

She ran her hands up her stomach, back down over her hips, and then back up to her breasts. She wanted to go back to feel his hands on her again, to feel his kiss against her lips, and to taste his skin.

Silliness, Lilly. You simply want to smell him again. She grinned. Indeed, there was that, too. His smell alone made her insides flutter.

Only a simpleton would even attempt to venture back to that house; and Lilly might be foolish, but she was not daft in the attic.

She could write him a letter. She shook her head. That would be totally improper. Any contact with him truly could cause scandal. Her brother would no doubt find out and then her life, as well as his, would become a bumblebroth. She sighed.

She couldn't really approach him out in public and thank him for what he'd shown her. Sweet Jesus, she could see the conversation as she strode down the Serpentine and crossed his path with his new wife on his arm.

"Pardon me, St. Jerome. I wanted to apologize for lacking fortitude and telling you to your face that I was pure. I know it certainly is shocking, but I thank you for educating me the other night. Oh, and my brother wants to kill you to avenge our honor."

His new bride's face would drain of all color and Lilly would beam at her, wishing she were the one on his arm.

"Educating you? Who are you?" St. Jerome would respond.

"Veronica. The woman you futtered the other night who then fled you."

His wolf eyes would glint with remembrance, "I had wondered where you went. I am glad you are well." He would urge his new wife to keep walking, not wanting her to know any of what his prior life entailed.

"Indeed, it was quite an insightful evening and I shall always remember your smell," she would say as they slowly began to turn away from her.

"You are very welcome." He would tip his hat to her and Lilly would watch them fade off into the distance, knowing full well what she would be missing for the rest of her life.

Lilly sighed. Ridiculous! Jealousy of a man she could never have because of how they met. She wasted good creative energy on that thought. He didn't even know her real name.

She didn't care. She wanted to see him again. Her heart beat painfully in her breast. She needed a plan to cross his path, something that would seem entirely innocent and inconspicuous.

She couldn't let him go without telling him who she was and that she appreciated him. Her heart sank.

No, Lilly, you want him to know you are smitten with him. Her lower lip trembled as emotions threatened to overtake her. She shook that thought from her head.

She indeed needed a plan or she would forever regret leaving Emma Drundle's home. *Think, Lilly, think. . . .*

St. Jerome said he was attending a musicale tomorrow to start his quest for a bride. Maybe her brother had an invitation as well.

The hairs on her neck stood. It was a bit of a far-reaching idea, but maybe it would work. . . .

If Brian did hold an invitation and she attended, then that night would be her introduction not only to St. Jerome, but to the entire ton as Lady Lillian. She would need a gown and bucketfuls of fortitude.

Well, she proved tonight she had a well of spirit to pull from when she thought she hadn't had any.

Lady Lillian. If she wanted St. Jerome to know who she was, then she needed to be who she was raised to be.

She cringed and cold sweat pierced her brow. Throughout her life, that title had felt wrong. Everything she thought of as being a lady—sophisticated, beautiful, graceful—she was not. She simply was . . . Lilly.

18

Grace

Winston stretched out on the mattress and small bits of wax poked and tugged at his skin. *Hmmm.* He ached delightfully. He had not futtered since he left India, and a fortnight before he had left on his journey for home had passed without any passion.

He slept the deepest he had in months. Futter was the perfect elixir to his tormented sleep patterns. When in a new place, he was kept awake by the sights, smells, noises, and new energies around him. He flexed his shoulders. He was alive and alert, and the desire to hunt pulsed in his veins.

Grace's soft curves and laughing tone came to mind. He inhaled and her scent teased his nostrils. He reached his hand out and cold sheets met his fingertips. Her warmth was missing from the bed. His eyes fluttered open to the dim glow of the richly decorated room he had rented in Lars Petersen's home.

He lay in bed alone. He stared at the ceiling and went over the evening's events. His cock pulsed in want of Grace's sweet lips licking and sucking him to a delicious morning spend. Where was Grace?

He pushed up to sitting. The wax remained on his groin and on the bed. The use of wax as an intensifier of sensations while futtering intoxicated him. Seeing the remnants of their time together on his groin and sheets warmed him thoroughly.

He slid his legs over the side and stood. From childhood he remembered Grace liked to be alone when she needed to think. He was similar. His most intense and meaningful thoughts were attained when alone: long walks in the forest, with the scents and sights of nature surrounding him. Wisdom practically floated on the breeze.

He hoped the situation was the same and *not* that she had left his bed because of his profession of love.

He had never told a woman he loved her before and his choice to do so at that moment surprised him. The compulsion to let his feeling be known to her had certainly trumped his need for control and emotional reserve. He sighed. Where was she?

He truly had feelings for Grace. He simply needed to convince her that she did for him as well. His fingernails caught the edges of the wax on his stomach and he peeled the remains of the cool wax from his skin. The sting of his hair pulled away as the wax let loose enlivened him. This was a moment for joy, not melancholy. Grasping his breeches from the floor, he slid them on over his scar. That damned scar. A chill gripped him.

Had she see his jagged scar before she left the bed? Or had she slid away as quickly as possible?

A small part of him hoped she had not seen the hideous red flesh. The memory of the stupidity of the event returned to him every time he viewed the disfigurement. A bigger part wanted her to see all of him now and always.

He pulled his white cotton shirt on over his head and headed for the door. She was somewhere in this house. What was she thinking and feeling about the event that happened between them? He had always seen Grace as a simple English miss, his friend, and the source of many boyhood fascinations. Finding her again shook his views of her mightily. His desire for a wife of passion and filled with adventure collided with his view of her. He wanted her. He simply needed to make sure she was well, then let her be to figure things out. No matter how hard it would be for him to leave things to play out as they should, he needed to let them go. Let her come to him on her own time.

Walking out into the hallway, he headed down the long, winding steps. He strode back along the staircase and opened the wood door. The main section of the house lay beyond. He stepped inside and closed the door. Two women's hushed voices came from around the other side of the stairs. One of them was Grace.

Introspection, mixed with longing, rippled from her voice. *Let her be, Winston. You know where she is now. And listening to her thoughts with her friend will not get you anything substantial. Walk forward and let her converse in private.*

He couldn't.

The need to know she was well wouldn't let his feet move. *One sentence, Winston. One! Know she is well and move on.*

He stood very still and concentrated on their voices. . . .

"Tell him. I have a feeling, from the way he looked at you, he already knows, but tell him," a young woman with a deeper voice than Grace's said.

"I—I shall." Grace's tone held a bit more lightness.

Winston sighed. What was she to tell? And to whom? He needed to know more. He strained to hear.

"I fear I told a lie. No, I did tell a lie . . . and I fear what the consequences of such a deception will be. I need to leave here, Grace." The other woman's voice sounded panicked and shamed.

157

Damn! They moved on to the other woman's issues. Winston's teeth clenched tight.

You should not be listening to their conversation anyway, Winston. Stop acting so common. Listening for any sign of acceptance from her is pathetic for a man of your travels. He shook his head. *You know better. That kind of behavior only leads to more and more suspicions. Move on. Grace will be done shortly. She will return to your room when she is ready to. Give her some time. You need faith in her, Winston. You know she desires you. Be patient, she will come to you.*

Winston nodded to himself. Indeed. She would never leave the house without a more in-depth conversation with him, and he was positive the "him" in the one line he overheard referred to him.

He strode down the hall toward the main ballroom and the back stairs to the second floor. As he turned and entered the main room, people danced all about.

The revelries certainly were well on their way. Most of the people who stood, danced, and futtered were fully in their cups. The sounds of clinking glasses, laughter, and music did little to enliven his spirits and loosen the grip wrapped about his heart.

A woman and man passed him, embraced in a different sort of waltz. Her hair was half down, and her breasts were clear to anyone who noticed.

The man groped and squeezed her nipples. Their mouths pressed, tongues licked. The woman's hands fluttered about his shoulders. Their hips rose and fell as their feet tapped and shuffled to the sounds of the orchestra.

Winston frowned. Only the English would consider such an act while doing other pleasurable activities. No, the French would as well. In India they would find a spot on one of the large benches. Doing so would make their goal attainable and more enjoyable. Dancing and futtering simply didn't mix.

He had left England to chart a different path for his life, and this house and the debauchery swirling about him confirmed his wisdom in doing so. How had Markus convinced him to let a room here?

The man lifted the woman and she wrapped her legs about his waist. As she clung to him, he fumbled with his flap beneath her. She lowered herself down and his pego disappeared within her. She cried out.

Winston's eyes widened.

Maybe the act while dancing *was* possible. Winston shook his head. Enough of this. He headed toward the back room and the refreshments. He needed a stiff drink to right his balance again.

He would drink a glass of port or whatever spirit could be found before he headed back to his bedchamber.

He walked around the edge of the dance floor, avoiding as many people as possible, and entered the back room. Men sat about, drinking and smoking and catering to women whom they wished to persuade into contracts with them.

He grasped a glass and a carafe of port with shaking hands. Pulling the stopper from the stem, he shakily splashed three fingers' worth of the deep cherry-colored liquid into the tumbler and raised the crystal to his lips.

"Where is Lady Wentland, Greydon?"

Winston swallowed the strong wine and glanced over his shoulder. Lord Brummelton stood to his side. "She is talking to a woman in the hall, Markus." Winston turned to face his friend.

Markus nodded his head. "Ah, very well. I was pleased to see you two together. She is a dear woman and you are a close friend."

"Indeed. Grace and I have known each other since childhood.

That is long before you set eyes and whatever else on her."
Winston raised his glass and sucked in a mouthful of the thick,
strong liquid.

Markus smiled. "You jest!"

"No, actually. I was close with her brother most of our lace
years."

"A better match than I imagined then. I am truly glad I talked
you both into coming here this evening." He winked at him.

"You talked her into coming?" Winston didn't know whether
to challenge him to fisticuffs or thank him. Had Grace futtered
Markus? It certainly was possible. It was likely. Winston frowned.

"Indeed. Since Wentland passed, she secluded herself. I happened into one of the smaller events and saw her this night. I
could not let her waste away with people who don't understand
her as well as I do."

"And what is that, Markus?" Winston's teeth clenched.

"She will tell you in time, Greydon."

"I don't plan on letting her leave this place without her acceptance of me as her husband, Markus."

"I certainly give you my blessing. Though I suppose it is her
brother you should have this conversation with." His brow
drew tight. "Remember where you are, Greydon. You are not
at church."

"I will obtain his blessing after I have her consent. I don't
see any issues with him. She, on the other hand—"

"Ah, indeed. Grace has a very colorful past, Greydon. She is
an amazing woman. Her marriage was a disappointment and
far from kind to her. You need to understand her many vibrant
facets. You could do her no further disservice than to paint her
in a corner as a schoolgirl. You and she are both here tonight.
Both of your own accord. Don't act like a proper saint when
you are here, just as the rest of us are."

"I have had that inkling, Markus. I am more than willing to accept her, as well as my sensual sides."

"Very well, I shall tell you one small piece of information, Winston. Her husband never bedded her. Not in the sense I am sure you have this night."

"Pardon?" She certainly was no virgin. What was Markus talking about? Winston tilted his head to the side in silent question for more.

"No rise. He was much older, as you know."

"Ah. Indeed." Poor Grace, she married and never futtered the man she wed. Winston's heart ached for her misfortune. He shook his head. "So he did other things with her then?"

"More than any normal husband would ever wish of his wife, and less than any normal husband would ever do with his wife." He smiled with sadness in his eyes. "She will tell you one day. In that time, you will know more about Grace than I ever shall. She has a love-hate relationship with his chair."

" 'His chair'?"

"Indeed. Her entire expression changes when she thinks about it." He chuckled. "She is an amazing woman."

"Why have you not taken her then, Markus."

"My relationship with her started because of a settling of a debt to Lord Wentland. A debt she never knew about and still does not. No matter how much I enjoyed her and care about her now, I could never wed a reminder of such."

Winston stared at Markus. *Debt?* The look on Markus's face told Winston, *Don't even ask him.*

He knew so little about Lord Wentland. When Grace's betrothal was announced, Winston was on a boat sailing around the southern tip of Africa.

Winston raised the glass of port to his lips and swallowed the sweet, strong wine to the last drop.

"Thank you for this information, Markus. I will not tell a soul what you have confided in me."

"I know you won't, Greydon. I would not have said a word to you if I thought otherwise." Markus turned and walked away.

Winston set down the glass and headed to the stairs. He strode up, two at a time. He hoped Grace was back in the room; he had so much to talk about with her.

19

Grace

Grace grabbed the door handle to Winston's room and pushed open the heavy wood. Her heart pounded in her chest. What awaited her within? She turned and quietly closed the door behind her.

The room was as she had left it, glowing with candlelight and smelling of spice. She walked to the bed. All that remained was a pile of blankets where they had lain. Small flecks of wax scattered here and there spread over the sheets. No Winston. Where did he go?

She turned about in the room and a tray with wine perched upon it sat next to the bed. It must have been a recent delivery. She reached down and poured a glass full of the deep cherry-colored liquid, then snuggled up on the bed to wait for Winston's return. She pulled the blankets up over herself and raised the glass. The sweet tartness of the wine filled her nose. She placed her lips on the edge of the glass and drank a long swallow.

And another.

And another.

Until the glass lay empty in her grasp. Her head fogged, and her vision grew hazy. A yawn passed her lips. She set the glass back on the table.

She would tell Winston . . .

She would tell him that she loved him, always had. Spending her life with him was a dream she had, and every time life set unbearable things in her way, she wished he were there to make her laugh and smile. She sighed.

Chills raced along her neck as her heart remembered the longing she had for Oscar's touch. She would never again long for someone the way she had for Oscar. She was afraid to show Winston how she loved him. Afraid her emotions would over-power her. For years her emotions lay behind a wall she had constructed: the yearnings, the desires, the disappointment, and the pain. However, Winston tempted her so. She wanted to let the wall down and see where things went.

She scooted down on the bed, into a position where she could see the door. She would wait here for him. Her eyelids hung heavy, then closed her in blackness.

The soothing warmth of Winston's hands rubbed up her back. She jumped and glanced over her shoulder.

Winston was not there.

A dream, Grace. Now stay awake. You need to tell him when he comes back. Her eyelids closed again and her legs twitched. He would return, and she would simply tell him . . . *I love you, too.*

What happened after that . . . would be . . .

Grace lay on her bed, staring at the cherrywood chair. The door opened, closed, and footsteps fell on the carpet.

"Good evening, Lady Wentland."

Oscar? No, it was not Oscar. The voice soothed her be-yond recognition. Though she could not turn to see who was there, she could only see the chair.

The mattress depressed and heat warmer than the sun wrapped about her. A smooth, hot male chest pressed to her back, tucking into her body. A sleek, ridged cock was pressed to the crack of her bum.

She rubbed back against the hard length. Her pussy throbbed, wanting only to be filled. Who had Oscar sent this time? Why was Oscar not perched in the chair, staring at her with hard eyes? This was, after all, his desire. Why was he not present to enjoy that which he gave away so freely?

She reached her hand back and wrapped her arm about his torso. Her fingertips pressed into the crack of his bum.

"I will never watch you from that chair. It simply is not close enough to you."

Whose voice was that? She needed to know.

His cock slid between her legs and directly into her slick cunny. She cried out and dug her nails into the crease of his bum.

"Good, Grace. I want to sleep joined with you, nothing more."

Winston . . . Winston would never watch her from that chair.

Grace awoke to the glow of a single, sputtering candle in the candelabrum, which stood by the tub. She rolled on her side and stared at the dimly lit empty room. She dreamed about Winston . . . Winston's blue eyes . . . Winston's warm hands and body pressed to hers as they slumbered deeply. His cock was still joined with her, as if the wax held them fast.

Where was Winston? She pushed up to sitting and slid her legs over the side of the mattress. How long had she slept? Time was irrelevant in this house. Pleasure was the only thing that mattered. People came and went as they pleased. No one cared about the hands of the clock.

She crossed her arms and rubbed her biceps with her hands in a vain attempt to warm her skin. Walking to the door, she pulled on the handle and exited into the hallway.

Maybe he went back to the ballroom in search of her? Maybe he was angry because she quietly left the bed to think? Hopefully, that was not the emotion coursing through him. He had known of her propensity to think alone, if he remembered such a detail about her.

She headed down the stairs toward the ballroom. Reaching the bottom, she turned toward the door that led toward the back of the house.

Violin music came from the ballroom. One of the ceremonies or theatrics had started. She always enjoyed watching them, but the need to find Winston crept through her. Winston could be anywhere.

She would try the common rooms first before venturing into the large hall.

She entered the first room on her left, only a few candles lit the space. On the edges of the room stood several chairs and in the center was a table. On the table's surface was placed a range of implements, as well as food and wine.

From this distance, Grace made out a wooden paddle, a long buggy whip, wooden hobbles, two wooden spoons, and a bundle of silk. The food was even more intriguing. Some sort of pie, a bowl of whipped cream, butter, two plugged carafes of oil, and another with wine.

What an interesting combination. She had, of course, seen implements used in play, and appetites did increase after a good session of futter. The food, though, she was certain was not for that purpose.

A deep moan drew her gaze to the side of the room—a moan she had heard many times a night when she performed for Oscar. Markus was seated in a high-back chair as a small woman dragged long, painted nails down his chest. Her petite body was draped simply in crimson silk.

Markus pushed women to take the lead in bed. He was a powerful man, who was the most passionate man Grace had ever known . . . well, before she futtered Winston. Her lips quirked up. Goodness, if anyone heard her thoughts, they would think her a wanton dove!

Markus enjoyed it when a woman was bold enough to grasp the lead, allowing him to be seduced. He also enjoyed seducing a woman, like he had with Grace. That was precisely what he did for Oscar.

Grace couldn't help but watch this woman. Her movements showed how experienced she was at the art of seducing a man. Maybe Grace could learn something from her.

Grace stepped to the side, out of the open doorway. She slowly lowered herself to the floor and sat in a position that allowed her to watch them, but not intrude.

Grace had never seen this woman before. Was she Markus's new dove? Grace didn't think so.

Her long, black hair hung down to her waist, and as she tilted her head back, her lips shone a dramatic red, matching her silk drape.

She was dressed like an erotic princess and her confidence mesmerized Grace. The woman touched a tip of one of her nails to Markus's forehead, then dragged the tip down to the bridge of his nose. Between his eyes, she tapped. He closed his eyes.

No verbal request was made and he did what she requested? Grace's brow pulled tight. Markus had played with this woman before.

The woman stepped off him, wrapped her hands about his wrists, and pulled.

Markus stood, his eyes still closed. He had no shirt on and his boots were off, his pantaloons were amiss as well. The woman grasped his pants and untied them. The cotton slid down his body to display his stiff prick, with the small ripe plum head.

A very nice phallus indeed.

Sensations of futtering Markus, his hardness sliding into her cunny as she lay on her back and gripped her thighs wide, came back to her. His cock parted her folds and slid deep . . . all so Oscar could watch. Never again would she futter a man she didn't have an emotional connection to. Winston had shown her what the difference was in doing so. . . . Oh, Winston. Tingles shot through her pussy. *Goodness, Grace, you just futtered thoroughly a few hours past.*

The woman grasped the length of silk on the table. Starting at the center of his torso, she wrapped the length of silk about his body once and then twice. The width was such that with one wrap it covered from his shoulders to just above his navel. Having the cloth wrapped repeatedly about his torso held his arms firmly to his sides. The last two wraps of the silk narrowed in width. The woman circled his pego with the tails and tied them in a pretty bow about his cock and sac.

Grace held in a snicker. He was all wrapped up as if a present for this woman or someone. The woman pressed a hand to his shoulder. He dropped to his knees before her. She wrapped her arm around his back and assisted him lying on a large padded blanket on the floor.

Grace watched with fascination. Never had she seen such a thing done to a man. She certainly could never do such a thing to Winston. She glanced at the door to see if anyone else had entered to watch. No one else resided in the room. Her gaze went back to Markus.

He lay on his back, his cock standing straight up from his body. The tip was an intense red in color.

The woman walked back to the table. There she picked up one of the carafes of oil and walked back to him. She unplugged the carafe and poured a thick golden stream down upon his toes. She moved her hand back and forth; the oil trailed up his feet to his ankles. A slight mint smell filled the air.

Mint oil? Now, that will tingle the skin. Grace smiled. It would feel good to use mint oil on someone.

The woman placed the carafe back on the table and returned to his feet. She kneeled and her fingers glided over his skin. Markus's muscles jumped, and as she hardened her touch, Markus moaned.

The woman shifted her body so she straddled one of his feet. She untied her silk wrap to expose an equally brilliant crimson corset. With her fingers, she stroked his foot and her pussy.

My God, what did that oil feel like on one's sensitive flesh? Grace's cunny pouted with moisture. The woman slowly lowered herself down onto Markus's foot. Grace's eyes widened.

The woman's head tilted back. The muscles in Markus's leg flexed, moving his toes back and forth in her cunny. The woman moaned and rocked her hips as if riding a horse.

Marcus's feet were covered with the mint oil. Grace wondered what the sensation was like. Not the feet part, but the oil. The oil would tingle, a burning sensation, which would flood the cunny flesh with blood, making the motions of futtering more acute. That would be delightful.

The woman shuddered and shook, her breath increased, and suddenly she stood. Her legs trembled and her hips continued to rock slightly, a primal motion of her body's search for release, which was denied. A motion Grace understood well. When she wanted more futtering her hips did the same—almost of their own accord.

The woman turned and sat on the floor between Markus's feet. She took her oily hands and rubbed her own feet with the oil, concentrating on the soft center flesh of the bottom of the foot. She stretched out her feet and, bending her knees out in the shape of a bow, she placed Markus's hard cock between her feet.

She moved her feet in a singular motion up to the head of his cock. He sucked in a breath and arched his hips up slightly. The woman slid her feet back down and his cock head turned purple. She continued to stroke him. From each stroke, Markus groaned. His upper body remained motionless and his lower continued to thrust and thrust with the motions of her feet.

Grace frowned. This scene reminded her that all she wanted was Winston. His tenderness and emotions for her while they futtered showed her there was so much more than this. . . . In truth, this had always left her feeling empty, as if she were hollow inside and simply going through the motions. Winston's hard cock and the way he cared for her showed in each touch he pressed upon her. He truly wished her to grow to face her own fears. The flesh of Grace's cunny throbbed—she needed Winston.

The dark-haired woman stopped as Markus's prick throbbed, nearing a certain spend. She stood and strode to the table, where she picked up the wooden spoon and the pie. She kneeled back down between Markus's legs.

Grace stared at the pie. She didn't want to see whatever this woman did to Markus with the pastry. She needed to find Winston and tell him all.

She turned and slowly crawled out into the hallway. Once there she pushed up to standing and leaned against the wall. She had no idea people did such . . . Wine, yes; oil, sure. But feet and pies? The hairs on the back of her neck rose and a chill raced along her skin. She certainly never would have thought.

Enough, Grace. You need to find Winston.

She pushed from her spot on the wall and headed to the next set of open doors.

* * *

Grace headed into the game room. St. Jerome sat with Lord Cunnington.

He glanced at her and then started. Placing his glass on the table between him and Cunnington, he stood, then strode toward her with determination.

"Who is she?" he growled at her.

"I—I don't know actually." She backed up a step. She supposed he should be angry with her, but he seemed positively livid.

"You know more than I." His eyes softened. "I need to find her."

She had always liked St. Jerome—down deep he had a kind heart. "I honestly thought you would have caught her before she left in my carriage. I am sincerely disappointed to see you here."

His eyebrows rose. "Your carriage? Where did your carriage take her?"

"You are a quick wit." She glanced over to Cunnington. "Veronica's" brother was a decent man as well, even if he spent most events in the cups. She sincerely hoped this night showed the girl not all so-called rogues were bad.

She stared at St. Jerome. Her bluish green eyes locked to his gray. Concern and desire etched his features. "Burber Place," she whispered, near silently.

St. Jerome's jaw set and he closed his eyes. He sighed and opened his eyes once more. "I had almost convinced myself she was indeed *not* related to him."

"My sincerest apologies, St. Jerome." She smiled a half smile at him. He would find her. . . . She, on the other hand, had no inkling where Winston had gone. Maybe St. Jerome could help her, too. "I am actually looking for someone myself, St. Jerome. Have you seen Winston Greydon?"

"I don't believe we have ever been introduced, so I would have no idea if I had seen him or not."

"He is tall, with fair hair that is significantly longer than yours." She inwardly rolled her eyes. St. Jerome's hair was unfashionably short.

"Are you looking for me?"

Winston's voice rolled over her body and her nipples pebbled hard. She licked her lips.

St. Jerome's brows rose and he smirked.

Grace turned around. Winston stood two feet from her. "Winston Greydon." She grinned at him, then turned her palm up toward St. Jerome. "Vincent St. Jerome."

"It is a pleasure." St. Jerome inclined his head.

"Indeed." Winston inclined his head back. "May I speak with you, Lady Wentland?"

"Pardon me, St. Jerome."

"I believe I have a lady to catch—though I do know the destination, so I suppose it is truly not a chase." He grinned.

The corners of Grace's lips curled up even farther. He would catch her, race or not.

Winston held out his arm to Grace and she wrapped her fingers about his hard, muscular forearm. Where had he been? He probably wondered the same of her.

"I just came from the room, Winston. I fell asleep as I was waiting for you to return." She nervously bit the inside of her cheek. Would he believe her?

"I know, Grace. I joined you in slumber for a time, then decided to do something for you."

"You did something for me?"

"Indeed. You talk in your sleep and mentioned something that I most certainly would find the utmost pleasure in doing."

She talked in her sleep! No one had ever told her she talked in her sleep before. Oh, God, had she mentioned the chair? Was her dream real? Winston had been behind her in bed and she dreamed about the chair and him. The words from her dream— *"I will never watch you from that chair"*—repeated in her mind.

"W-what did I say in my sleep, Winston?"

"You will see."

They walked together down the hallway to the wicked room with the red ribbon on the door. He pushed it open and stood holding it for her from the outside. "After you, Grace."

She stepped into the room and he followed right behind her. No one resided in the room. She stared at the tree settee in the center. Her fantasy when she first saw that seat flooded back to her:

Her hands were pushed back against the wood tree and the leather straps tied tight about her wrist as a man, with gold hair, bit her neck and breasts. His hands spread her thighs wide as his rough fingers slid up her soft skin heading toward her core.

Chills of excitement raced about her skin and her nipples pointed. She glanced at Winston. Winston's gold hair . . . Winston was that man. Her chest tightened and heat rose to her face.

"You have an intensely naughty mind, Grace. A beautiful mind."

Oh, my! Her cheeks grew warm. He was going to tie her to the tree. With her arms tied above her head, he would lick and lave every inch of her body with his tongue. Her body trembled.

"Indeed, such a naughty mind."

Before he pleasured her, she needed to explain to him why she feared him.

"Winston, before we do this, I need to say something to you."

"Very well." He studied her with kind blue eyes.

"I—I . . ." Her heart swelled in her chest and tears welled, pushing at her eyelids.

"Shhh, Grace." He walked to her. His hand rose and brushed a tear away, then cupped her chin in his fingers. "You don't have to say it, Grace. I know."

"You know?" Her lip trembled.

"Yes, I know you have been hurt in the past but loved anyway. I know that pain has festered, chewed and twisted your insides so you, at times, don't know the person who resides there anymore. I know you love me. I will do all I can to guide you back through the tangled web you have wrapped about you. I will never harm you, Grace. There is no fear in loving me."

Grace swallowed hard, but she didn't say a word. He understood her well enough to see all that without her saying a word. A happy glow spread through her belly and up about her heart.

"Not speaking again, eh? In moments you will be making plenty of noise." He winked at her.

He placed his hand on the small of her back, his heat a brand on her skin. Awareness skittered deep into her lungs, and her breath deepened.

He stepped forward and forced her to the settee. She chewed the inside of her cheek. What would he do with her, once he had her tied up?

He grabbed the hem of her shift and pulled it up and over her head in a single pull. "Sit, Grace."

Her body trembled as his voice caused every fine hair on her body to rise. She turned and sat on the gold upholstery, the smooth, carved wood of the tree at her back.

"Raise your hands above your head, Grace."

She reached her hand up, straight above her head. His fingers gently wrapped her wrist. He turned her left palm inward to lay flat against the tree branches, then her right palm. The muscles on her forearms stretched and burned anew. He stood so close, all she wanted to do was reach out and touch him, to feel his heat against the tips of her fingers.

The leather tether attached to the tree wrapped about her fingers one at a time, then secured her wrists. Being at Winston's will, tied with nowhere to go, thrilled her.

He stepped back, his heat slowly evaporating from the air about her. With each step he took farther and farther from her, her heartbeat increased. What was he doing? He grabbed a chair from the wall opposite her and centered it in her view, then sat.

A chair? Icy sweat pierced her brow. How could it be that he was setting up a chair?

He leaned back in the chair and placed his elbow on the arm, then perched his cheek on his knuckles.

His blue eyes sparkled with desire from beneath lazy eyelids. "You are beautiful, Grace."

Heat washed her face at his words and she lowered her eyes shyly from his face. His gaze still fixed on her. Fever sprang across her skin, erasing all the fear that had resided there.

She stared at the exposed ivory skin of her thighs. He wanted to see *her*—not her with another man.

She slowly relaxed the muscles of her thighs, allowing the legs to rotate to the outside and display most wantonly her newly shaved pussy. She clenched and relaxed the muscles of her sex.

"Umm. Indeed. Your cunny is beautiful, too. Peach-hued ruffles, hiding a succulent honeypot."

A ripple of gooseflesh prickled her skin anew. God, she wanted him to touch her. She whimpered beneath her breath. *Please, please, sit forward, slide your fingers into my oiled cunny, and spread my lips wide.* She held in the words that pushed to tumble from her tongue. Her arousal filled her senses as wetness slipped from her womb.

"Grace, time has changed us. As you have your fears, your

emotional scars, I have scars of my own—physical scars. I wish to show you."

She worked her throat, trying to find her voice. "Yes." The word came out a whisper.

Winston stood up and unbuttoned the flap to his breeches, then pushed them down his legs to pool at his ankles. "Look at my thigh, Grace."

Her gaze settled on the firm, defined muscle of his upper thigh, then slowly lowered. Above his right knee was a tea-plate-sized bumpy red scar. "Does that hurt?"

"Sometimes the skin itches. Sometimes the flesh is numb."

"How did it happen?"

"A dog in India." He shook his head. "A few of us were out late one evening at one of the parlors and were entirely in our cups. A friend lost his biscuits on the street in a rather wealthy part of town. A guard dog came at my friend and I stepped in to protect him as he heaved his stomach out on the lane. The dog got a nice chunk of my thigh—though I have to say, I did well against him. My canine foe whimpered away."

He pulled his breeches back up over his legs, leaving the flap open. "I seldom do not wear trousers, Grace."

A dog attacked him—he wore pants in the tub; he turned away from her to take off his wet pants, then put dry ones on. It was more than a physical scar. It was something he didn't like about his body. He was embarrassed by his wound, self-conscious of the ugliness of the flesh.

Her heart ached for him. "Winston, you are the most stunning man I have ever known. Your bravery when your friend needed you speaks to your good character. I always feel safe and protected when in your presence."

He kneeled before her, his sapphire eyes even with hers, and smiled. "Grace, I want to show you how much pleasure I get from touching you, from controlling you in futter."

Her body trembled. . . . *Pleasure from touching me—. . . controlling me in futter. . . .*

Control in futter—fear crystallized the blood in her veins and seized her every breath. Maybe having control of her in futter meant he would share her? Every fine hair on her body stood stiff as icicles. *Stop it, Grace. He is a good man. He will be good to you. Let go of your fears and give all of your love to him. He loves you.*

"I see your fear, Grace. Tell me."

"I—I fear you will share me."

Winston sighed an exasperated sigh, and grazed his hands along her thighs.

"Men are rather simple, Grace. We like something to relate to, something nice to look at, and something that can give us a bit of an emotional boost. All of those things can be accomplished simply by flirting with someone . . . including your wife. I realize from all you have seen, and the particular strains of your marriage, that you might conclude that I, too, desire more than one woman. I do not. I am a different man, Grace. I will do my best to build us a lifetime of happy moments."

"Wife?"

"Indeed, Grace, I can't very well leave here this night and not have you promised to me. I don't want to leave here this night without you coming to my bed. But realize that is improper and would cause scandal for you, me, and your brother."

Grace couldn't tear her gaze from his fingers on her thighs. She couldn't look at him. My God, her dreams could come true. . . . He tempted her heart to spill her secrets to him.

"I need you, Grace. I hadn't known that need until I saw you in the ballroom, but I do. I will not and could not ever share you. Simply put, the thought of someone else touching you angers me."

"I love you, Winston. I—I want to confess my secrets, but

doing so will take time and patience." Lots of patience to share her twisted thoughts about that damn chair. Oddly, she really did want to share her deepest secrets with him. He may understand her better than anyone else she knew.

Winston's fingers flexed on her thighs. "I will listen to all you have to say, Grace. I will help you find your way once again. We always did fit like two opposite halves. We balance each other. Now, on to my feast."

His hands slid farther up her legs to her hips, fingers wrapped her sides and he pulled her forward.

"*Eek!*" Her bottom teetered on the edge of the seat, while the rest of her body was on an incline, peaked by her hands above her head.

He chuckled, then leaned in toward her. His face was next to hers, his body pressed to her front. Wet tongue traced the curve of her ear, down to the lobe, and the plump drop sucked into his moisture. His breath blew against her ear, and every fine hair on her arms rose.

"You are amazing, Grace, amazing." The words came out a mumbled whisper. "Sexy and hot. A lady and a vixen."

Winston's tongue traveled lower, gathering up every ounce of her flavors. Salt and sweetness, everything that was Grace from childhood combined with every spicy skill she had learned as an adult. She was a woman whom any man would fall for and wish to please.

He needed her. He needed to make her moan and show her how much he loved her, so she would give herself wholeheartedly to him without reservations.

In her childhood heart, Grace was his . . . had always been.

Her adult mind feared that heart, though.

He would show her that she was safe in heart, mind, body, and soul. His mouth slid lower and lower. The taste of her skin flooded his veins, and the skin of his cock filled. Stiff and straight, his heated flesh pressed against her thigh.

The muscles of her leg jumped and she moaned. His teeth grabbed hold of the soft, textured flesh of her nipple and he suckled hard.

Her body arched off the bench and into his, her legs gripped his hips. He would shatter her walls, make her see, make her want more than anything to be his . . . his wife.

He continued to suck and applied pressure with his teeth to the hard tip.

A moan bordering on a scream burst from her lips, and he soothed her ache by rolling his tongue around the tip.

From her every motion, he could tell she struggled with letting go. She fought the sensations until they overpowered her and then she let them fly. She feared them and delighted in them all at once.

He slid his tongue to the other breast and swirled his spit about it.

She moaned and pressed her breast up toward his mouth. She was pleading with her body for him to take more, give more.

"Good, Grace, I want more. . . . Give me all of you."

"Yes."

He sucked her nipple hard into his mouth without letting the pressure go as he rolled his tongue over and over the flesh. She squirmed and her legs gripped him to her as her body washed in heat and sensations.

He pulled back and rocked the bud between his teeth. "Yes, what, Grace?" He would not be letting go of her flesh.

"Yes, I promise to be yours, Winston." Her entire body sparked to life on the words. She shook and rocked and moaned against him.

"Indeed."

He let the tip of her nipple loose and slid his tongue down her belly, swirling into her navel, then lower. Over the freshly shaved skin of her mound, he traced a path of love. Lower and lower still, he lapped. His cock strained to be buried deep in her, but he wouldn't. No, not this time—this was about her. He held himself in check with an ironclad will.

He slid his tongue down the crease of her thigh, tasting the salty sweat that pooled there. His hands splayed upon her inner thighs and pushed them wide.

The muscles beneath his hands trembled and he flexed his fingers to soothe her. His tongue flicked and lapped at her. The scent of her arousal—her slick folds and honey—overwhelmed his nose, and his lungs locked. His heart hammered in his chest. He would taste her.

He flicked his tongue sideways to her hole. Catching her labia, he flicked and flicked the sensual flesh.

Grace erupted, squirming and panting. "Oh, Winston!" she screamed as wetness leaked from her core and onto his tongue.

She tasted delicious, seductive, heady. The tart, earthy, sweet tang tingled his taste buds and left him wanting more . . .

More . . . of her squirming, more of her calling out his name.

His tongue slid up to the hard button of flesh that poked out from her body so impatiently. Indeed, he would take care of her needs. Again and again.

Her hips arched into his lick as he caressed one side of the button and then the other. He stayed away from the top, which he discovered so many women found too intense a sensation.

He circled down and around her entrance. The flesh beneath his touch wept and throbbed. He slid to the hard section of flesh between her holes. He so wanted to make her squirm. Flicking his tongue downward, he gently caught the puckered flesh of her bottom.

She wiggled and tried to pull her bottom away from him and his hands stayed her retreat.

He hummed, his tongue vibrating her lush, pouting flesh with each lick.

Squirming and panting, she rocked her legs against him. *Oh, indeed, that's it, Grace. Let go.* Her stomach muscles clenched and jumped. His sac pulled up tight to his body, pushing him to take her, to bury himself deep in the oiled velvet of her cunt.

He thrust his tongue deep into her weeping honeyed walls, licking, lapping, and savoring every squirm his tongue created. Once more he circled the bud, then dove deep to flick her pucker before plunging back into her. The walls of her oiled pot clenched his tongue.

She shattered. "Winston . . . Winston . . . Oh, Winston!" Her walls crumbled. Her body pulled and thrashed against the ropes, with which he'd tied her to the tree, as she spent. Her belly muscles jumped, quivered, and clenched hard. His cock wept for release, while wanting to spray his seed all over her.

He placed his hand on the flat of her stomach and stared, waiting until her muscles relaxed.

"Are you well, Grace?"

Her eyelids hung heavy and he searched her face for any sign of discomfort. Quiver after quiver racked her body. Her breath labored in and out. Slowly she returned to a calm state.

"Yes. I am quite well, Winston."

He stood up and slid his hand down his cock and back up to the tip. His hand stayed at his pleasure points on the ridge. His thumb and forefinger wiggled and wiggled. His body shook and he gasped as his seed rose quickly. "Tell me, Grace. Tell me again."

"Winston, I love you I am yours . . . yours to do with as you wish, to teach me, to love me . . . and I will do all I can to please you. Do with me what you will."

Heat rushed through his belly. Her words *"Do with me what you will"* repeated in his mind. His finger worked quicker and harder, tingles rushed through his bullocks and contracted. His seed sprayed from his body in a fevered relief. "Oh . . . oh . . . oh . . ."

His sticky, slick custard covered her belly and breasts. His legs shook and he stumbled back and crumpled down to kneeling before her.

He panted and his fingers slid up her belly, spreading his seed over her skin. He wanted it everywhere . . . a thin film of him, of his seed, clinging to her. The smell of him would linger beneath her clothes later that day. He leaned and kissed the soft flesh on the inside of her thigh. Not only would he teach Grace how to get past her fears, but she would bring him pleasure beyond anything he knew. How? Simply by loving him.

20

Grace

Grace floated up the stairs in a bliss she had never known. Winston's heat radiated from her side. His arms possessively wrapped about her. She wanted to confess all about her life and her marriage. The story of how she had come to know of this world of sin and futter was not easy for her to tell.

He kissed the top of her head and pushed open the door to his bedchamber.

"Winston, how did you come to this house? I never imagined I would see you here. I had not really imagined bumping into you in any way, in some time."

He laughed lightly. "Markus. I believe he talked you into coming here as well. I walked off the boat. Met up with my brother and he invited me to club with him. While there, Markus and I reacquainted ourselves. He shared my very first boat from England. That was a fun journey of cards and drinking, the likes of which I had never experienced. We became friends after that." He smiled one of those boyhood smiles, which nearly spread to his toes, and shrugged, jostling her. "He told me about this event. Said I should stay in the house for the evening, and if I was interested to let him know." He gently sat her on the bed and covered her with the warm blanket. "I tend to be a light sleeper, so I contemplated not doing this, but I knew what I wanted, Grace. So I said yes."

"You knew what you wanted?"

"Indeed, a woman who was not afraid of being sensual and wicked in the bedchamber, but a lady in the public eye."

"Oh."

"Indeed. You, Grace, shocked my senses when I saw you dancing with Emma."

Grace's lips curled up. "How did dancing with Emma shock you, Winston?"

He stripped off his pants and crawled into bed beside her. "I had not seen you in years, yet instantly recognized you." He ran his hand down the curve of her hip. "I still thought of you as the proper lady you were raised to be. I know that may seem silly now. It may even be sillier when we consider all the time that has passed. At the same time, we all hold on to memories that we cherish."

"Life changes people, Winston."

"Indeed. I know." He pressed on her shoulder and she lay flat on her back, gazing up at his beautiful blue eyes. "I learned so much in India, Grace. Not only about how to make wealth, but how to live as who I am. My journey secured my future and stature and helped me know what I liked and wanted in my life."

"Tell me how you learned to futter the way you do, of the sensations you learned, the wax."

"Ah, you do indeed like wax. Each time I drizzled some on you, your cunny grew slicker for me."

Her face grew warm. "Quite so. The sensation heightened all of my senses and made me focus on you and what you did to me."

He smiled and his fingers lazily drew circles on her stomach and breasts. "Your breath." He blew out through his lips. "I learned that from a woman named Vijyuma. She had the typical black hair and dark skin, but she was a teacher. An elder woman, they have many different things they do before enjoying futter. Bathing is one. I enjoyed shaving you." His hands traveled down her belly to the shaved bone of her Venus. "Vijyuma enjoyed the concentration breath games instilled. She explained the focus involved in the one holding the breath, and how if done during futtering, the mind shuts down and you end up only feeling. Did you experience that when I had you hold yours, Grace?"

Memories of the bathtub assaulted her: the lavender scent, the hot water, and standing on her tiptoes. The water dripping from her face and hair. How Winston's phallus slid so easily into her bottom and filled her. She quivered. She had many memories of Oscar, and none of them held only good things. This memory with Winston she would never forget, for it brought her only joy.

"I see you are reliving some of what we did. There is so much I wish to teach you, Grace. What we experienced last night was only a taste. Before I show you more of what I learned, I need to know more about your experiences. I know there is so much to tell, so only share what you feel comfortable with tonight. The rest can come out in time."

"I need to tell you, Winston. I don't wish to go into the details just yet. You know about the chair." Her cheeks grew warm. She couldn't believe she confided this to Winston. "Oscar could not get stiff. No matter what he or I did, nothing would work—though he enjoyed the rush of emotions that came with watching someone he loved perform with others.

"Oscar would leer. Oscar spun his webs from that infernal chair. I, of course, knew nothing about this before I wed him.

His first wife bore him his heir. After her death, something happened to him, which he refused to tell me about. He no longer could rise. With his second wife, he tried a false wooden harness. He despised the device and refused to use the attachment with me." Chills raced along her spine. Like the rush of a river on a new spring day, recollections of her life with Oscar simply babbled out from her. "I often wished he had, I so longed for his touch. I thought for some time that his incapacity to rise was my fault. In time I realized this was an ailment to which there was no cure."

She swallowed hard. She knew this was necessary. Winston needed to know all that happened to her. She wanted him to know.

"Can you continue, Grace?"

"I have no choice, Winston. I have been carrying this burden for years. Unless I let go of the past and release these emotions and memories, I won't be free to allow myself a life as I know it can be." She swallowed again. "The short answer is, Oscar never bedded me in my marriage. He touched me, undressed me, finger frigged me in the first few months of our marriage only . . . and he watched. Always watched from that damn chair." Grace frowned and her brow pinched tight.

"Indeed, that chair. I am looking forward to seeing the torture device." He ran his fingers along her side, and her muscles twitched and jumped. "Markus is right. When you think of the piece of damned furniture, your entire body tenses. I do hope one day you will remove that chair from your life."

"H-he had me futter with other men as he watched me—men and women. Couples and singles. He enjoyed when they made me scream. Both in ecstasy and in pain. After every single encounter, he would require me to spread my legs. With them spread, he would kneel between them, undo his flap, and piddle on my cunny. The first time he did this I was utterly confused."

Winston's finger stopped in the trail he mapped on her skin. "Did he speak to you as he did so, Grace?"

"He did. He would call me an unclean little girl who needed her pussy washed." Her face grew impossibly hot. She closed her eyes. My God, her heart pounded in her chest. She just told Winston about the strangeness of her marriage. "He said it was the only thing he could do that was physical with me."

Winston blew out a disgusted breath. "Physical, yes. Humiliating was a thrill to him, Grace. Many find this kind of behavior arousing." His fingers trailed down to her cunt and slid deep inside her. "It appears you do."

Oh! She pushed down on his fingers' invasion. "I grew to like any attention he would bestow on me. Besides undressing me, that act was the only physical thing he would do to me."

Winston pushed his fingers deep into her and cupped them back toward him. Grace's hips arched up and she squirmed. He loved using his fingers to search for that special place he had learned about from his Indian teacher. If he could locate that spot in Grace, she would spend like she had never done before.

He never expected that confession about Oscar. Lord Wentland had a wicked streak. The good thing was, Grace had grown to enjoy that kind of attention. He pulled his fingers back out until the tips brushed her button, then thrust them back into her spongy warmth. "You were an excellent pupil for Oscar, Grace. Are you willing to put aside and learn anything I wish to teach you?"

"Quite so, Winston." Her body trembled in lust.

"I thought of you often on my journeys, Grace. Starved for the opportunity to touch on the long journey by boat to India, my mind conjured up elaborate scenarios of us wedding, of the passion we would share." He leaned in and kissed the soft skin below her ear. "I then received news you were betrothed to

Wentland. My hopes dashed, I turned to the passions within. Simple couplings quickly became something I detested. I turned to anything that would add a grain of spice to my fevered dreams. India is an ancient culture. The women are well schooled in the arts of Venus. When I would conjure up visions of what I had learned, I often thought of you. It was natural that I should, in the beginning. As the months turned to years, those visions faded and were replaced by those that reflected where I was."

Grace arched her hips as he continued to breathe his words and story against her skin. "Roll over on your stomach, Grace."

Grace rolled to comply. Tension radiated through her in waves. The slender muscles of her spine and the taut muscles of her bottom clenched and released in anticipation. "Relax, Grace, you will enjoy this."

He kneeled by her feet and grasped the thin pieces of leather tied to the elephant trunks carved into the posts of the bed. Winston ran his fingertips along her calf and circled her left ankle. Lifting her foot, he tied the thin leather restraint. "Spread your legs, Grace."

She slowly slid the free right foot away from the left one, which was held secure.

Winston then tied the right ankle. Moving slowly, he trailed his finger up her legs to her bottom.

Grace moaned and her muscles quivered.

He continued up her back to her shoulders. There he leaned in and kneaded the tense flesh. Her muscles relaxed and her eyes fluttered shut. "I will pamper you as often as I pleasure you, Grace. I will give you everything." He lifted her arms up above her head and tied them to the headboard with the leather straps hanging in the middle. He moved to the side of her.

Her bluish green eyes slit open and stared at him. Standing at the side of the bed, he savored her body. The shadows from the candles played on her crevices; nothing could hide the beauty of her. "You are amazing, Grace." He moved slowly to the foot of the bed and her legs spread wide.

Her pussy lips were slightly open, revealing dew curled in her blushing skin. His cock hardened. She was at his will's delight. She squirmed, lifted her head, and looked back at him with desire and submission in her eyes.

"Winston, thank you for whatever you are about to do to me."

His lips quirked up. "You will enjoy this, Grace."

"I have no doubt, Winston. I simply wanted you to know in case I fall asleep after. I am so very tired."

He laughed outright.

She certainly would enjoy this. He leaned down and lifted a long feather he had placed beside the bed. Lifting the feather up into the air, he dragged the edges down the center of her spine.

Grace giggled and pulled against her restraints.

"See, I told you." He dragged the feather down her sides and along the outside of her legs. He lightly tapped the fluttery tip of the feather against her feet.

Grace squealed and thrashed against the leather. He couldn't contain his own joy at hearing her squirm. He laughed, a soul-deep sound.

"Do you want me to join with you, Grace? To feel my hard cock slide deep in your wet pot?"

Grace shivered but said nothing.

Winston smiled. "Your cunny is held so open to me, Grace. Do you wish me to part your folds and slide deep inside?"

Her muscles trembled, but still no sound.

Winston raised his hand into the air and brought his palm down against her left buttock. *Crack!*

"Ouch!"

"Do you wish me to fill you with my pego, Grace?"

She squirmed her bottom and pushed it up in invitation to him.

Crack! His palm hit her right buttock this time.

"Oh!"

The flesh of his palm burned and he gazed down upon her weeping cunt.

"Answer me, Grace."

"Winston, please fill me."

"Good, Grace." A smile he felt deep in his soul erupted on his face.

She was a good girl. He climbed up on the bed behind her. The dull red imprint of his palm lay on her right bottom cheek. He loved the look of his handprint on her bum.

His cock twitched as the image of her bottom—bright red from his hand spanking—came to mind.

He grasped his cock in his hand and slid the skin back. Parting her bum cheeks, he leaned down and entered her. Her slick cunt slid down his pego and encased him.

"Oh!" She wiggled her bottom against his probe.

"Oh, indeed, Grace."

Grace giggled.

Nothing in the world could match that sound. He pulled out to the tip and thrust back into her.

He slid back to the tip and glided the head of his glans along her slick, wet cleft. Grace's pussy quivered and the muscles of her bottom trembled against him. He rubbed his cock against her clit and then pushed deep into her hole once more. He would futter her every evening and every morning.

He bucked into her. His hands braced himself on the bed and his lips came down on the soft flesh of her shoulder. He greedily lapped at her salty skin.

Grace moaned.

Pulling his cock back to the tip of her swollen lips, he thrust back into her stifling heat. His sac contracted and tingles shot up his belly. Grace arched her back and pushed her bottom up into him, meeting each of his thrusts with a matching one of her own. He slipped in and out of her velvet oils in long, steady thrusts. Her cunny contracted about his hard flesh. She cried out as waves of pleasure washed over and over his pego. His muscles shook and his breath came out ragged. His insides flipped over and burst out of him as he sprayed his seed inside her succulent cunt.

He collapsed on top of her. They both rasped and gasped for breath. Her eyes closed and she sighed.

"I love you, Grace." He kissed her mouth, her shoulders, her ears, her neck, and her cheeks in a series of pecks.

Her breathing deepened and her muscles twitched and jumped lightly.

He grinned against her skin. She slept. He gently untied her hands, while still lying on top of her. He slowly dislodged his soft cock from her womb. He sat back and untied her ankles. He pulled the blanket up over her and him. As he pulled her into him, Grace mumbled, "I love you, Winston. Thank you."

21

Lilly

Lilly stepped on wobbling legs from the carriage.

"Sweet Lil, you ready to see some of society?"

Her fingers wrapped around her brother's arm. Sweet Jesus, no, but St. Jerome would be here and she had her plan. All she needed was to bump into him and he would know. . . . She could then politely apologize for her clumsiness and thank him for last night.

She glanced down at her white dress with silver embroidery about her neckline, waist, and hem. She spent the entire day in front of the mirror, readying herself for this night. Her short corset dug uncomfortably into her hips and belly, and she wiggled, trying to find relief.

The home they were to enter in Mayfair was grand. Her eyes grew round as she stared up at the tall building and the doors that stood open to the entrance hall.

"Lil, are you well?" Her brother stopped her on the steps and stared down at her.

"Quite so, I am simply nervous." She smiled up at her brother.

Nervous to see St. Jerome here. . . . Nervous she would not see him here. She simply wanted to turn around and run.

"You know all we do at these things is drink punch, eat cakes, and then listen to music that makes half the crowd fall asleep. You will see people drool, snore, and twitch. Nothing to be nervous about." He chuckled.

Lilly laughed. He was trying to relax her. "Remember our governess, Samantha, and the flower?"

"Who could forget? She was a stone too heavy, and as you practiced on the harp, she would snore so loud her bosom would shake. That flower simply needed a little tug."

"What I still don't understand is how you got it between her breasts and back to your seat without her even flinching."

"That is a secret I shall never tell." He winked at her.

They reached the top of the steps and entered the small entranceway. "Lord Cunnington and Lady Lillian Grey."

She walked forward, her hand anxiously clutching her brother's forearm. Where would she see St. Jerome?

A well-dressed woman in her late forties approached them. "Lady Lillian, such a delight to have you at our small musicale. My sweet daughter is playing the cello and I know she will be delighted to know she is not the only one new to crowds in the room."

"I am delighted to be here, my lady. Thank you for the kind invitation to my brother and me."

"It is our pleasure. There are drinks and snacks through the doors." She turned her hand over and indicated the large doors that stood to the left of them.

Her brother guided them through the doors, and Lilly glanced around. Hardly anyone resided in the room, a few couples stood in hushed conversations, standing here and there. At the front of the room, chairs were arranged in a circular fashion, with a single chair in the middle for the young woman to sit on as she played. Lilly smiled. She never was good at anything musical.

Turning back toward her brother, Lilly stopped still. Her feet wouldn't move and all the blood drained from her face.

A stunning woman, about ten years her senior, stood with her hand wrapped about St. Jerome's arm. Her brown hair was swept up and tucked beneath a red feather cap. Her eyes, a steely gray, stared at him with such adoration. Her heart sank to the bowels of her stomach. She wanted to leave. She was not here even a tick of the clock and she wanted to run.

"Lil, what is it?"

She glanced up at her brother. "Umm." Sweet Jesus, she would go straight to hell for all the lies and sins she had done in this past day. And all for what? To know her brother a bit better? To know herself a bit more? To have her heart shattered. . . .

"My nerves. I need to use the washroom." Her throat closed off and she swallowed hard.

"It is down the hall."

"I will be fine, Brian."

He winked at her. "I know you will be."

She turned on her heel and headed down the hall to the washroom. She opened the door and closed the paneled wood. Leaning her forehead against the cool surface, she inhaled a deep breath, and tears welled to her eyes. He was with a woman, a very pretty older woman. What was she to do?

She had not planned on him being here with someone. *Take another deep breath, Lilly.* In some ways, St. Jerome being here with another woman made things easier.

She simply would make her apology and say her thank-you and that would be all. Quite so.

She squared her shoulders, ran her hands down the front of her gown, and opened the door. Indeed, that was what she needed to do. That, or simply ignore him.

She walked back into the room and headed straight for the refreshment table. She grasped a glass of lemonade, wishing it were wine. *You can do it, Lilly. Simply head in his direction and trip. Bump into him and spill your lemonade on yourself and on him, and then say your apologies.*

She stepped in his direction. *Hold your head high, Lilly. Shoulders straight. Yes, that's it. You have fortitude.* Her brother stepped in front of her.

"Sweet Jesus," she mumbled, almost spilling the lemonade on his nice evening blacks.

He chuckled. "You are nervous. I have reserved us two seats in the middle. I figure that way we can doze off and no one will likely notice."

Damn. Lilly cringed. *Stop that, Lilly. You know that you have to play the social game. Music is why everyone is here.*

"Middle not what you had in mind, Lil?"

"Oh, no, that will do. It is . . ." She dropped her gaze from her brother—maybe he could help her. "There is a man over there that appears familiar to me, Brian. I hoped to gain an introduction to see if he is indeed who I am thinking of."

"Which man, Lil? All you have to do is ask me." Protection rang in his tone.

She should have known this would not go as she had planned. *Silly fool, Lilly.* Her ideas never panned out. Just look at what happened last night! "The medium-build man with very short black hair standing—"

"St. Jerome, Lil." Her brother's tone cut her off, saying, *Leave him be.* "I can't imagine you know him, though I do believe you have heard that name."

Lilly couldn't look her brother in the eyes and stared at a spot on his cravat.

"Many consider him a scoundrel of the worst sort. A few know he is generous and kind. I am fortunate to know he is both, but I would never wish his publicly scandalous past on any woman."

"St. Jerome." She tried to feign dumb. Then she inwardly cringed as her brother tilted his head at her and narrowed his eyes.

"Lil, what is afoot?"

"I . . . um . . . nothing."

"Lilly"—the word was whispered but harsh—"you have never been good at lying. Do you know St. Jerome?"

She stared at her brother, then glanced over to see St. Jerome staring at her. The woman who was with him had gone from his side. His gaze slid down her body, as if his hands had made the caress. She trembled and heat bloomed in her face. Sweet Jesus, how did he do that and not even touch her?

"You—you were at the party last night."

Her gaze jumped back to her brother.

His eyebrows were pulled together and his mouth was in a tight frown. "St. Jerome asked about a woman who fit your description, who was looking for me." Brian glanced to St. Jerome, then back to her. "He was the one who suggested I bring you here. I—I—" Her brother's face turned bright red and his jaw twitched in rage. "I'll kill him." His voice came out as a lethal whisper. "I swear I will. We are leaving, Lil. Immediately."

Panic clawed at her and she glanced around. No one stared at them. "No, please, Brian." Her hand reached out and clutched his forearm. "I know I have a lot of explaining to do, but, please, can you simply introduce us here so that I can say what I need to him? Then—then I will tell you all you wish to know."

"No." The word held no possible sway. "That scoundrel. To think I trusted him. To think I sat last night and had brandy with him. That is it." He spun about and headed straight for St. Jerome.

Lilly cringed and glanced quickly around the room once

more. Guests still wandered into the hall and no one stood close enough to hear their conversation. Sweet Jesus, her brother had a temper, and when it went off, he did not think straight. This would ruin her, him, and St. Jerome. She dashed after him, watching in horror as his fists clenched and reclenched at his sides. He reached St. Jerome, Lilly only two steps behind him.

"How dare you! We have business to discuss. I have a mind to have my second call on yours to make arrangements for tomorrow!"

"Keep your tone down, Cunnington. Do not ruin us all when you have no idea of the particulars I need to discuss with you."

"Particulars? Particulars? You call seducing my sister a small matter. You will marry her or I will take you out with my sword."

"Those are the particulars I wanted to discuss with you, Cunnington. I simply needed to see . . ." He glanced at Lilly, his eyes questioning.

"See what, St. Jerome? I have a feeling"—Brian's voice dropped to an even quieter whisper—"you saw all of her last night."

Lilly held in a startled breath.

"Hold your tongue, Cunnington. She is *my* future. . . . I will not have you ruining her reputation here."

"*She is* my *future*. . . ."

"*She is* my *future*. . . ."

Lilly's head grew light. He intended to wed her.

She swallowed hard. She had never considered marriage as the outcome. Even if it was what she had wanted. How did he know who she was?

"You will wed her then?" Her brother's hands unclenched.

"Indeed. I will be by on the morrow to discuss this." He searched Lilly's face again. "May we please enjoy the music this night, as people are starting to wonder what this conversation is about?"

Brian didn't move. He stared at St. Jerome with glossed-over eyes. "We are leaving, St. Jerome. Lady Lillian is not feeling well. I shall see you at eight sharp. If you fail to show, you will have only one more decision to make—swords or pistols."

"Indeed." He reached out and grasped Lilly's hand and raised her fingers to his mouth. His lips brushed across the silk of her gloved knuckles. "Lady Lillian." He smiled and lowered her hand.

Her name from his lips. She sighed and her heart leapt.

Her brother turned and, in a polished and refined move, grasped Lilly's hand from St. Jerome, then placed her fingers on his sleeve. They walked from the room and out of the house.

He signaled to the coachman. It would be a few moments for him to maneuver to the front of the house to pick them up.

"Brian—"

He held up a hand, effectively staying her words. "I wish to know how you feel. I am simply crushed my friend lied to me, Lil. You shocked me. . . . I need a few moments to contemplate. You lied to me as well, Lil. You know if Pa were alive, St. Jerome would be done for, too."

"Let me tell you, Brian, what . . . well, why I was there. How we met. I really think you will understand he had no idea it was me."

"He knew the moment I said he had described my sister that you were indeed my sister whom he futtered." He shook his head. "I had so hoped, Lil, that you—that you would have married for love. Not for some mistake of lustfulness. Not for duty." He closed his eyes. "I need to think a bit. I am going to walk home. I will put you in the coach and see you back at Burber Place. Then we will work this through."

He grabbed her hand and raised it to his lips.

"Lil, come on, I will put you in the coach. This is taking far too long. I need to walk this out."

199

They walked down the steps and the short distance to the coach. "Take her home. I shall walk."

He handed her up into the coach. "I will have a plan for all this mess."

Lilly sat back in the coach as her brother closed the door behind her. She had never seen Brian look so shaken. She had disappointed her brother. A frown touched her lips and her heart pinched.

St. Jerome wanted to wed her and she had no issues with that prospect. Her brother did, however. She closed her eyes.

Brian . . .

St. Jerome . . .

He wished to wed her . . . her. The plain, small, silly lady no one had ever seen. Her lips curled up in amazement, but then her brow pulled tight. How could that be?

22

Lilly

St. Jerome pulled open the door to the carriage and pounced in, shutting the small door behind him.

"Lady Lillian, eh?" He sat on the bench opposite her.

With huge brown eyes, Lilly stared at him from across the cab.

She was unmasked, and he could see her entire face. Stunning. Her small nose matched every other dainty part of her—well, everything besides her enormous brown eyes. She truly was a gem.

"St. Jerome, what are you doing?"

"I knew your brother would walk home. I needed to talk to you tonight before tomorrow's particulars with your brother." He reached across the cab and grabbed her hands in his. By Jove, she was small. Her hands fit in the palm of his. "I had no idea until I saw the evidence on my pantaloons that you gave yourself to me. Lady Lillian, are you well?"

A pretty blush bloomed on her cheeks. My God, she was all his. He couldn't quite believe his fortune. Shy, spirited, determined, and with a passion that consumed whoever was near.

"I am quite well, St. Jerome. I am a bit sore, but nothing, I imagine, that is avoidable in instances such as what we did."

"No, not entirely." He ran his thumb over the back of her hands. "I could have been much gentler with you. I am quite large."

She shyly lowered her eyes from his. "My only experience in seeing that part of the male body was last night, and yours was wider than the others I saw. Size did not seem to matter much in anyone's enjoyment, though."

"I suppose not, though many think thickness is better."

The carriage jolted forward and they were on the way back to Burber Place. The streets were crowded with people going to evening events and the journey would be slow.

He glanced across the cab at her. She was nervous. He wanted to see her smile.

"Veronica—pardon, Lady Lillian—I had no inkling I would find my bride at my last Emma Drundle event." A smile curved his lips. "Oh, the scandal we would cause if anyone were to find out."

Not one smile, or even a twitch, came from her lips.

"Please call me Lilly. I have never liked being called Lady Lillian. The name never really suited me. It is such a beautiful, sophisticated name, and, well, you are the only person besides my mother who has ever called me beautiful."

He stared at her as she fisted her hands in her lap. She truly believed she was not lovely. "You are beautiful, Lilly. Stunning, fact be told. Didn't you notice all the women and men watching you last night?"

"No." She wouldn't raise her eyes to his.

"They did. You have a quality in your spirit that is mesmerizing, Lilly. I am happy you bestowed your favors on me. Am even more delighted that you will be my wife."

"Are you sure, St. Jerome? With little prodding, my brother could be talked out of forcing you to wed me."

He leaned across the cab and grasped her chin, turning her face and eyes to meet his. His lips were a breath from hers. "Lilly, sweet Lilly." His lips pressed against her plush softness and she sighed into him.

Her taste—oh, so sweet, so deliciously innocent.

So deliciously *his.*

Never would he have thought he would have fallen so quickly for someone; yet here he was, sitting across from a woman, a perfectly respectable woman, and all he wished was to open his chest and give her his heart.

By Jove, for her—for his Lilly—he would become a besotted fool in no time. His lips curved into a smile against hers. He would enjoy every minute of it.

He moved his hands up to the silken skin on top of her breasts. He lightly brushed the back of his hand over her bosom. Her body trembled and she arched against him, encouraging him to do more than touch. He dragged his lips across her cheek and down her neck to her chest.

His lips thirsted on the milk of her skin. His fingers dipped below the fabric and into her dress. He found the hard bud and thumbed it. Her body quaked and her breath deepened. He slid the fabric on her shoulder down and continued to kiss her.

Each stroke of his tongue, each flick of his thumb, against her puckered flesh elicited purr after purr from deep in her chest.

His fingers slipped below the lush curve of her breast and he pulled her. He bent his head and greedily sucked on her deep coral nipples. She was salty with a hint of lavender. He groaned at the first taste of her forbidden flesh.

"Oh! Oh! Please, St. Jerome." She thrust her chest forward, pressing her nipple farther into his mouth.

By Jove, she was truly a minx. His cock strained in his drawers. Sweet innocence covered untutored, wanton passion, like none he had ever seen.

Her shaking hand slid out and straight to his waistband.

She tugged at the material with unsure fingers. Her hand trembled against his stomach and she quickly unfastened the buttons to his trousers. Her fingers slid in and wrapped about his solid length, then pulled him out.

"Oh, Lilly!" He wanted her skin on his, touching him all over. He wanted to explore her every naked crevice. His need for her was raw, primal, and complete.

Her trembling hand against his hard cock urged him further. He ached from holding back. Her hands gripped him below the ridge to his head and she slid the skin back. He clenched his teeth, and tingles shot straight to his sac and through his bum. His control slid quickly beyond his grasp. He needed to be inside her. He yanked up her skirt.

Giggling, she wiggled her hips to move the fabric out of his way. He glanced up at her face. That smile would shine on him every day for the rest of his life. He grinned back at her, happy through to his soul.

His fingers probed into the slick yearning folds of her cunny, and his lips recaptured hers as she screamed. His mouth ravished hers in an urgent need, which he could not, would not, deny. He boldly stroked the inside of her mouth with his tongue until they both were dizzy and panting.

She slid her legs farther apart on the seat and arched her hips toward the edge.

My God, what was she doing?

She gently tugged at him, using his cock as if it were a leash to lead a dog home. Oh, God, he was about to futter her here, for a second time in a totally untraditional place. His hips arched forward, his body wanting to go where she led. He cursed to himself. Damn it, he couldn't deny her.

He slid forward and the tip of his cock touched the sweet, oiled petals of her cunt. A groan vibrated deep in his throat as he thrust into her guiding hand. The tip of his cock stroked into her warm, wet cunt.

"Please, please, St. Jerome."

Damn it, he wanted to hear his Christian name from her lips. He continued to thrust harder into her hands, his crown penetrating her deeper with each press. She trembled and shook her body, an utter quake of sensations.

"Remove your hands and call me Vincent from here forth."

Her hands slid away from his erection. "Please, please, Vincent."

He slid all the way into her. The tight skin of her folds opened and gripped him all the way to his testicles. He held himself there and tried to regain control of the sensations assaulting his body. He couldn't. Warmth speared up his gut and the hairs on his neck stood. He pulled out and thrust back into her, hard.

"Vincent!"

His aroused flesh encased in her deep oiled warmth, he rocked his hips, pushing his groin against her sensitive bud.

A groan of pleasure erupted from her.

His body shook. "Am I hurting you, Lilly?"

She leaned forward, her breath rasping against his ear. "Hurting me? No," she said hoarsely. "This is so pleasurable, so different from yesterday. I feel like I am flying—like, with one more move, I will simply explode." Her body squirmed and writhed beneath him, and her hands clutched and tensed on the smooth fabric of his back.

"One more movement, eh?" He pulled his cock out a fraction.

"Sweet . . . Jesus!" Her cunny muscles clamped about him and she spent.

He increased his pace. His seed rose quickly with each clasp of her swollen, oiled flesh against his hardness. Wave upon wave of sensations crested through him and he groaned. "Oh, God, Lilly." He pushed back in, then pulled out ever so slowly.

He savored the feel of the tight stretch of her cunny over the ridge of his cock. Every move of his cock inside her elicited ripple after ripple—spasms surging from deep in her womb.

God, he made her feel good. He made her spend and spend. His emotions soared.

Lilly's body relaxed, and she licked a trail to his ear, swirling her tongue into the cup.

He pushed hard into her and increased his stroke. "You're so tight, so wet. It feels so good to be inside you again . . . oh!" His cock thrust in and his balls tightened. "I am going to spend."

His cock exploded. Pinpricks of pleasure washed from the top of his head all the way to his toes. The soles of his feet tingled and he jumped. His entire body was hypersensitive. What had she done to him?

"There is definitely no way we cannot wed now," Lilly said humorously as he panted, his forehead resting against her shoulder.

"There was no way I would not want you as my wife before this moment, Lilly. I struggled from the first moment I met you. You are, *my* sweet. You are mine. All mine. I will protect you, guide you, and show you the world."

Lilly smiled against his ear. "Indeed, I would like that. I gave you my innocence, St. Jerome. I also gave you my heart."

St. Jerome's arms squeezed her tightly. "Thank you, Lilly. For you stole mine yesterday, it is only fair I get yours in return."

She laughed. Her heart flipped in her chest.

The carriage came to a halt. Lilly pulled back from St. Jerome and quickly pushed her breasts back into her dress. "If we see Brian, how will we explain to him why you are in the coach?" She straightened her skirts back over her legs.

St. Jerome tucked his cock back into his drawers and the footman opened the door and held it wide. Brian stood beyond.

Damn. He glanced at Lilly and then back to Brian. "Believe me, Lilly, he already knows."

Lilly stared at her brother, her eyes growing round. Cunnington's expression thundered.

"Lilly!" He stood back and glared at them.

Vincent knew what would come next. He would need to persuade Cunnington not to kill him and not to shun his sister. He jumped down from the carriage and offered his hand to Lilly. She placed her trembling hand in his and stepped down onto the cobbled walk.

He turned her toward him and raised her fingers to his lips.

"All will be well, sweet Lilly, but I need to speak with your brother alone."

"Enough, St. Jerome."

Cunnington's steely glare raised the fine hairs on Vincent's neck. He had never seen his friend so angry. Then again, if Lilly were his sister and he found Cunnington with her . . . there would be pistols at dawn.

"Cunnington." He bowed his head at his friend and strode toward him.

Cunnington turned on heel without saying a word and they walked together into the main hall of Burber Place. Lilly entered the house on their heels, but she stayed in the hallway.

Vincent followed Cunnington into his study and closed the door behind him.

Vincent turned about. "I am sincerely—"

Cunnington's fist slammed into his chin, knocking his head to the side. His teeth bit down on impact and his lip split wide. The warm, salty tang of blood filled his mouth.

"Damn." His fingers touched his lip, sending sparks flashing before his eyes. He wiggled his jaw and blinked.

"You deserve so much worse, St. Jerome. She is my sister. Damn it. If I could not see the love in her eyes, it would be a bullet smashing into your head, and not my fist."

"Indeed, she is your sister, and I am one of your close friends. When she gave herself to me, I had no idea—"

"Hold your words." Cunnington held up a hand. "I don't want to know any of the details, St. Jerome." He walked over to the window and stared out at the night. "I saw how you both looked at each other. I know you fancy one another. You simply should have told me."

He was correct of course. He should have. . . . Their friendship had lasted through so many years of women, drinks, and fights. How did one address the topic of futtering a friend's sister? He simply had not known how to handle the situation.

"Yes, I should have told you. By the time I thought I knew who she was, I didn't quite know how to tell you, Cunnington. I think I hoped that you would simply consent to what needs to be."

Cunnington turned around and stared at him with a mix of anger and compassion in his eyes. "I know you are a decent man, St. Jerome." His words were harsh and not soothing. "I also can recognize that you two will do well together. My sister needs someone like you . . . someone to guide her in life. You do a pretty decent job at that."

Vincent walked toward his friend. "I do promise to take very good care of her, Cunnington." By Jove, his head hurt. He wiggled his jaw once more and slid his tongue across the puffed split in his lip. "Damn, I forgot how one of your punches feels, you nearly uncorked me."

A satisfied smile curved Cunnington's lips. "As I said, you deserved a stone more. My sister's love is what is keeping you in this world."

"Indeed, and I know if I ever do anything out of line, you will see fit to uncork me at first shot."

"Indeed."

"I am surprised you have kept Lilly a secret, Cunnington. Your sister is beyond handsome."

"My father was overly protective of her and my mother. He never let either out of his sight. She was home tutored and then cared for our mother when ma was ill. She is a sweet girl, St. Jerome, and not worldly."

"I know. It is those qualities that make me want to guide her, protect her, and cherish her always."

"Very well then. See that you do so or I will slice you through with my sword."

Lilly lay in her bed, her covers pulled up to her chin. *Knock! Knock!*

She rolled over and stared at the door. "Yes?"

"Lil, may I come in?"

"Of course. Please come in, Brian."

The door cracked open and Brian walked into the room, leaving the door ajar. He strode to the window and pulled back the curtains. Moonlight flooded the room and his figure. He turned. "Couldn't see a blast thing. Sorry, Lil."

"No worries, Brian." She chewed on her lip. What had happened? Was everything well? She fisted her hands in the sheets.

"St. Jerome will wed you, Lil."

A smile turned her lips. Brian had consented! The alternative to this news had turned her stomach since the moment they left the carriage.

"What I still do not understand, Lil, is why you were at Emma's event in the first place."

"I went in search of you, Brian. I had heard so many of the townsfolk back in Bedfordshire say that you were a scandalous rogue and I just couldn't understand how anyone could be so mistaken about you. You are my brother—sweet, loving, kind. You are a good man."

"Oh, Lil." Brian blew out a loud breath.

"I hid in the carriage blanket box." Her lips curled up. "Not a very smart thing to do. I do not recommend it."

"You what?"

"I knew you were coming to the capital and I crawled into the blanket box."

"Lilly." Brian closed his eyes.

"It is okay, Brian. I understand so much more now. I met this wonderful woman. She gave me her carriage to come home in last night. She helped me to understand that you are still all of the things that you have always been to me, but you are what that place is, too."

He kept his eyes closed. "Lil, I go to those events—"

"It doesn't really matter to me why you were there, Brian. I love you no matter what you choose to do or enjoy."

He nodded his head and grasped her hand in his. "Thank you, Lil. You always have had a good head on your shoulders and a warm, forgiving heart." He stood, then leaned down and kissed her on the forehead.

Epilogue

Lilly sat in the morning room as the sun shone through the windows. It surely was a beautiful day. She turned and smiled shyly at Grace. Her new friend had become so dear to her. She had opened her mind and let her see a part of the world she had never known existed. "I can't believe we are both to be wed."

Grace glanced down at her hands and then back to Lilly. "I am so very happy, Lady Lillian. Winston is such an amazing and wonderful man. He tempted my heart. In giving him my soul, he gave me the sun, the moon, and all of the stars." She raised her cup to her lips and sipped. "My brother was thrilled Winston asked for me. When we were young, we had all been quite close. Of course Winston didn't say anything to him about *where* we saw each other again." She tilted her head to the side and stared at Lilly. "How did your brother take to you and St. Jerome? I know they are friends."

Lilly sighed, then frowned. "Extremely upset at first. St. Jerome kept what happened from him on that night. After the carriage last night, I thought he was truly going to run St. Jerome through." She grimaced as that image played over in her mind. "You should

213

have seen the rage in his eyes. He didn't say a word to me, simply walked with St. Jerome to his study." She, in turn, had gone to her room. "I have no idea what was said, don't really think I wish to know, but he obviously saw how much we are enamored with each other, because he consented."

Grace smiled at her. "He knows what kind of man St. Jerome is. He is a good man, from all I have witnessed. He will do well by you."

"I feel he shall. You and I will have to shop for some . . ." Heat rose to Lilly's cheeks. "Some fun items for our wedding trips. I never knew one could purchase bloomers and masks the like that I saw women wear at that ball." Lilly raised her cup to her lips and smiled. Bloomers, corsets, capes, and wicked masks . . . sweet Jesus, the things she was now willing to talk about over tea! Two days ago, if this topic had come up, she would have stayed quiet and turned the color of a strawberry.

"Winston has every detail planned, and *all* of them sinful. I would be delighted to shop with you and show you all the best places. I am glad our paths crossed, Lady Lillian."

"Please call me Lilly, Grace." She reached across the table and wrapped her fingers about her friend's hand. "Do you know where you are going? Or has he kept that a secret?"

"He said he would plan the entire thing, Lilly. Honestly, it does not matter to me where he takes me."

"I have no idea where St. Jerome would like to take me. I have seen so little of the world, even Bath seems like an exotic place."

Grace laughed out loud. "Indeed, an exotic place that smells horrendous because of the healing properties of the water. Lord Wentland and I went there once, and, my goodness, I simply can't imagine bathing in them."

"I never would have known."

"I have a feeling we will from here forth be fast friends, Lilly.

214

We are opposites in many ways, but similar in others. I enjoy your company." Grace squeezed Lilly's hand back.

Lilly stared at her friend. Her heart was overfilled with all the love she had found in the past two nights. "Indeed, Grace, I do believe we are, and shall continue to be . . . different but *wickedly* alike."

Please turn the page for an exciting sneak peek of
Lacy Danes's
short story,
"Lust's Vow," from
WHAT SHE CRAVES
now on sale at bookstores everywhere!

1

Longing

Surrey, England, 1815

"Come on, Emma, hit him harder."

WAACK.

"Uhhh."

"Oh . . . God . . . good girl, Emma, good girl. Again."

She shouldn't listen to this. Hannah's brows drew together as she strained to hear the voices coming from Lord Brummelton's secluded summerhouse.

What were they up to?

The tone of their voices intrigued her. She stepped forward to continue on her daily ritual to the mill—*blast*, she couldn't get her feet to move. She needed to know what mischief was about.

Her maid, Gertie, said Mr. Roland arrived back from the war with friends but—

WHACK!

Another pleasure-filled groan floated on the fall breeze.

She stared at the octagon-shaped structure. Floor-to-ceiling

219

windows that faced the river reflected the dappled light of the late-afternoon sun, marring the view within. Nothing. She couldn't see a thing.

"Oh God, Emma, his arse is so red. Reach around and touch his prick."

Hannah's eyes widened. *Oh my.* They were engaged in a sexual act.

"He's not ready, Rupert," Emma said in an exasperated voice. "Even though you could spend, I want this to last." Emma's squeaky voice paused. "Isn't Kenneth supposed to join us?"

"Who cares about Kenneth? Get on with it, woman!"

Biting her lip, Hannah hesitated. Maybe at a different angle she could see . . . something. Her heart pounded in her chest as she stepped forward.

CRUNCH.

She stopped. Blast. Fallen leaves. The sound was so loud to her ears in the silence of the woods. They would surely hear.

The leaves scattered in a thick carpet all around the structure. She frowned. There was no way she could approach silently, but if they were engrossed in the love act, they might not notice.

A groan came from a man with a baritone voice, and shivers cascaded down her arms. Hannah closed her eyes. Good Lord, she longed for that sensation.

She didn't care if they heard. She needed to learn how to pleasure a man. At least two men were in that summerhouse engaged in wicked futter and were thoroughly enjoying it. Enjoying the act as her husband never had with her. Surely she would learn to pleasure a man if she could see them, and if by chance they saw her . . . Well, she didn't give a damn.

Hairs on her arms and neck stood in anticipation as she determinedly crept forward, shuffling her feet so as not to make a sound. She would finally understand what made Simon leave her bed.

The path that followed the river went directly in front of the summerhouse. *Please let there be no reflection on the glass at a different angle.* Her heart sped in her chest as another groan filtered through the trees.

Once in front of the structure, she scooted behind a birch tree. The width was a bit narrow, but she could hide her face if she needed to. She inhaled the crisp fall air and closed her eyes. *Please let me learn.* Then she peeked through the windows of the cottage. Oh my. Her eyes bulged in shock.

A man with pale skin knelt on the floor, his breeches pushed down past his knees. A blond woman, younger than herself, stood behind him, a long, thin switch in hand. She held the birch out to the side, and *swoosh*, the twig hit his bottom with a loud crack. Ouch. That's not what she expected.

The kneeling man flinched from the impact and groaned. Another deep groan came from a man who stood farther back in the structure.

He watched them as she did.

While giving orders to Emma, his penis jutted out of his pants. His long fingers stroked the length, settled at the tip, and then rolled. Hannah bit her lip. His well-proportioned hands stroked in a musical rhythm. Beautiful. His hands held an artistic quality.

In her mind, those big, graceful hands slid down her body, working their magic on her bare skin. She trembled and her eyelids fluttered. *Oh my!* His fingers caressed her breasts, tapping as if playing a fine instrument. Then circled her nipples and he scraped his nail over the hard peak. Her nipples budded into the confines of her corset and she sucked in a tight breath with longing for his touch.

His hands slid up her inner thighs. The heat of him seeped through her dress as he jerked her legs apart, lifting her skirt so he could access every part of her.

221

She groaned and remembered the pictures from the books she read. Engravings of a man placing his tongue where his phallus normally fit. How she desired to experience a touch like such.

If this man lifted her skirts just like so, and kneeled between her legs he could give her that experience and more. His hair would tickle her inner thighs. His hands would burn marks into her bottom as he lifted her sex opening to his mouth. Her heart pounded against her ribs. Oh, how she wanted to feel a man's tongue tasting her inner core.

Her insides quivered. What would lying with this man be like? His hand slid over his prick again in a controlled move. Amazing. His expertise in this act shone in every motion. She licked her lips, wanting him to touch her, and create that wonderful tingling sensation in her body with his hands. What a shocking, yet delightful thought.

The man on the floor did not cry out in pain as the switch hit him again, but moaned in pleasure.

How could anyone find pleasure from a spank? Her eyes narrowed, and she tilted her head to the side. Surely she missed something. She blinked again. Yes, he found pleasure. His breath puffed in and out, and his bluish-red penis stood stiff as whalebone between his legs. Amazing. Strangely the sight aroused her. Her eyes widened. How could she like watching such an act?

She tried to take in the whole scene, but she couldn't stop staring at both men's sex. The man who knelt possessed a long narrow phallus, much narrower than the two of her experience, but a good thumb longer than Simon's.

The other of her comparison was a vague memory of beauty and satiny skin, to which neither of these could compare. Her heart sped and her skin heated as she remembered her youthful hand trembling, rubbing down the hot skin and plum-shaped head. She shook herself and pushed the pleasant memory from her mind.

WHACK!

Hannah flinched. She couldn't imagine Simon finding pleasure from a spank, but then again nothing she did pleased him, so maybe she was wrong. He only found excitement in his whores and at his clubs.

The man moved from the back of the cottage into a better view. Hannah ducked behind the old birch tree and closed her eyes.

God, she was mad. She gasped for air.

The five lonely years since Simon's death had made her crazy with the urge to learn to please a man. First she had lowered herself to purchasing all sorts of bawdy books, books that talked of things such as this. And now . . . Now she ogled Mr. Roland and invaded his privacy.

Her chest tightened. The reality was she would never hold the skill to master such pleasure. God, this was agony. She needed to leave before one of them noticed her. Indeed . . . Her shoulders slumped. Oh poppiedust. She turned and stepped in the direction of Huntington Cottage.

"Emma, dear, I want to feel your hot cunt while you frig Kit with your mouth."

Hannah flung around. This she couldn't resist. She read about kissing a man's sex in the *Perfumed Garden* and wondered if men and women truly found pleasure that way.

Emma knelt on cushions on the floor. Kit lay in front of her, his phallus standing straight as the trees that surrounded her.

Hannah's hands brushed the smooth trunk of the large birch tree. Imagining the hotness of smooth male flesh as her hands ran across rough cool bark, she slid her hands out to the edges, then up and down. In her mind her hands explored every ridge and vein of his sex. Her pulse increased, and her chest tightened. God, she needed to feel a man again. Her hands trembled.

With all the books she'd read, the next time a man joined her in bed she hoped she would have an idea what to do.

Emma leaned down and her tongue traced the head of the man's penis. Kit groaned.

"Umm . . ." Hannah's tongue slid out and traced her lips. She imagined the salty flavor of skin and the tapered shape of prick head as an erection pressed into her mouth. Her nipples peaked hard beneath her corset.

The other man, Rupert, knelt behind Emma. Flipping her skirt and petticoat up onto her back, he ran his hands down the swell of her creamy bottom. "Good girl, Emma. Take Kit in," he murmured, then slid his hand between her spheres. Hannah whimpered. Oh how she wanted rough male hands on her bum again.

"No, Emma. Pleasure Kit. Concentrate on nothing but him."

Kit groaned and thrust his hips up as Emma lowered her head down. Half his shaft slid into her mouth. As she pulled her head up to the tip, his shaft shimmered with her saliva.

Hannah's mouth watered. She wanted this, wanted to be Emma as she slid hot male flesh into her mouth and another man caressed her. She swallowed hard. How scandalous.

Emma's tongue slid out and traced the ridge; she puckered her lips, and slid back down the length.

Hannah could feel the pressure of a phallus as the head slid into her mouth. Saliva pooled and dribbled down the length of the prick as it throbbed and twitched. Her lips caressed the ridge and popped to the tip. Wetness dewed her skin, and her sex pulsed as a moan caught in her throat. She crossed her legs in an attempt to control the building desire and slickness slid down her leg.

Good Lord, she should tear her gaze away. Her chest tightened and her skin tingled. Too many years . . . how she needed a man's touch. She had no prospects, no admirers. This was madness. Her lip trembled.

Kit groaned, and tears sprang to her eyes. She would never, could never, possess the ability to pleasure a man this way, but still she stood and watched. She was a fool.

Tingles slid across her body with every caress the threesome made. Her nipples strained against her corset as Rupert grasped his large stiff prick. He ran his hand along the length, then laid his prick in the crack of Emma's bum. Not between her legs, but in the crevice. He rocked his staff back and forth, sliding the head up and down the valley. His gaze fixed on the sight.

"Oh, Em, you have the most glorious arse." Gripping the base of his shaft, he slid his hand forward and back in the same motion as he rocked.

Simon had never done such a thing to her. In the short month he shared her bed, he always joined her in the same position. Him on top, with her legs spread wide.

Viewing such an animalistic position caused a hunger to seep through her. She could almost feel the hot skin as the head of a penis slid between the spheres of her bum, stretching her sex, spearing her womb. A man's muscles shaking against her bottom as he pumped into her like an animal in the fields.

Her sex spasmed and she arched her back in search of the imaginary prick. She wanted Rupert's penis to fill her, to bring her the blissful release she only created with her fingers on her own, but there was nothing there. She gritted her teeth.

Oh, how she wanted to diddle a man in that position. This man. Shifting her stance, she gasped, and her nubbin throbbed.

His hands flexed, gripping Emma's bum and she imagined his fingers on the soft flesh of her bottom, gripping her hard. His arms jerking her back into his hips with controlled precise moves as his penis pushed into her sex again and again.

The delightful friction of her flesh stretching to fit him as he mated with her made her knees weak. One of his hands slowly trailed her hip to her stomach and then dipped to the curls at the peak of her thighs. Forging through the coarseness he fingered her dripping flesh and touched where they joined.

Her entire body trembled at the thought of touching the spot where they fused together. Slick and wet as he thrust into her, she would drag her fingers across his smooth burning skin and caress his sac as it hit her bottom on each thrust.

She clamped her leg muscles tighter, trying to capture the sensation in her mind, and the delicious ache between her legs spiraled. *Good Lord.*

Emma continued to devour Kit's penis. She licked and sucked until on a groan Kit thrust his hips with abandon. Her mouth slid farther down his length, and he cried out in pleasure. His hands gripped Emma's curly hair as his face contorted in ecstasy.

Pain ripped at her heart and she closed her eyes. *Please let me have the chance to make a man cry out in pleasure the way this woman did.*

Her eyes fluttered open. Oh! Juices slid down Hannah's leg as Rupert slid his prick into Emma from behind. Blast it. She wanted to feel the delight they shared, but the only way to do that would be to touch herself. Trembling, she tried to restrain her hands as they slid down her dress. Her sex pounded with the beat of her heart as her face flamed with heat. What if someone saw?

Rupert pumped and flexed his ass as his penis speared into Emma between her bum cheeks. She could hear the wetness as he slid in again and again. Her fingers found the place between her thighs and pressed her skirts between them.

The fabric of her shift dampened and clung to the lips of her sex. She wanted to feel their slickness with her bare touch, but she didn't dare lift her skirts in the open and touch herself.

Imagining her fingers were Rupert's, she caressed the swollen folds through the muslin and brushed over the hard bud between. Lightning shot through her body and a groan bubbled up her throat. Every muscle in her body strained for release.

Rupert's breath labored and Emma whimpered with each stroke. His phallus shimmered with wetness and the head and skin shone an intense red each time his penis pulled out.

Hannah pressed the fabric into her opening, mimicking Rupert's stroke, and rubbed hard against her blissful nubbin. Her eyes barely slit open, she watched as Rupert grew closer to spending in Emma.

Rupert grunted, then cried out a deep thrilling sound that was music to Hannah's ears and body. Splendid contractions wracked her, starting from womb and spreading through her entire being. Her knees weakened and she braced herself with her shoulder against the tree. How she wished this magic coursing through her was created from his prick.

Kenneth Walker plodded down the path toward the river. He refused to stall any longer. They needed to be ready for the members when they arrived for the masque. The masters would be excited about the event and ready for bawdy play. If they weren't there to greet them when they arrived, things would get out of control.

Damn Rupert for not restraining himself until the festivities for a bit of nifty. Last night finally proved to Kenneth that he preferred his loving one-on-one. Emma had favored him, much to Rupert's annoyance, then all but wrapped her legs around him this morning before the group could rise.

He refused to be any woman's plaything. Just the idea that

Emma was Rupert's and preferred other men made his skin crawl. Out of respect for Rupert, he let this morning's flirtation pass without comment.

Memories of his father's sobs in his aunt's library as his mother coldly told him she would not give up her lover chilled his spine. His jaw clenched and his cheek twitched. How she reduced the powerful Duke of Deventon to a slobbering lump still puzzled him. He shook himself to rid the thought.

Never, never would he let himself fall prey to that kind of humiliation or, more precisely, to that kind of woman for more than one night.

He rounded the turn in the path, and the summerhouse lay ahead.

"Emma, dear, I want to feel your hot cunt while you frig Kit with your mouth."

Shit. He stopped in his tracks. So much for his dallying. Turning toward the river, he beheld black hair and a deep blue dress peeking out from behind a white birch tree.

Well, well. His lips curved up. Someone peeped on Rupert and his games. He held in a chuckle. If Rupert knew, he would perform to the fullest and probably spill his seed within a second.

The woman's face slid out from behind the tree and gazed into the summerhouse. Her hands slid up and down the rough bark as if she stroked a large cock.

Damn, what a pretty thing. And oddly familiar. He glanced at her hands again as they clenched the edges of the bark. His chest tightened. Could it be? He stared back at her, black hair and a round face with pale clear skin.

God, that tiny nose and those lush lips occasioned his dreams. A groan caught in his throat as he stiffened. What stood behind that tree would be just as magnificent as it had been twelve years ago. Even better, she would have matured into a woman, soft, with flesh in all the right places.

Hannah Hay, the Marquess of Wolverland's eldest daughter and the first woman to touch his cock, stood watching his friends as she stroked a tree-sized prick in her mind. Only her imagination could make such a leap. His smile grew bigger and his cock throbbed. Lolling his head back, his fingers found the ridge that pressed against his buckskins and he stroked.

Hannah's hands had been so small and soft against the tender flesh of his youthful prick. His body shook. He had longed to touch her for weeks. When she finally consented, he had been so aroused that he spent after one stroke of her silky hand.

His fingers tightened upon the ridge of his straining shaft, and he forced his eyes open to watch her as she spied on Rupert in awe and fascination. Her face was still so easy to read: curiosity, pleasure, and arousal showed clear as day on her china-doll features.

Her pink tongue slid out and traced her lips, then her mouth opened as if taking a prick between their fullness. Damn, those lush lips would feel amazing on his cock. Wetness seeped into his pants and his prick strained. Closing her eyes, she sucked in the sides of her cheeks.

Good God! Without a doubt Emma sucked Kit right now, and Hannah wanted to suck someone too. Raw need flooded his body, and he stepped forward. He would walk to her and offer his body like he did all those years ago.

His boyish voice came back to him. *"Come now, Hannah. Let me tickle you."*

She had been awkward then, just as he had. His mouth watered as he touched his boyhood tongue to the crevice at the base of her throat and tasted her skin. She would taste the same. He knew it.

The smell of her perfume and the sound of her laughter. Shaking hands, trembling bodies, and sloppy, urgent kisses. His throat constricted. God, the way she had looked at him and gently touched his face. No woman since had been able to measure to her genuine kindness when his world shattered. This time what they shared would be different; no one would force him to leave. This time he would bed her and bed her well.

"Ahhhha!"

The cry of passion snapped him back to the sight at hand. Emma moaned and whimpered. Kit surely spent and now stroked her as Rupert had his way. They would be done soon, and he wanted Hannah to know he watched her watching them.

He cleared his throat loud enough for Rupert to hear in the cottage.

Hannah did not budge, but her hands slid down the front of her dress.

He shook his head and smiled. Just like her to be so absorbed. She probably wouldn't notice if a herd of sheep wandered through. Bending down, he picked up a stick and tossed the twig at the tree she stood behind. The foot-long branch hit square against the trunk and she jumped. Her gaze flew to him as he stood in the path to the summerhouse. He grinned. *Yes, dear, someone is watching you.*

The trail was the only way she could go. If she went past the summerhouse, Rupert would see. She glanced at the house, then at the path. Her face flamed crimson.

Ah, Hannah, how you flatter me. He did not know there were still people around who blushed at such things. With her head lowered, she turned on her heel and cut through the trees to the riverbank.

Oh no, you don't, my sweet Hannah. In five long strides, he came up behind her and clasped her arm.

She pulled, but his grasp held firm. "Let go of me, you beast!"

"Sweet, sweet Hannah . . ."

Hannah's eyes widened. "Do I know you, sir? Please unhand me." Yanking her arm again, his grip eased but did not fall from her body.

Her heart pounded so hard the beat made her hands shake. How could someone have seen her? Good Lord. This was the man Emma mentioned when Hannah first spied on them. He knew what she watched. Her cheeks grew hotter. She averted her gaze to the riverbed and stepped away from him.

"Not so quickly, sweet." His hand stroked her arm, and lightning slid through her veins straight to the place between her thighs. *Not now, blast you, damn body.* She closed her eyes and tried to quell the shiver his caress caused, but failed. His muscles stiffened in return.

"Don't say you don't remember me." The man shook his head at her as she tried once again to yank her arm free.

"Damn you, sir, let go of—"

"I believe I was the first man to ever touch you."

"P-pardon?"

He inclined his head and raised his eyebrows.

Her mouth dropped open. "Kenny . . . Kenny Walker?"

He smiled. Then laughed. "Haven't been called Kenny in ages, but, yes."

Was this truly him? The young man with whom twelve years ago she had spent her most memorable summer. They had run through the woods, played hide-and-seek, and swum in the lake with her sisters and his brother. Her first infatuation, her first kiss. Good Lord. The young man who by just saying "Hannah" had made her heart pound and heat grace her cheeks with wicked thoughts.

She searched his face. His strong straight nose, angled cheeks, and dimpled chin were the same. His eyes, the same smoky brown that you could get lost in, stared back at her with intense heat. Her body dewed, remembering all that that hungry stare promised.

She studied his body. Oh my! His shoulders had broadened, and his chest, encased in a tight-fitting coat, left little to the imagination. Her breath hitched at sculpted thighs encased in tight buckskin breeches. A lump formed in her throat, and she swallowed hard, envisioning those legs tangled in hers.

A very fit, attractive, and well-muscled man stood before her. God, he was much taller than she remembered. Her memories . . . oh. Her eyes closed. His fingers as they slid up her skirts and into her wet folds, making her tremble in such a way she thought she would die.

Kenny gently stroked her arm and with his thumb traced circles in the fabric of her sleeve. Her nipples ached, pebbled hard, wanting the circular motion.

His hasty departure from his aunt's after a summer of friendship and flirtation and his last words, *"I will bed you one day, dear sweet Hannah,"* slid through her mind.

She stared at his breeches where his erection bulged. He didn't even try to conceal his arousal. He journeyed to the summerhouse today to have relations with his friends. He, like her husband, was a rake, with a bad enough reputation that she had heard of his adventures.

A deep rumble of a laugh came from him, and his erection twitched beneath the leather of his pants. Her cheeks grew warm, but she was unable to pull her stare from the bulge. All she wanted was to touch that ridge. God, she was mad.

"Let me tickle you, my sweet," he said as he slid his finger beneath her chin and raised her eyes.

Eyes blazing with need met hers. Her sex clenched and she

groaned. His words, the same he used all those years ago. She bit her lip. Her body knew the promise in those words. But what if she was as bad as her husband claimed? Kenny had been with many women since their encounter . . .

"Hannah? Please . . ." His voice, filled with raspy desire, caressed her nerves. She needed to be touched, and who better to touch her than the man who initiated her to the act of coitus?

"Yes, Kenny, touch me. Touch me."

Please turn the page for an exciting sneak peek of
Lacy Danes's
"Martin"
from ANIMAL LUST
now on sale at bookstores everywhere!

1

Cumberland, England, 1800

Sweet mother! What a blunder she'd made! Jane's hand shot to her mouth, and she bit the skin of her palm.

Jonathan had never loved her. He lied.

Tears blurred her vision and streamed down her cheeks. She tripped and stumbled, barely seeing the wooded trail before her. The flesh of her sex burned, and her legs ached. How she needed a nice long soak in a tub and time to sort this out. Dash it!

When had she misunderstood his intentions? They had been secretly touching and kissing behind his tavern for months. The whole town thought they would marry. Then, today at the fair, they'd snuck into the woods.

"Lovely, lovely Jane, ye give me a tickle, won't ye, love?" *The smell of the ale from his breath wafted about her.*

She shouldn't, but how she fancied him. What could it matter?

"You will marry me?" she breathed into his hair, her head spinning in aroused bliss.

He grunted as her touch ran down his muscled back.

He'd grunted! Her teeth ground together as she ran without seeing the trail before her. Sweet mother! He had never said he would wed her. She had craved his touch and the feelings he created in her so madly she'd mistaken the grunt as an affirmation of his designs.

She'd given her innocence to a man who had no intentions of wedding her. Her fingers clutched her stomach. She could be with child, and she had no way to take care of a babe nor herself. Daft, truly daft.

Her head spun. She gasped for air as her legs tangled in her skirts, and she tripped, landing, limbs spread wide on the hard, damp earth. Oh. She lay, lungs burning, unable to breathe, and closed her eyes. Her entire life had changed in one act of wanton misdeed. She would pull herself together. She would find a way if she carried a child, but for now . . . she would grieve while no one could see her.

"Lovely Jane." He buttoned up his trousers as he inhaled a deep breath, the crisp air clouding as he exhaled. "Not bad for a green tickle, and no worries about the clap."

The clap. He'd rutted with her like she was no better than a tavern wench. He loved her. He said he loved her. Her eyes closed as tears welled.

" 'Twas lovely, Jane. Ye have a sweet little honeypot. Take good care of it and we'll come out here again sometime." He turned and headed off into the trees.

By God. What had she done?

With her face down in the dirt, tears silently ran down her face. Her limbs trembled, and her head spun. She hadn't cried in an age. The act depleted and exhausted her. *Pull yourself together, Jane.* With a sob, she straightened and got to her feet on shaking legs. She was a wealthy merchant's daughter. He was friends with her pa. How dare he treat her ill?

Panic grabbed at her heart.

This act ruined her prospects of a normal life and brought shame on her family name. Her father's business would suffer. How could she be so selfish? Her family, she held dear.

Frantic, her gaze darted around the forest. Nothing but trees. *Think, think, you fool. . . .*

Her fingers pinched the bridge of her nose. She would go to Jonathan and beg him not to say a word. Dash it all. Her eyes squeezed shut.

If she could only figure a way out of the woods. She held her breath, listening for any sounds from the fair. Nothing. What is the rule? Follow the sun and it will lead you to the north. . . . No. . . . Sweet mother, she should have listened to her father when he talked about directions.

She stepped toward the setting sun; pain spread through her ankle and up her leg, and her temples throbbed. Ouch! She put weight on her leg and swayed. She could limp but not far.

The forest grew darker. Where was she? She hobbled up the path. Dash it all. Lost, that's where. She picked up her pace. Frost eased up around her heart, and she pushed aching dreams down. Just ahead, a road loomed, and the sun dipped below the horizon. The lane, rutted and ill used, surely led somewhere. . . .

Thunder cracked in the distance as she stared up at the large wooden door. Darkness brewed, and she passed not a soul on the road to this place. The house stood four stories tall, with huge spires that reached to the sky. She had resided in Cumberland for five years, and not once had she heard of an estate such as this. Lifting her hand, she knocked as rain plummeted to the earth in large wet thunks behind her.

She knocked again; shivers raced over her skin. The door creaked open.

"May I help you, ma'am?"

"Oh, indeed." She practically jumped at the man sticking his head out of the small crack. "I'm lost and injured." She pointed to her ankle. "And, well, you see, it is beginning to rain. Would it be possible for me to stay here this night? I could sleep in the kitchen or . . . or . . . the barn. I shan't be any trouble."

The man's eyes went wide behind his round spectacles, and his face twisted in what looked like horror.

"I . . . I . . . know this is highly irregular, but please?"

He schooled his features back to a serious line. "I'm sorry, ma'am. There is no safe way for you to stay here."

Safe? "Pardon?" *Oh, please just let me in.*

The wind whipped up and blew down the last of her pinned-up hair. A shiver racked her body, and her teeth chattered.

"Oh . . . Oh . . ." He glanced into the house. "Very well, ma'am. You will do as I say, do my bidding exclusively. Without fail. Women should not be in this house."

He was concerned about propriety? What a jest! She was ruined. Tears touched her eyes in shame, and she shook them away. What silliness! This man possessed no way of knowing that.

"I will do as you wish, sir." She had no choice. Either she stepped into this house and escaped drowning in one of Cumberland's deluges, or she would try to find her way back in the dark and probably die. She cringed. That was a bit too pessimistic, but she just couldn't go another step this night.

He hesitated and then opened the door just enough to admit her. She slid into the darkened hall and glanced around. A grand staircase stood twisting up to the roof. Dim light shone through a window above the door and illuminated the entry and the paintings that covered the walls. Where did the stair lead? An eerie chill raced up her spine, and she stepped forward, eager to see what lay at their end.

"This way, miss."

Startled, she spun around and followed the servant down a hall that went off to the left of the entry.

"I will put you in the east wing. You will lock your door. Every bolt. I will bring you warm water to wash. After, admit no one to your room."

A bit protective for a servant, but then again, maybe his master was a real curmudgeon. The last thing she wanted was to end up back out in the rain now. "Very well, sir. I have no wish for you to lose your post. I can surely sleep in the kitchen."

"No!" His voice was a sharp shrill.

Her brows drew together as her eyes adjusted to the dim light in the hall they trod down. Why was he so nervous?

"Until I tell Lord Tremarctos you are staying with us, you will stay out of sight." The man swallowed hard. His hand moved upward as though to tweak his collar and then stopped midair as he glanced at her from the corner of his eye.

Odd! Surely she had nothing to fear. Besides, tiredness ruled her, and the events from the day shook her so terribly it would be no problem to stay locked behind a door in this house.

This house. . . . Her gaze darted around the hall, and she almost stopped and spun on the spot. What a beautiful house! The floors shone of a dark, polished marble. The doors stood floor to ceiling with massive iron hinges bigger than anything she had ever seen.

In the dim light she could tell that the house shone with delights she would never see again. Truly a pity. She wished she could see every detail. They turned a corner, and she followed the man up three flights of narrow servants' stairs. At the top of the hall another male servant approached, and the man who let her in waved his hand, calling him to them.

"Bring me hot water, a pitcher, and have Jack send up tea with cheese and biscuits."

"Sir." The man inclined his head and stared at her as she passed.

Her attire was a mess! Nevertheless, politeness dictated that he shouldn't stare. Her fingers picked at the mud that covered her dress, and her gaze settled on her dirt-splattered hands. She rolled her eyes. Just her luck! Finally she saw the inside of a fancy house, and she looked as if she'd spent the day gathering greens from the garden.

Halfway down the hall, they stopped and he pushed open a door. She stepped across the threshold and stopped. Her eyes widened, settling on the well-appointed room. "Oh, sir, a servant's room will suffice."

"No, ma'am. None of the servants' rooms have doors. And . . . well, you promised to lock yourself in."

She turned as he bent to light the fire in the grate. The sputtering flame cast more light into the dark room. Oh, how she wanted to get warm, wash the filth from her body, and curl up in that huge, heavenly bed. Her mouth dropped open. My goodness, the mattress was enormous; the posters were carved but with such dim light she couldn't see the design.

The linens looked a scrumptious deep shade, too dark to discern in the glow from the fire. The image of her lying on deep scarlet silk, naked, flashed before her. Her hair spread across the pillows as a lover caressed her thighs, his head between her legs, licking the entrance to her womb. Her knees wobbled as tingles scorched through her sex. Oh, my! Her hand shot to her mouth in shock, and she shook herself, trying to erase the image from her mind.

Never in her life had such thoughts entered her head. When she imagined the act with Jonathan, loving never involved a bed, and never with his mouth there. Her hand smoothed down the front of her dress to the apex of her thighs. Would kissing there be pleasurable? Her cheeks flushed warm, and she snatched her hand away. Thank goodness no one could see her thoughts!

She was tired; that was all. The man who had passed them brought up water and filled a tub for her to wash in; he was followed by a gentleman with a tea tray. She waited until they left, bolted the door as requested, and then sat down on the chair by the fire. Tears trickled down her face; they were the last she would allow because of Jonathan. Tomorrow would be a new day, and she would find a way out of this mess. But tonight . . . she let herself cry once more.

A noise pierced her slumber. What was that?

The sound increased as her eyes fluttered open to darkness. The fire in the fireplace burned no more, and the rain outside fell in a deafening pour.

Crack.

Lightning lit the edges of the curtain as a scratching from the other side of the door grew louder. Her heart increased to a fast beat. What was that? A dog?

She pushed back the covers, scrambled to her feet, and crossed the icy room to the door.

She shivered as she stood before the white painted wood. Her gaze scanned the line of eight locks the servant had requested she bolt. She had felt silly when she listened to him, but his nervousness about letting a woman stay here made her wonder what lay beyond that door. Leaning toward the door she placed her ear to the crack.

Sniff, sniff. A low rumble of a growl came from the opposite side. "I can smell you." *Sniff.* "The virgin's blood, the semen, dripping from you."

She jumped and scrambled back, an arm's reach from the door in outrage. How . . . how could anyone know what she did today? She had washed . . . thoroughly. There was no possible way anyone could smell her folly. Was this a dream?

"Who . . . who is there?" Her voice wavered as she reached out and touched the bolts she had thrown that night.

"Let me in." The growl, so low and throaty, made the hairs on her neck stand. "Let me taste what you have so freely given to another."

She continued to stare at the door; shame and panic boiled through her body until her body shook. The scratching increased. The sniffs echoed as if the person outside her door stood beside her. "Let me in. . . . Let me in. . . ." the raspy growl rang, and sweat slid down her back.

It would not give up. Somehow she sensed it.

The sound of something dragging widened her eyes, and with a bang, the door shook on its hinges. "Let me in, damn you!" It howled in outrage. "I will have you. There will be no denying me."

"No. . . . Go. Leave me be!" She yelled into the blackness and stepped back from the door as the wood once again shook and creaked with the weight of the pounding.

This surely was a dream. Nothing like this could be real.

Her body shook, her gaze stuck on the door. *Please let the locks hold firm.*

A sharp cry of pain came from the other side of the door, and a breath tickled her neck. Her hand shot to that spot as she spun, expecting to see someone there. Nothing. The curtains blew, and the window snapped open with a crack.

Dash it all! She jumped and hurried for the window. The wind howled, blowing her hair back from her face in a gust. She grasped the sodden wood in her hands and tugged; she stared out at the night. Rain came down in sheets, and as the wood frame clicked shut, lightning lit up the gardens below.

A figure clung to the wall at the base of the building. Crimson eyes stared up at her. She gasped, bolted the window, and pushed away from the glass, the curtain falling back as—she swore—the eyes emerged above the edge of the sill.

The cry rang in her head once more. Her heart pounding, she spun and stared at the door.

Nothing. Not a sound except the pounding in her heart. Her body shook uncontrollably as every shadow in the room moved, alive and coming for her.

This is just a dream.

Close your eyes and things will all get better.

She jumped, nerves taut as she stumbled back to the bed and crawled up on the mattress. Her eyes darted back and forth between the window and the door, searching for anything she could make out in the black, but all stayed still.

Just close your eyes and things will be well. In the morning you can leave this place for home.

As she forced her lids shut, quiet met her.

2

The warmth of smooth silk surrounded her, and a pleasant aroma tickled her nose. Mmmm. She inhaled again.

Cinnamon.

Her mother's baking. She loved her pastries. Jane's stomach rumbled, and she lazily stretched, scooting her bum to roll on her side.

Firm pressure compressed her into the mattress, not allowing her further motions. What? She strained again as her eyes fluttered open to darkness. She was not home. This was not her bed.

She pulled, and her muscles strained as her gaze shot around the darkness. Her eyes gaped as she sighted the vague outline of the door. The white painted wood stood, unlatched and open into the room. Her heart rapidly sped. Jerking her body, she frantically strained. She couldn't move. Her muscles shook. Yet nothing restrained her. Another dream; this was just another dream. She squeezed her lids shut.

Sniff, sniff, sniff. Warm air tickled her stomach.

Sweet mother, that was real. Her eyes shot open. Still, she saw nothing. The bedclothes lay flat, but beneath the covers her shift slid up her torso to her breasts. What . . . "Stop! Don't touch me!"

She squirmed. Warm silk touched the peak of her nipple, and her lungs locked.

"Please!" Panic gripped her, and her body turned clammy. *This is what happens when you willingly participate in the act outside of marriage. You go mad with nightmares and dreams of carnal desire.* She squeezed her lids shut, and warm, moist air puffed up her neck to her ear.

"I said there would be no denying me."

The smell of cinnamon grew stronger, and her whole body trembled.

"What do you want from me?" She strained and pulled to move but couldn't.

Silence met her.

"Why can't I see you? Is this a dream?"

Still nothing. Chills raced her skin; she squirmed and strained her muscles. Warm smoothness dragged down her stomach, and her body trembled in the touch's wake. Heat flooded her core.

"I will not harm you," the male voice cooed softly, reassuring her. "To whom did you give your gift?" The warm cloth dragged up to her breasts and circled her nipples.

"Oh, God. . . ." Her breasts grew heavy, and she groaned. Why . . . how . . . Oh, why did her body respond to this bizarre touch? "That is no concern of yours." This had to be a dream—a pleasant yet strange dream.

"Ah, but if this is a dream, what does it matter?"

"I—I guess that is true," she said tentatively. "But if this is a dream, why would you say such?"

A low rumble of a laugh shook her body as smooth wetness pressed to her neck, kissing her racing heartbeat. "You are beautiful. Your eyes . . . I have never seen such a shade."

Her body grew warm at the comment. "Thank you. They are my mother's."

He grunted as his lip reconnected with the skin at the base of her throat. Shivers of pleasure pulsed across her skin. What did it matter if she told him of her folly? This surely was a dream.

"I gave my innocence to the tavern owner in Sudhamly."

The pressure holding her tightened, and the air grew thick. A low gruntal growl pressed to her throat, and a tongue licked her neck from base to ear.

A burst of warm air caressed her earlobe. "You are very brave." His tongue swirled into the curve. "What did he give you in return?"

Her body shook, and she pulled her head away from the invasion. "I—I don't understand. The only thing he gave me was his seed and an aching heart."

A deep, angry hiss slid down her spine, and her body quaked. "You love each other?" His voice sounded strangled.

"I—I thought so . . . but he did not." Her chest tightened as she said the words aloud. A true statement, and she needed to face that fact.

"He should have returned your gift. It is required to give something in return, especially when one gives her innocence."

"I'm sorry, I—I don't understand. What do you speak of? Who are you?"

The warm cloth circling her nipples vanished, and his mouth sealed upon her breast in a vise. Pain shot through the tissue into her breast, and her body arched off the mattress. He nibbled, and the ache swirled to intense pleasure, tingling down her belly to the flesh between her legs.

"Oh, God, what . . . what are you doing?" Her lips trembled as his tongue swirled the nipple.

He growled.

"I will give you the gift your mate stole from you."

"The gift?"

His warm breath slid down her belly, and a puff of steam touched the curls at that apex of her thighs.

Oh, my stars! This dream was exactly what she had envisioned would happen on this bed when she first glimpsed the monstrosity. The warmth of velvet brushed her thighs, and she bit the inside of her lip. After parting her legs farther, the spongy slickness of muscled tongue slid along the slit of her sex, and her womb clenched.

Virgin's blood, echoed in her mind. *Seed that does not belong.* The warmth pressed into her womb, and her body arched once more off the mattress.

Yes, enjoy the gift he denied you.

The tongue swirled the crevice, licking and sucking, as if he tried to remove every last ounce of the evidence from her folly. Oh, if she could only remove the memory from her mind!

Her heart pounded in her chest, and teeth grazed the flesh of the opening to her womb. Intense pleasure spiraled through the muscles of her legs, tightening them. Her toes curled, and her womb contracted, spending juice from her core. "Oh . . . oh!"

His tongue traveled across her scored flesh and lapped the honey that now flowed freely from her. Fierce sensation shot, arching her hips off the mattress. She rubbed her curls against the large head and wide shoulders she now felt pressed between her legs and bore down on his tongue. Oh, there truly resided a man between her legs!

Blissful tingling grasped every nerve of her body. Her fist clenched tight; blinding light flashed as every muscle in her body thrashed in wave upon wave. She screamed and then shook, her legs bucking to the touch of his tongue. He licked her clean from anus to curls as her muscles jumped and pulled away from the too intense caress.

"What . . . what was that?" Her gaze focused on the figure of an extremely large man who, without a doubt, knelt between her legs. She squeezed her eyes shut. Oh, she'd gone daft!

"Your pleasure. For allowing a boar to mount you."

"Pardon? The gift," she whispered and squeezed her legs together about his thighs. Indeed, he was there.

"Yes." His large hands gripped her thighs and gently squeezed.

A howl pierced the air from down the hall. She started, and a swirl of air washed across her. The warmth of silk and body heat gradually faded, and the faint smell of cinnamon clung in the air.

She trembled and pulled the covers up close to her body. Was this a dream? She reached down and slid her finger into the slick flesh of her sex. It surely was.

Raising her hand to her nose, the smell of cinnamon clung stronger than her scent. How strange and too odd to think about. Her gaze shot to the closed door to the hall. In the faint light she counted eight thrown bolts. Exhaustion fluttered her eyelids shut, and she drifted into a strange and blissful sleep.

Tap, tap, tap, tap.
"Ma'am. Ma'am."

Jane woke with a start. Scrambling her body to the upright position, she stared at the door. She scrutinized the line of eight securely latched locks and then pinched the bridge of her nose. It had all been a dream.

"Ma'am, I have your laundered garments."

"One moment." She pushed off the bed and headed for the door. Sliding each latch open, she turned the knob. Surely a dream.

"Pardon, ma'am." A hand thrust through the opening; it was holding her dark gray wool dress, stockings, petticoat, and corset. She clutched them. "Thank you." Then she peeked her head through the crack in the door.

"Lord Tremarctos has been informed of your stay with us and wishes you to take breakfast with the family." He swallowed hard, his Adam's apple bobbing. "I will send Jerome up in a quarter of an hour to escort you to the hall."

"Very well." She shut the door and bolted the locks. All she wanted to do was depart and straighten out this whole day with Jonathan, but she would like to see the house in daylight. Leaving an hour later would not change the situation one whit. She frowned.

Turning back toward the bed, she gasped. Across the chair she had sat in the night before, a stunning pale green muslin dress lay. The color exactly matched her eyes. "Where did that come from?"

She raised her hand to touch the smooth, expensive fabric and noticed her hand wavering. She clenched her fingers into a fist. He had said he loved her eyes. It had been a dream, right? She turned away from the temptation and studied the room. No one could have gotten in. There was one door, and the window . . .

She rushed to the drapes and pulled them back. Rain came down steadily beyond the panes of clear glass, but the bolt remained latched. Certainly the dress had been there last night. How strange she had not noticed the garment. Then again, her mind had swum in other issues last night.

She glanced at the bed; the color of the linens shone a deep crimson in the daylight. The carvings entwining the posts depicted beautifully detailed bears.

Her fingers glided along the carved figure of one bear. Smooth and cool, the bear stood on its hind legs and fought with paws and mouth the next bear carved into the richly hued wood.

She bit her lip as her fingers stilled on the interlocking paws and mouth. Her stomach fluttered, and her other hand spread across the taut surface. How odd! Surely her stomach rumbled because of hunger. She needed to dress and feed her rumbling middle.

She gazed at the gray wool draped over her arm and then glanced longingly at the fine muslin stretched across the back of the chair. How silly to long for a piece of clothing. She had never owned such a fine-looking garment. Yet that dress pulled at her.

She wanted to put on the garment, to feel the slip of the fine fabric down her body. Would it be as smooth and as warm as the touch of her lover? She gasped and turned away from the dress. Nonsense, just nonsense.

"Bruno, are you sure she remained bolted in when you asked her to come to me this morning?" Lord Tremarctos shifted, agitated in his seat behind his desk.

"Yes, your grace. I heard the bolts slide. There is no way she could have faked it."

Very interesting. His brows lowered, and the corner of his lip curved up in concentration. His boars were all on edge this sunrise. The disquiet surely came from the smell of a woman inside the walls of Tremarctos.

"Still, none of this sits well. Does it, Bruno?"

"No, your grace."

With the torrential rain, she would not leave until the ill weather ceased. "Make sure all my boars are at breakfast. I don't want one of them coming across her without the knowledge that she is our guest. Or for her to be caught off guard by one of us." *If we are all in the same room, the situation will arise without much prodding.* Then he could decide what needed to be done.

"Yes, your grace. I will rouse them."

Lord Tremarctos stared after Bruno as he shut the door to his study. His fist clenched, breaking his quill in half. Please let the knife in his gut be for sane reasons, not for the dread that came to him in his sleep last night. Oscar. His teeth clenched. No . . . they all would surely want to fuck her. Even if she was not a mate, the smell of innocence shed pulled at even him. Let his unease be only that. His fist hit the desk with a loud thud.

Ursus . . . please stay dormant—he squeezed his eyes shut—and let his sons choose a mate without the turmoil that had stayed with him for a lifetime.

3

Beautiful. Jane stepped across the threshold into a magnificent dining room. Along one wall stood large windows partially covered by thick black drapes. In the center of the room, a large black-stained wooden table stood polished to a slick shine, surrounded by substantial black and gray upholstered chairs. She could see the dinner guests, in their fancy dresses, sitting in the large chairs. They laughed and sipped spiced wine. Sweet mother! The room glittered with the polish and sophistication of the moneyed.

With not a sound in the room, her slippers echoed throughout on the black polished floor. She glanced down at her gray wool once again and cringed. She looked frumpy and so out of place in such surroundings. Jerome, who escorted her, held out a seat for her halfway down the table. She smiled and sat. "Thank you," she whispered, afraid to break the tranquil atmosphere.

"What do you take for repast?"

"Tea and something sweet—no, cinnamon, if you have it." She could still smell the scent from her dream.

"Ma'am." He scurried to the sideboard and brought her a

teapot and cup. She picked up the pot and poured the steaming liquid. Setting the pot back on the table, she glanced down at her lap. My stars! The chair made her dainty, and she was far from small.

"Now behave." A deep voice came from out in the hall, and her gaze shot to the door. An elegant, massive man paused at the doorway; then he entered the room with an air of control.

"Welcome to Tremarctos, ma'am." He held up a hand. "Stay seated. I am Lord Tremarctos, and these are my boars." The elegant, gray-haired man pointed to the door as man after large man entered the room behind him. All of them possessed something from the elder. Boars surely meant sons.

Boar? The word felt oddly familiar.

"What is Tremarctos?"

"Why, this place," the youngest-looking one replied as he slid out the chair beside her. "Devon Ursus at your service, ma'am."

His blond hair, pulled back from his face, displayed striking angles that lit up when he smiled. His icy blue eyes assessed her as if gazing straight through to her soul. Her blood heated with wicked sensations. He tore his gaze away, leaving a chill in her bones.

"And you are?"

Jane jumped and turned toward the voice that came from the other side of her. Another of the large men sat down, and awareness skittered through her body. "Oh, pardon . . . I am Miss Jane Milton."

The heat of the two enormous male bodies surrounding her tangled her emotions. How she wanted one of them to touch her—yet she feared that touch at the same time. Any one of them could crush her like a fly.

"Miss Milton. I am Mac, and that rogue there," he lifted his hand and pointed to his brother standing against the wall, "is Martin, my twin."

They did look remarkably alike yet different. Both possessed thick, dark brown, wavy hair—tucked back behind their ears—that brushed their shoulders. But their eyes . . . Mac's were a hard green, startling in intensity, and Martin's were a cottony pale brown, shining with the kind of gentleness she could get lost in.

Jerome leaned in and placed a plate, a sugary cinnamon roll perched atop, in front of her. She glanced up and smiled at him. The smell, so delicious, captured her senses as she stared at the cinnamon stickiness and licked her lips.

"Miss Milton, the last introduction is of my eldest son and heir." The father's tone sounded as if it scolded.

"Ma'am, I am Lord Orin Arctos." He stood formally at the side of the table, bowed to her, and then sat. Never once did he truly look at her.

Martin pushed from the wall, capturing her attention. With a small cup in his hand, he pulled the chair opposite her from the table and sat. Her gaze fixed on that cup. The same cup she held in her hand was dwarfed by his grasp. Hmph. Small cup indeed.

What kind of men were these? She had never seen such big, burly men. She glanced up, and Martin's gaze briefly touched hers. Lightning shot down her spine. Wh—what was that? Her teacup shuddered in her clutch.

"Orin is a bit formal, but nothing to fear," Devon whispered, mistaking the reason for her shaking hand.

"Oh, surely." She couldn't tear her gaze from Martin across the table; his brows stooped over his eyes as he assessed her, and her heart beat so hard in her chest she swore she visibly pulsed to the beat. What was wrong with her?

Her body had gone mad since yesterday. Each man's gaze created startling effects on her. Though the act of giving her innocence had been painful at best, her body now craved scandalous and wanton things. She shook herself. Maybe she had a fever, though she felt fine. Her fingers briefly brushed her cool forehead.

"Are you well, Miss Milton?" Mac's long, thick fingers pressed her forearm.

Martin stood up with alarming haste, his chair clattering to the floor. Everyone jumped; their gazes snapped to him.

"Sit now, boar, and behave," the father said from the head of the table as he studied his knife in indifference.

My stars! Was this kind of behavior common among these men? The air grew thick with tension, and Martin's cheek twitched as his gaze fixed on Mac's hands, which were still settled on her arm.

"Pardon, Father." Martin inclined his head. "I—I need to leave."

"Very well. Say your farewell." Lord Tremarctos's cool blue gaze slid over Martin and then shot to Jane and narrowed, only to settle on Mac.

Mac leaned back in his chair, and the corner of his lips crooked up. Good Lord! She had no experience with brothers. Maybe all male siblings regarded one another this way?

"Good day, miss." Martin bowed his head swiftly and headed for the door. What a strange and odd occurrence! Such hostility did not welcome her. She didn't feel safe at all. The time had arrived to leave.

"Your lordship, I—I am sorry to disrupt you . . ."

When the boars had all followed their father into the dining hall for the morning repast, Martin could just barely contain his rage as Mac had sat next to Jane at the table. Martin had schooled his features as her virgin blood heated in his veins. Last night had changed him.

Her openness about her feelings and the caring emotions that poured from her for the man in town shook him. She would

258

make a good mother and excellent mate if he could only get her to accept him. He had wanted so much more from her last night, but he had barely escaped and bolted the door before Mac came raging up the hall, howling at her scent.

They always fought about women, and with the Ursus's healthy sexual appetite, squabbles happened frequently. Martin accepted the challenges, the wrestling. In most cases, he enjoyed the pleasure of the adrenaline of the fight . . . but Jane was not any woman to fight over. She was a possible mate for him, not a mere sexual release, and it remained unseen if Mac wanted more from her, too.

He had leaned against the wall in the dining hall and sipped his thick black coffee as he surveyed the situation. Her beautiful lower lip caught between her teeth. Her blond hair, down, pulled back from her slightly tanned skin, held him. She was utterly intoxicating.

What a sight they all made! Five men the size of oxen, sitting in substantial chairs dwarfed by their physical size. He'd wanted to show himself to her last night, but just couldn't bring himself to. His sure size would have sent her screaming in the night. So he'd used his mind to block her from seeing him.

As it was, she would notice his scent if he ventured too close. Dammit! No matter how he wanted to, he couldn't reveal his intentions in front of his brothers. She would surely leave if the claws came out, and he wanted nothing more than for her to stay . . . for a lifetime.

What did she think of him? Her gaze had scrutinized him as Mac introduced him. He had wanted to slip into her mind as he had last night, but his family would know the instant he did, and he couldn't hint at his desire. Not yet.

Repressing his intentions went against every lesson his father had instilled in him. Eventually his instincts would take him, and his family would know. But, for now, he needed knowledge, so he had sat back and watched . . . waited to see if one of his brothers desired more than mere sexual conquest.

Jerome had then leaned in and placed a cinnamon roll in front of her, and Martin smiled. She craved him. Devon caught his grin and winked. Yes, Martin did have a chance with her. Yet Devon had no idea Martin had already tasted her.

Orin finally sat, brooding in his usual silent way.

Martin had pushed from the wall and seated himself opposite Jane. Her gaze touched his, and the hairs on his neck lifted. She would be his . . . had to be. His instinct never raged this strong for a possible mate. He fucked several but never wished to start the mating ritual of Orsse. Jane. . . . Making her his was the one thought pulsing through his brain.

Mac had leaned toward her; his hand had risen bit by bit, heading in the direction of Jane's arm. Martin's blood had pounded through him; teeth clenched, his muscles had strained as he tried to control the will to defend her.

He would not permit his brother to touch her. She belonged to him. Dammit! He had tasted her. She infused each breath he took. Mac's hand landed on her forearm, and Martin's muscles had sprung him to action. His chair had clattered to the floor in alarming speed. He had barely suppressed a raging hiss as his vision hazed.

"Sit now, boar, and behave," his father had said from the head of the table as he feigned studying his knife.

Martin couldn't keep his rage controlled. Every thread that he held taut quaked. "Pardon, Father." His voice deepened and wavered in rage. "I–I need to leave."

"Very well. Say your farewell." *Gain your control, Martin, and say your farewell with grace.*

Of course, his father would test him.

His father's cool blue gaze had slid over Martin and assessed the situation in one glance. Then his father's eyes had shot to Jane and narrowed. What problems this caused! If either Martin or Mac were not sent from this house, another disaster like the one his father had initiated with Uncle Oscar would come full circle.

Mac had then leaned back, the corner of his lips inching up, mocking him. Damn him! Martin had wanted to jump over the table and tackle him to the floor. If he touched her again in any form, he would kill him. His fists clenched as the bone of his knuckles rose; his claws unsheathed. Damn him!

"Good day, miss." Martin had bowed his head, swiftly absorbing her beautiful pouting lips and deep honey-colored hair. His blood pounded through his ears. He tried to control this overwhelming desire for her and smashed his teeth together, snagging his tongue in the process. The salty taste of the virgin's blood that he had forced to flow anew last night flooded his mouth, and his semistiff erection hardened to full.

He had stepped forward. He needed her; she possessed him. His hands fisted, and his claws extended through his skin. *No! Get control of yourself! The green grass, the river* . . . He had inhaled a wavering breath in an attempt to gain control.

His muscles shook forcefully as he restrained himself from pouncing on his brother. He turned, leaving the room in haste. Striding down the hall, he picked out the tone of her voice. He stopped, anxious to know her thoughts, her feelings, and listened to her songlike tone.

"Your lordship, I—I am sorry to disrupt you and your family. I would like conveyance in your carriage. I wish to return home."

Damn it all. . . . She wanted to leave. Of course she did! What sane woman would stay in this madhouse? His hands shook with the need to possess her, lock her away, and make her accept him. His inner bear cried out in pain. Leaving was the only way to control this. . . . He would go for a ride. The rain, the smells of nature would calm him.

261

Lacy Danes

* * *

Jane sat at the table and waited for his lordship to answer. He stared after Martin, a deep, worried frown etching his face.

"My lord?"

His gaze slid to her and caressed her form. "I am sorry, Miss Milton, but our carriage needs repair, and with the rain so heavy, you will have to stay with us until the storm stops."

The same piercing cry from the night before rang out in her head. My stars! She did not think she could handle another night in this strange house.

Something of importance had happened between the twins in the moment when Martin had left the room. Her heart still sped when she thought of how fierce Martin had been; his soft eyes had changed intensity, and she'd half expected him to howl. The transformation had frightened her. All five of the men towered above her, their shoulders as wide as a door and arms as big as the trees by the river. She was so small, so helpless surrounded by them. She did not for one instant think herself safe, as the butler had said, "in this house."